THE IRON WATER

An Inspector Tom Harper Novel

Chris Nickson

This first world edition published 2016
in Great Britain and the USA by
SEVERN HOUSE PUBLISHERS LTD of
19 Cedar Road, Sutton, Surrey, England, SM2 5DA.
Trade paperback edition first published
in Great Britain and the USA 2016 by
SEVERN HOUSE PUBLISHERS LTD

British Library Cataloguing in Publication Data
A CIP catalogue record for this title is available from the British Library.

ISBN-13: 978-0-7278-8643-9 (cased)
ISBN-13: 978-1-84751-744-9 (trade paper)
ISBN-13: 978-1-78010-809-4 (e-book)

Typeset by Palimpsest Book Production Ltd.,
Falkirk, Stirlingshire, Scotland.

To the Memory of Ian Hallewell
Gentleman,
Reader

ONE

Leeds, July 1893

Tom Harper held his breath and counted. One second, two . . . three. All the way to ten.

Then the wooden boat exploded. Two shattering blasts that echoed off the hills. Pieces of the vessel flew high in the air, almost in slow motion, the boards and splinters crashing down into the lake. Hundreds of them. Thousands, speckling the surface until only ripples remained.

'Very good,' he heard one of the men in top hats say. 'Very good indeed.'

'Something for tomorrow at Roundhay Park,' Superintendent Kendall had told him as he put the letter on his desk. 'I want you there representing Leeds Police.'

'Yes, sir,' Detective Inspector Harper replied. He read the first couple of lines and looked up. 'Torpedoes? What in God's name are they?'

Kendall shook his head. His hair had gone greyer in the last two years, the lines deeper on his face. 'Some sort of rocket, from what I can gather, except they go underwater. A new weapon for the Navy, evidently. It's a demonstration for some government people, all very experimental and secret. We're going to have bobbies closing the roads into the park. Only names on the list admitted.'

'Why are they doing it on Waterloo Lake?' Harper asked. He didn't understand; it seemed like a bizarre choice. If these were naval weapons, why not somewhere out at sea?

The superintendent rolled his eyes. 'Don't ask me, Tom. I'm just the messenger here. Make sure you're there well ahead of time. And be on your best behaviour. There are going to be some important people there.'

'Yes, sir.'

*   *   *

'First thing tomorrow?' Annabelle asked as she settled back against him and closed her eyes with a contented sigh. 'What time?'

'Up there by five.' He'd need to leave by four to walk the distance, before the trams were even running.

'Let's hope she doesn't wake us during the night.' She looked over at the crib next to the bed. Mary was sleeping soundly. Fourteen months old on Wednesday. Mary Grace Harper. Her smile, her hair, her eyes, her laugh . . . from him and Annabelle.

As soon as the pregnancy was common knowledge, the women around Sheepscar had frowned and clucked and tutted. She was too old to have a bairn. Something would be wrong. A list of the problems that could happen. If he'd believed it he'd have been terrified for her. But that was the way here, always some mutterings under all the care and the smiles. In the end everything had gone smoothly. The labour had been long, but the midwife had done her job and mother and daughter emerged hearty and hale. He could still scarcely believe it when he looked at Mary. She was his, a part of him, named for the girl who'd been his wife's best friend as she grew up. Dead now, but living on this way.

'Shhh, don't tempt fate,' he whispered. Since she'd passed three months and the colic went, their daughter had been a good sleeper. Growing so fast, a hefty weight when he picked her up after arriving back from work. No real illness, touch wood; the worry always remained at the back of his mind.

Annabelle had insisted on feeding the baby herself. No wet nurse; she'd never even considered the idea. 'Why wouldn't I give her the breast?' she asked as if it was the most obvious thing in the world. 'I have milk, that's what it's there for.' And that was what she did until she weaned their daughter at nine months.

No nanny either, and no talk of one. They could afford it, but she wasn't interested. When she went to one of the bakeries she owned, she pushed the child in a baby carriage, wrapped up against the weather.

'I'll not have people saying I'm getting above myself,' she insisted. 'There's enough round here work all the hours God sends and still bring up families. If they can do it, so can I.'

He was proud of her. Of both of them. He loved his wife; even now he was still astonished that she'd agreed to marry him. But until Mary was born he hadn't known how loudly his heart could sing.

Annabelle curled against him. She'd been out this evening at a meeting; the new Independent Labour Party. He couldn't understand how she found the time for it all. Running the Victoria pub downstairs, keeping an eye on her three bakeries, a baby, and her politics. She'd turned down the chance to become part of the committee of the local Suffrage Society, but she was still very active locally, helping to organize and speaking at meetings. Sometimes she took Mary with her, enjoying the fuss everyone made of the child. This time, though, she'd gone alone and he'd had his little one to himself for two hours, the first time she'd trusted him.

'The experience will be good for you,' Annabelle had told him briskly before she left. 'I showed you what to do, Tom. Just you remember, women have been doing it for thousands of years. I think a man can cope for a little while. Oh,' she added, 'when you change her, there's some lard to use as cream on her bum.' She gave him a big smile.

He managed, even bathing Mary before reading to her from *The Water Babies*, watching as her eyes gently closed.

Early July, barely dawn as he strode up Roundhay Road in his best suit, the soft grey wool, his present from Annabelle three Christmases before. Already men were starting to emerge from the streets of back-to-back houses, on their way to the early shift. By the time he reached Harehills the air began to smell cleaner, the houses larger and more prosperous. Out beyond that was wealth. Oakwood was nothing more than a hamlet, a few houses by the road and the terminus for the electric tram by the arched entrance to the park. A copper saluted him as he approached.

'Anyone here yet?' Harper asked.

'They brought the ordnance a few minutes ago. Along the Wetherby Road and the Carriage Drive. And a fire engine right behind it. I daresay the toffs will show up in their own good time. No reporters allowed at this one, sir.'

He strolled along Park Avenue, relishing the quiet and the soft early light. Along the hillside, a few large houses stood back from the road, only the servants up and around at this hour.

There was plenty of activity by the lake, men manoeuvring a wagon into place with a welter of shouting and swearing. The brass of the fire engine glittered in the early sunlight, the horses that drew it enjoying their feed bags. And Harper spotted a familiar figure.

'Hello, Billy.'

Inspector Billy Reed of the Fire Brigade, looking uncomfortable in his best blue uniform. Detective Sergeant Reed once, until he transferred over and earned his promotion.

'Hello, Tom.' They shook hands. 'Here for the spectacle?'

He nodded. 'Whatever it is. How about you? For show, or just in case there's a problem?'

'We've been involved from the start.' He pointed along the length of the lake and explained, 'They'll tow the boat out soon. If everything goes to plan, at seven they'll fire two of those rocket-powered torpedoes and they'll destroy it.'

'Sounds simple enough.'

Reed snorted. 'As long as the damn things work. Half the time they fizzle out. Are you showing the flag for the police?'

'Something like that. I'm not even sure why they need me.'

'They just like us all on our toes.' A small pause. 'How's crime? Are they keeping you busy?'

Harper shrugged. 'It never stops. You know what it's like.' He should, they worked together for several years. 'And then there's always Mary.'

'How is she?' He smiled. Reed's wife, Elizabeth, was the manageress for Annabelle's bakeries; the two women were close.

'Wonderful.' It felt like a stilted, awkward conversation, like two friends who hadn't met in years and realizing they had little in common any more. 'I think I'll take a walk and see this boat.'

By a quarter to seven the important folk had arrived in their carriages. Sir James Kitson, from the engineering company, top hat gleaming. Charles Parsons, an industry grandee, greeted with proper deference. The Lord Mayor and men in the bright braid of naval uniforms. Harper bowed as he was introduced, then kept his distance.

It all seemed like a waste of his time. The toffs were making an early picnic of the event, wicker baskets full of food, popping bottles of champagne. Enough to remind him that he hadn't eaten yet. And no one was offering him a bite. Of course.

Then the sharp whistle blew and the men were making their final adjustment to the metal torpedoes, checking the angle and the fuses. Finally, exactly on the order, the missiles were launched, vanishing into Waterloo Lake. All that remained was a thin wake through water the colour of iron, bubbles rising to the surface.

And then the explosion.

Three hundred yards and it was still loud enough to make his ears ring. Complete destruction. My God, Harper thought, is that what war at sea was going to be like in future? How would anyone survive? He glanced across at Billy; the man's face was impassive. Reed had been a soldier, he'd fought with the West Yorkshires in Afghanistan.

'What do you think of that?'

'Impressive, I suppose.' He hesitated for a second. 'Dreadful, too.' He turned and walked away towards the fire engine.

Harper was lost in his thoughts for a few seconds. Then he heard shouting in the distance. Somewhere along the bank of the lake. Even with the hearing almost gone in his right ear he could make out one of the words: 'Police.'

He started to run.

TWO

He was out of breath by the time he reached the men. They were standing by a rowing boat, still shouting and babbling and gazing out at the water.

'I'm Detective Inspector Harper,' he told them, the words coming in a rush. 'What is it?'

'Out there,' one of them told him, pointing.

He looked. At first he could only make out fragments of the destroyed vessel bobbing on the lake. Planks, half a mast, part of the deck. Then he spotted something pale. An arm. It moved slightly, as if it might be alive. More of the body surfaced. Someone's back, naked, the flesh white and dead.

It floated about twenty yards from the shore, rising and dipping with the swell. Too large for a woman, he thought, too muscled, but it was impossible to be certain.

'You,' Harper ordered one of the men, 'and you. Get out there and drag it in.'

'I'm not touching anything dead,' the man objected. He was large, strong, his face set.

'You called for the police. Now get yourself out there.'

The inspector was aware of others coming up behind him and turned as the pair settled in the boat and began to row. Billy, followed by a few of the men who'd been watching the performance.

'Stand back please,' Harper instructed, gently shooing them off. As soon as they spotted the corpse they seemed happy to obey, retreating to the top of the hill.

'Looks like you got more than you expected, Tom,' Reed said grimly.

'I thought this was supposed to be straightforward.' He shook his head. 'I could use a hand for a few minutes . . .'

'I might as well. The engine can't leave yet, anyway.'

A man. He'd been right about that, and naked as the day he was born, except for the rope tied around his belly, twelve inches or more left dangling from the knot, then cleanly cut.

The corpse had been turned on his back, dark hair slick and wet against the skull, dripping on the grass of the bank. The fish had been at him, but most of everything was left. The body was only just beginning to bloat; he hadn't been down there too long.

'Anything familiar?' Harper asked, kneeling to gaze at the face for something he might recognize. A scar, anything at all.

'Not to me,' Reed said, lighting a cigarette to mask the smell.

'Nor me.' He sighed. 'More's the bloody pity.'

The dead man couldn't have been in the boat the torpedoes hit.

'We looked it over proper before we towed it out,' one of the rowers insisted. 'Just to be certain.'

'How many of you checked?' Three hands went up. That idea was a dead end. It meant only one thing. Someone had dropped the naked corpse into Waterloo Lake a few days before. Weighted down, by the look of it. One of the splinters from the explosion must have sheared the rope, and the body had risen.

'That knot,' the rower said.

'What about it?' Harper asked.

'That's a bowline. Good and strong. A sailor's knot.'

One slim piece of information. But that was how it always began. Some tiny thing and it built from there. Coppers were on their way to start searching the area. A hearse had been requested to take the man to Dr King, the police surgeon, for a post-mortem. There wasn't much more he could do here.

'What do you think, Billy?'

'Your guess is as good as mine. I don't envy you the job, though.'

Reed was in charge of fire investigations now, given the job after Dick Hill moved down to Oxford for a promotion there. The brigade was part of the police force, but there was nothing here to involve him professionally.

Harper assessed the situation. No one could tell him anything worthwhile, nobody could identify the corpse.

'I might as well go back to the station and get this investigation started,' he said.

'I'll walk to the engine with you.'

They talked about small, inconsequential things: the weather, children. At least the resentment and bad blood that had replaced friendship seemed long in the past now. He was grateful for that, at least. Small mercies.

By the time he caught the tram back into town, sitting on the open top deck, his mind was firmly on the dead man. Who? And why there in the lake? Transporting someone all the way out to the park then rowing out on the water couldn't be an easy job. It must have happened late at night; there'd be too many people around otherwise.

As the vehicle turned the corner at the bottom of Roundhay Road he glanced into the windows of the Victoria. Were Annabelle and Mary inside or had they gone for a walk? Then his thoughts flickered and moved back to the corpse.

A quick nod to Sergeant Tollman as he entered Millgarth Police

Station and Harper walked through into the office. Neither Ash nor the new detective constable, Wharton, was there.

Superintendent Kendall was sitting at his desk, neat in his black suit and high collar. Thick mutton chop whiskers sprouted from his face. The air was heavy with the smell of his hair pomade.

'I've already heard about it,' he said. 'Give me the details, Tom.'

He recounted the little he knew.

'You're absolutely positive he wasn't on the boat they blew up?' The superintendent frowned.

'The men who towed it out swore they checked it fully. And his body would be more damaged if he'd been on board. Then there's the rope around his waist . . .'

'Where is he now?'

'On the way to Hunslet.' The police mortuary, in the cellar of the police station there.

'How long before Dr King will get to it, do you think?'

He made a quick calculation. 'Two hours, at least. Probably a little longer.'

Kendall rubbed his face wearily and shook his head. 'The papers are going to love this one. "Mystery corpse unearthed by war experiment."'

'We'll do what we can.'

'Solve it.' The words were an order. He understood. Journalists from London would be up here. The Admiralty would keep a close eye on things. Leeds would be in the news. After years of clamouring it had finally become a city at the start of the year. Now they'd have to prove they were worthy of the title.

'Yes, sir.' No other answer was acceptable.

'Since you have some time before King will be able to tell us anything, I have another job for you . . .'

There was a crowd gathered on the riverbank above Crown Point Bridge. A strange-looking boat was tied up at the wharf, six coppers around it, talking to men who might have been the crew. A few nosy parkers had gathered, keeping their distance as they tried to find out what was happening. And in the middle, a head taller than the others, Ash.

Detective Sergeant Ash he was now, promoted the year before and worth his weight in diamonds. He was a natural detective, a man who made connections well, who could think on his feet. Harper had pushed for him to be given his stripes; he deserved them. He wasn't Billy Reed, but he was clever and genial. Standing close behind him, eyes darting round nervously as he took it all in, was DC Wharton. He'd only moved into plain clothes the month before; it was too soon to tell how good he might become. But everyone had to start somewhere and learn.

'What do we have?' the inspector asked as he pushed through the small crowd. Kendall had told him nothing.

Under his moustache, Ash smiled. 'A little bit of excitement, sir.' He used his thumb to point at the vessel bobbing on the water. 'They're dredging the river, started up past the railway stations a few days ago. That floated to the surface an hour ago.' He indicated something on the cobbles, covered by a piece of sacking.

Harper looked at him questioningly, knelt, and drew back the hessian.

A leg. A woman's leg, still in its stocking and boot, clumsily severed near the top of the thigh. He looked for a few seconds then replaced the covering.

'Where was it?' he asked.

'Just downstream.' It was one of the crew from the boat who answered, a bantam of a man with dark curly hair, his chest stuck out like a challenge. But his words were subdued and all the colour was gone from his face. 'You see over there, where the river and the canal separate? A little before there.'

'Thank you. Who are you?'

'Will Horsfield. I'm the mate here.' He patted the gunwale of the boat then shook his head sadly. 'Been doing this job ten years and never had owt like this before.'

'Have you taken any statements yet?' Harper asked Ash.

'The uniforms got everything, sir.'

He gazed out at the river. It was deep brown, filled with choppy little waves, all the mud and silt churned up by the dredging, stinking from all that flowed into it from the factories. Nothing like the placid grey of Waterloo Lake.

He'd been a copper for fourteen years and never had a corpse emerge from the water before. Now there were two in a single morning. What about this one? Another murder? Suicide? Accident? With only a leg they couldn't tell a damned thing.

'Right,' he said after a minute and turned to Wharton.

'Get that wrapped up properly and take it to Dr King with my compliments. Tell him I'll be over later and I'd appreciate anything he can tell me. Warn him he has something else coming, too.'

'Yes, sir.' The young man looked slightly stunned.

'After that go back to Millgarth and look through all the reports of missing women for the last month.' That would be a start.

'What about us?' Horsfield wondered.

'You can help us look for the rest of whoever she was,' the inspector told him. 'Go over every inch you've covered this morning.'

As people dispersed, he heard the sergeant cough. 'Dr King's going to be busy, sir?'

'Yes. It's been a strange morning . . .'

Two hours later he was walking across Crown Point Bridge, Ash at his side, Wharton a pace behind them. The River Aire lapped at its banks as if nothing had happened. Barges were tied up at the wharves, two and three deep, loading and unloading cargo. The water stank, refuse floating, the corpse of a dead dog caught in the current. Summer, but the smoke from the factory chimneys kept the sunlight out, covering everything with a blanket of soot.

He saw the dredger moving slowly, men watching over the side.

On the way back to the station he told the sergeant about the torpedoes and the body that rose from the lake.

'Watery graves today,' Ash said. 'Not a pleasant place to end up, is it, sir?'

Wharton had discovered five women reported missing over the last few weeks. Any one of them could have ended up in the river. He'd need more before he could go any further.

They turned into the police station on Hunslet Lane and took the steps down to the cellar. Through a door and into a tiled corridor with its stench of carbolic. King's Kingdom.

Dr King had been the police surgeon for over thirty years. He was in his eighties now but showed no inclination to retire, his mind alert and acerbic, his body still spry. Loud, tuneless singing came from one of the rooms.

'He must have gone to see that Mozart opera at the Grand,' Ash said.

'Who?' Harper asked.

'A composer, sir. He's dead now. That's one of his arias.'

The body from Roundhay Park was on one table covered with a sheet; the leg from the river lay on another, still in its hessian. King wiped his hands on a dirty piece of linen as they entered. He beamed as he saw the policemen.

'I have to congratulate you, Inspector, you come up with the most interesting specimens. Two in one day, that's a record even for you. Both from the water, too. That's novel. And you're here with Sergeant Ash.'

'That was a good job on *Il Mio Tesoro*, sir.'

'Do you think so?' King brightened. 'Can't do it the way I used to. I sang it once in the Amateur Operatic Society.' He peered at Wharton. 'Ready for this, young man?' he asked with a dark smile.

'Have you examined the bodies yet?' Harper tried to herd them back to business.

'I thought we might enjoy that together, Inspector.' It was King's gruesome little test, making them watch the post-mortem and hoping they'd faint or be forced to leave. He unknotted the string around the limb.

'Well,' he began after a moment. 'This is fascinating.'

'What?'

'Where the leg's been severed.' He pointed. 'I've never seen anything quite like it. Take a look.'

The wound was ugly, almost as if someone had ripped the limb from the rest of the body.

'A dredger found her, is that correct?' King asked.

'Yes, sir,' Ash answered.

'That might explain it.' He seemed to be talking to himself, moving around, studying it from all angles. 'Yes. They have blunt blades.' King looked up. 'I can't think of anything else that might have caused it. This certainly wasn't done by an axe or a knife. That would have been a cleaner cut.'

The doctor unlaced the boot and removed it.

'It's cheap enough, mass produced,' he said. 'Worn at the heel.' Slowly he rolled down the sodden woollen stocking, then brought it close to his face. 'I'd say this is probably grey when it's dry. That might help you.'

'Anything would be useful,' Harper told him.

King began to examine the leg.

'She was quite young. No more than twenty-five, if that, but fully grown – say older than sixteen. There's no sign of varicose veins. It's impossible to tell just from this, but I don't believe she's been in the water more than ten days.' He stood back and rubbed his chin. 'No, that's all I can say on this one.'

He turned and pulled back the sheet covering the man from the lake like a conjurer revealing his trick.

It was easier to get a sense of the body now. His hair had dried mousy brown. It was long, over his ears and on to his neck. But he looked quite young, probably in his late twenties, with long sideboards down to the jawline, and a thin moustache.

'First we need to give him a name,' Harper said.

'Leonard Tench,' Ash replied without any hesitation as he stared into the corpse's face.

'What? Are you sure?'

'That I am, sir. He grew up next door but one from me. I've known him all my life.'

The examination didn't reveal much, but Harper wasn't giving it his full attention. He wanted to be back outside, asking Ash about Leonard Tench. At least the doctor's voice was loud enough that he didn't have to worry about missing anything.

'He didn't drown,' King said finally. 'He was put in the water after he was dead. He was probably only down there for a day, two at the most. Weighted down by something.'

'What killed him, sir?' Ash's voice was hoarse.

There was silence for a minute or more, then the doctor answered, 'A blow to the head. The usual blunt object, but this one was hard enough to cave in his skull.' He stood back, thinking, then looked at the chest and limbs. 'Yes. He was bitten by what-ever they have in the water there, but he wasn't stabbed. I'll send on my report later.'

'Thank you,' Harper told him, eager to escape into air that didn't rasp against his throat.

'How well did you know him?'

Ash hadn't spoken since they left Hunslet. He'd walked with his head down, staring at the flagstones on the pavement. Wharton kept with them, listening attentively.

'Best friends when we were nippers,' Ash said with a small, wan smile. 'In and out of each other's houses, our mams would clip us both round the ear. You know how it is, sir.'

He did. His own childhood had been the same way.

'And what happened to him?'

'We lost touch a few years back. Must have been . . . back in '84, I suppose, when we were eighteen.'

'Where was this?'

'Quarry Hill. Dufton Court, down there off Somerset Street.'

The place was no more than a loud shout from Millgarth. Filled with the poor and the Irish, cheek by jowl. Harper had been through it often enough. Plenty of places with two or more families to a room. Damp cellars where water ran down the walls, but people were glad to live in them anyway, because any roof was better than none.

'Do you have any idea what he might be doing now?'

'Not a jot, sir. I'm sorry.' Ash hesitated. 'It just took me back a bit, seeing Len like that.'

'We're going to need to find out everything about him. Do you know anyone who might be able to tell you?'

'I can ask. We moved up to Burmantofts when I was nine but both of us ended up working at the same place.'

'Where was that?' He wanted every tiny scrap of information.

'The chemic in Sheepscar.' Ash pursed his lips. 'Chemical works. I left as soon as I could. Joined the force.'

'You get busy. Discover everything you can.' He glanced towards the clock on the Parish Church. 'Meet me back at the station at five o'clock.'

Six hours, Harper thought. With a little luck that should be enough time to learn about the man. He turned to the constable. 'How many of the missing women come within the doctor's age range?'

'Two, sir.'

That narrowed it down – as long as the body wasn't a girl no one would miss or care about. 'How long has each of them been missing?'

Wharton fumbled in his jacket for his notebook and riffled through the pages. 'One's been gone ten days, the other just three days. Sir,' he added quickly.

'Who's the first one?'

'Charlotte Brooker,' he read. 'Aged nineteen. Her father's a manager at the gas works on York Street. She said she was going for a walk in the evening and never came back.'

'Right.' Harper carried on walking. 'What about the other one?'

'She's just sixteen. Emily Lacey. Lives in Holbeck. Works at Marshall's. She's run off before.'

The first one. That was what his gut told him. At least it was somewhere to start. And if it was Charlotte Brooker, her family would finally learn what had happened.

'Go and see Mrs Brooker,' he ordered. 'Don't tell her we found a leg. Say we might have a lead. I want you to find out whatever you can. Scars, identifying marks, anything like that. What she was wearing when she left.'

'Yes, sir,' Wharton said.

'Leonard Tench,' Harper said to Sergeant Tollman as he walked into Millgarth. 'Do you know him?'

Tollman rubbed his chin. 'It seems to ring a faint bell, sir,' he said eventually. 'Wait a minute.' The desk sergeant disappeared into a back room, waddling more than walking as his belly bulged against the shiny buttons of his uniform. He reappeared in a moment, carrying a heavy ledger. 'Got him. Shoplifting in '85. Looks like he worked up to a spot of burglary two years later. Nothing until '90, then we brought him in for beating someone. He got three months that time. Haven't seen him since. Why do you want to know, sir?'

'He's our man in the lake. What's the address we have for him?'

'Number three, Rugby Mount.'

Not far from the Victoria, Harper thought. Closer still to the chemical works.

'Thank you.'

So Tench was a thief and a man with a quick temper, he thought as he walked along the road. God knew there were enough like that in Leeds. But to die that way . . . he'd never heard of a killing like it. Not the murder itself, but weighing down the body in the lake. Someone hadn't wanted him to be found. That took planning. It took effort. Two men, at the very least, more likely three. And some important reason.

On Rugby Mount it was impossible to escape the choking smell of the chemical works. It burned his nostrils and throat as he breathed. A scrawny cat lazed on the cobbles as the inspector walked past and knocked on the door of number three.

The woman who answered was short, almost toothless, with wispy grey hair and clouded eyes. She had the pinched face and sunken cheeks of someone who'd never eaten well enough, and skin as wrinkled as tanned leather.

'What do you want, luv? We're full.'

A rooming house; that made sense.

'Leonard Tench,' he said.

'Left two days ago.' She paused and corrected herself. 'No, someone come for his things two days back. I've not seen him since Friday.' The woman shook her head. 'Some folk. Been here four year and then gone without a word.' She stared. 'Who are you, anyway?'

'Detective Inspector Harper, Leeds City Police.' He still wasn't used to the new name of the force.

'Why?' the woman cocked her head, suddenly sharp. 'Has summat happened to him?'

'I'm sorry to have to tell you, but he's dead.'

She crossed herself, muttering something under her breath.

'I'd like to see his room.'

The woman shook her head. 'Already someone in it. And there weren't a scrap left. I swept it out mesen. The man who came, he took everything.'

'Did he tell you his name?'

'No. I didn't ask.' She folded her arms under her bosom. 'Why would I? He just told me Len had found a job in Manchester and he'd offered to pack up his things and send them on.'

'Can you describe the man who came?'

She thought for a moment and shrugged. 'Ordinary. Red hair,
I remember that. Dark red, you know, like copper.'

'Was he young? Old? Tall? Short?'

'Middling. I don't know, a bit older than Len, I suppose. I'm
sorry, luv, I didn't really bother about him. Like I said, though,
I were surprised at Len, not coming back here to take care of
everything himself. He'd always been pleasant enough.'

'Was he paid up?'

'To the end of the week.'

'What was Len like, Mrs . . .?'

'Fisher. Not good, not bad, really. Just there. I'll tell you
summat for nowt, though, he must have had a strange job.'

'What do you mean?' He could feel the hairs on his arms
prickling.

'It weren't regular, like. He'd laze in of a morning like he had
a butler to take care of him. Then sometimes he'd be gone a day
or two. Often he weren't back while late. But he allus paid on
time. Not like some of them, wanting to let it slide.'

'You've no idea where he worked?'

'Used to be at the chemic, he said, and he smelled like it, an'
all. But they all have their shifts, like clockwork. So he weren't
there no more. As long as he handed over his money every week
and didn't cause no trouble, I never fussed about it.'

'What about his friends? Did you ever see any of them?'

'No,' Mrs Fisher answered, then hesitated. 'I've just remembered. It must have been last year. Maybe the one before. I asked
him why he lodged round here if he didn't work here. He said
he had a friend close by. That's all.'

He asked a few more questions, but she'd already told him
what little she knew. As he turned the corner on to Meanwood
Road he saw a familiar figure trudging towards him.

'Thank some good luck and Sergeant Tollman,' Harper
explained when Ash reached him. 'We're close to the Victoria.
Let's go there and see what we have.'

As soon as he walked into the parlour, Mary started toddling
quickly towards him. Stumbling at first, then almost running,
face full of joy as she threw herself against his legs. He could
hear Annabelle in the kitchen, humming quietly to herself. The

table was covered with books on politics, a few open, the others stacked high.

Harper picked up his daughter, kissed her nose and heard her giggle.

'I hadn't expected to see you during the day.' Annabelle came out, wiping her hands on a rag, then smiled. 'And Sergeant Ash.'

'Mrs Harper.' He clutched his battered bowler hat awkwardly in his hands.

'Annabelle,' she reminded him with a smile, 'how many times do I have to tell you?'

'We were nearby,' Harper explained.

'Have you eaten?'

'Not yet.'

'I'll have Ellen find you something. Do you mind looking after Mary for a few minutes? I need to go downstairs and talk to Dan.'

He hefted the child a little higher. 'I don't think she'll tell any police secrets.'

They waited until the footsteps had faded, Annabelle on her way to the pub below, before they began.

'What have you managed to find out?'

'Not as much as you, by the look of it, sir.'

Harper recounted what Mrs Fisher had told him. 'How does that fit with what you've learned?'

'I went to see my mother first.' Ash's face reddened slightly at the admission. 'I thought she'd be able to tell me about the family.'

'Did she?' He bounced Mary on his knee, grinning as she started to laugh.

'Seems Len's father wasn't above a bit of thieving when he could get away with it. Never caught, but everyone knew.'

And down on Dufton Court he wasn't alone. No one was likely to tell the coppers.

'So it runs in the family.'

'She told me Len's older brother has been in prison a few times. I never really knew him, can't even picture what he looked like. Then I went over to the chemic. He hasn't been there since '90, when he went to prison. Someone told me he'd been lodging on Rugby Mount. And that's where I saw you.'

'A troublemaker?' He combed his fingers through his daughter's hair.

'Not so much that.' He sighed. 'Things seemed to disappear when he was around. They could never prove it was Len, but it stopped after he'd gone.' He ran a hand over his head. 'It's funny, sir, it's not how I remember him at all.'

They heard someone climbing the stairs and fell silent. Ellen entered, carrying a tray with a plate of beef sandwiches and a pot of tea, Annabelle right behind her.

'What's got the pair of you around here? I thought you were at the park first thing.' She settled in the chair, watching the two of them before leaning over and scooping Mary into her arms and stroking her hair back into place.

'Trying to find out about someone,' Harper told her. 'His body turned up in Waterloo Lake this morning.'

'Someone from round here?' Annabelle asked. 'Who?'

'His name's Leonard Tench.'

'Len Tench?' she said in astonishment. 'He's dead?'

'Did you know him?' Harper seemed surprised.

'He used to be a customer.' She thought rapidly. 'Must have been . . . four years ago. Probably not long before I met you, Tom. I finally had to tell him not to come back. He'd have a few, then try to pick fights. I had to threaten him with the cudgel before he'd go.'

That was easy to imagine; Annabelle wasn't afraid of anyone.

'Do you know anything else about him?'

'Never wanted to,' she answered with a frown. 'It was good riddance as far as I was concerned.' She held Mary at arm's length and sniffed. 'Come on, you, I think you need changing.'

'Now we need to know what Tench has been up to recently,' Harper said as they ate.

'Whatever it was, it must have been bad for him to end up that way.' Ash shook his head. 'It's just hard to believe, sir. I remember him the way we were when we were lads. He liked some fun, but that was all.'

'People change. Not always for the better.'

'True enough.' He paused for a moment. 'By the way, how was the torpedo demonstration?'

'Impressive,' he answered after a moment. With everything else he'd forgotten all about it.

Before they left, Harper slipped into the bedroom. Mary was napping in her cot, her white gown flowing around her small body. He gazed at her for a moment.

'Lovely when they're asleep, aren't they?' Annabelle whispered. She was sitting in an armchair by the window, reading. 'I thought I'd give you two some peace while you were working.'

'No need. It was hardly secret.'

'When you get home later I want to talk to you about something.'

'Oh?'

'It's only an idea.'

'Fine,' he told her, baffled, then kissed her. 'I'll try not to be late, but . . .'

She laughed quietly. 'I know, Tom. Work.'

THREE

'Time to start talking to the narks,' Harper said as they sat on the top deck of the tram going back into Leeds. Down on the pavement a boy was shouting the headline about a disaster at Thornhill Colliery. One hundred and thirty-five dead in an underground explosion. So many it was impossible to imagine.

'I've been thinking the same, sir. It's strange, though . . .'

'What is?'

'It looks as if Len's been involved in crime for a while.'

'True.' With his record, money but no job, what other explanation could there be? Mrs Fisher told him that Tench always seemed to have money. Whatever he'd been doing was more than shoplifting and fights, that was certain. Something that paid.

'But we haven't come across him for a few years, sir. And it seems to me that we know most of them, one way or another.'

'Maybe he's been lucky,' Harper answered. 'Or we just haven't been looking in the right places.' He was certain that Tench hadn't been living on the straight and narrow.

'Possibly,' Ash agreed. But his voice sounded doubtful. 'We need to find Ted Bradley.'

'Who?'

'Len and me met him when we started at the chemic. Palled around a bit. He was a year or so older, knew the ropes. They became good pals. He might be able to tell us something.'

'Is he still at the works?'

The sergeant shook his head. 'Left around the same time as Len. I stopped off at the address they had for him but he's not been there for over two years now.'

'See if you can find him. With a little luck we'll know more after we talk to a few people. We'll meet at Millgarth later.'

But Pieman Peter, Herbert Drake, and seven others that he tracked down here and there all shook their heads when he mentioned Tench. None of them had ever heard of him. Walking up Briggate, Harper heard the paperboy yelling the fresh headline from the *Evening Post*, hot off the press:

'Torpedo brings up body!'

He paid his ha'penny and stopped to glance at the front page, the crowds on the streets swirling around him. For all they'd tried to stop reporters watching, one had an accurate account of the grand explosion on Waterloo Lake.

The article was sensational, but that was the way to sell papers, climaxing with the body rising to the surface. At least they had no details, just the mystery. Who was the corpse? How had he ended up in the water?

Harper rolled up the newspaper, carrying it like a baton. He had three more people he wanted to see, then he'd call it a day. He'd changed since Mary arrived and he knew it. No more endless hours working. Now he was happy to be at his own hearth. He'd never particularly desired children, never even thought about them. He'd been taken by surprise when Annabelle told him she was pregnant. But from the moment he saw Mary and picked her up as if she was the most delicate thing in the world, he had known everything was different.

He'd started out as a copper on a beat that took in the

yards and courts between Briggate and Lands Lane. He could probably still have walked them all with his eyes closed. But in the last few years, things there had altered. Many of the old places had been torn down to build Queen's Arcade. So new he sometimes felt he could still smell the paint on it. Leeds was becoming a different place. Modern, fast. How long before he felt left behind?

Boots slipping on the greasy cobbles, he cut through to Swan Street, and the White Swan, which stood behind the music hall. Horseshoe Harry had started drinking there the year before, moving after they finally demolished the old Rose and Crown.

Harper found him in the corner, over by the empty fireplace, a glass on the table in front of him, face set in a frown under a moustache that almost hid his mouth.

'You look down in the dumps.' He signalled the waiter for another beer and took a seat to Harry's right, keeping his good ear towards the man. At least he'd be able to hear him.

'Thunder had to be put down yesterday. I've known that horse since he were a colt. Sad days, Mr Harper.'

Harry was a farrier, shoeing half the horses that pulled carts around the centre of the city. It had been his family's trade for generations, forging and hammering, then fitting the horseshoes to the animals.

He was a big man with heavy, muscled arms covered in tiny burns and scars. There was a bigger scar on his left cheek where a mare had kicked him once, slicing him open from temple to jaw. It gave him a dangerous look; maybe that was why people told him things.

'Leonard Tench,' Harper said. There was a pause, less than a heartbeat, but long enough. Harry knew something, he was sure of it.

'Who?'

'Come on Harry, don't kid a kidder. You know, I can see it in your eyes.'

The man lowered his head, gazing at the drink before him. 'George Archer.'

The words were so quiet that Harper had to strain to make them out.

'And that's all I'm saying.'

He knew the name. He knew it too bloody well. Harper nodded, put down a shilling and walked off, back down Briggate and through towards Millgarth.

The police had been after Archer for years but they'd never found anyone brave enough to testify against him. The few who said they would either changed their minds later or disappeared from the city, never seen again, not even a body to be found.

And the thought took him back to Dufton Court, where Tench and Ash had been born.

Archer had grown up there too, in a house round the corner on Somerset Street. He was still a small boy when he'd started out as a runner for the local gang. As he grew, filling out, learning how to wield a cutthroat razor, he'd become the man who threatened and cut anyone who didn't do as he was told. By the time he was eighteen, Archer had worked his way up to be the leader of the gang and he'd stayed there ever since. Clever and ruthless; a dangerous combination. Business had boomed. Arson, murder, thefts, prostitution; the coppers knew he was behind them all if there was money to be made. People didn't cross him. They didn't refuse him. And they definitely didn't stand in court and give evidence against him.

He'd moved out to the suburbs somewhere. That was what the inspector had heard, and now he was trying to present himself as respectable. He could afford the best lawyers, not that he'd needed them too often; there was rarely enough evidence to take him to court, let alone put him away. If Archer was behind Leonard Tench's death, proving it was going to be a hard battle.

Wharton was waiting in the office when he opened the door. His report was already complete, lying on Harper's desk, the writing a neat copperplate.

'What did Mrs Brooker have to say to you?'

'It's all there, sir.'

'I know. That's for the record. I want to know what you made of her.' What ended up on paper was only half the story. It would be a good lesson for the lad: if you were working a case you needed everything you could find.

'She's terrified,' Wharton began after thinking for a few seconds. 'She's scared we'll find a body and scared we won't, if you know what I mean, sir.' The inspector nodded. 'I don't think she'd heard about the leg. But once she does she's going to put two and two together.'

'Is there anything to identify the girl?'

'There's a little scar on the back of her neck, that's all. Nothing on her legs.'

'What about her disappearance? What did she have to say about that?'

'Charlotte's never done it before, sir. The mother kept saying so. She was adamant. It's why she's sure something bad has happened.'

'What about young men? Has the girl been courting?'

'Not that Mrs Brooker knows, sir.' Wharton ran a nervous hand through his thick brush of hair. He smelled of old cabbage and tobacco.

But parents often didn't know the whole truth about their children; Harper had learned that long ago.

'Who else is in the family?'

'A sister, sir. Cordelia. She's a year younger.'

'Talk to her in the morning, she might know something. How had Charlotte been before she vanished? Happy? Melancholy?'

'Quite normal, according to Mrs Brooker.'

'Dig deeper into it tomorrow. There's not a lot we can do without a body, though. You might as well go home for now.' As the constable was leaving, he added, 'This is your case, Mr Wharton. I want you to work on it until you find some answers. Keep me informed, and come to me if you have any questions.'

'Thank you, sir.' His smile was a mix of gratitude and fear. 'I won't let you down.'

Harper stared over at Superintendent Kendall's office. He'd gone to a meeting, and wouldn't be back tonight. He'd need to know about George Archer.

Five minutes later Ash arrived.

'Nothing yet, sir,' he said. 'No luck on Bradley or anything else. I thought I'd go out again tonight and see who I can find.'

The inspector sat back in his chair. 'I've come up with a name to make you think. George Archer. Horseshoe Harry says he and Tench had something going.'

'Len with Archer?' The sergeant shook his head. 'I can't believe that, sir. Not the Len I knew.'

'People change,' Harper reminded him.

'I know, but . . .' The words tailed away. 'Well, maybe he did, at that.'

'We'll find out more in the morning. And I'll want a word with the super then, too.'

'You're off with the fairies again, Tom.'

'Sorry.' He smiled and sighed, pushing the plate away. Good steak and kidney pie, but he hadn't been hungry. The thoughts kept stirring and raging in his head.

Annabelle had Mary on her knee, spooning beef tea into the girl's mouth. She loved the taste, she'd enjoyed it from the first, reaching out to clutch the spoon with her pudgy little hands. Her brown hair had grown in thick curls they brushed every night, and her eyes seemed to take in and examine everything around her.

'What were you thinking?'

'Work,' he admitted and tried once more to shake it from his mind. Now he was home it was time to discover what was on hers. 'You said there was something you wanted to talk about.'

They could have cleared her books off the table before the meal. They'd even done it for a while. But each time, all the volumes quickly found their way back. Now it hardly seemed worth the effort. It was easier to move them around so there was a space to eat.

'There is,' Annabelle said. She wiped the baby's mouth and lowered her gently to the ground, watching her stagger determinedly away towards a doll on the rug. She'd begun to walk two months before, tentative at first, then suddenly more certain. 'I've been thinking about selling the bakeries.'

For a moment he didn't know what to say. He'd wondered what to expect, what was so important, but he'd never imagined this.

'What? Why?' He didn't understand; it seemed unlikely, impossible. She owned three of them, all local, built them up from scratch. She'd only opened the third shop two years before; he could remember the day quite clearly. They baked all the goods in a kitchen behind the Victoria, starting in the middle of each night.

'It just feels like the right time.'

He waited. He knew Annabelle; she'd never make a business decision just on feel. When it came to money, she was cunning as a fox. There had to be a deeper reason.

'Go on,' he said. 'There's more, isn't there?'

'Miss Ford's asked me to be the secretary of the Suffrage Society.'

'Do you want to do it?' Stupid question, he thought. Of course she did if she was considering selling the bakeries.

'I've already told them I will.' From the corner of her eye she saw Mary about to wander into the kitchen and hurried to pick her up. The little girl squirmed in her arms.

She'd been offered a post on the committee before. At that time she'd turned it down, once she discovered she was going to have a child.

'Miss Frobisher's retiring,' she continued with a smile. 'She's moving to Harrogate. Going for the spa water.'

'The last time you were offered something you said it would involve travel . . .'

'Not being the secretary. That's just local,' she told him. 'I made sure of that.'

Harper pursed his lips. 'I don't see why you need to sell the bakeries in order to do it, though.'

'Time.' He could hear her hesitation. 'It's going to take a few hours every day. Then there's the speaking at meetings. I'm not going to give that up. Mary. You. I won't be able to do everything.'

'What about Mary?' She'd settled down, curled happily in the crook of her mother's arm and inspecting her fingers. 'When you're working, I mean.'

'Most of the work will be here. And when I have to go round town I'll take her with me.'

Inside, he smiled. She'd already arranged the details. Annabelle had made up her mind and he had no desire to change it.

'Do you have someone lined up to buy the bakeries?'

'That's what I wanted to talk about. I had an idea . . .' she began slowly, looking at him through fluttering eyelashes. 'I thought maybe Elizabeth would be interested.'

Elizabeth Reed already managed all three of the shops. She knew how they worked, their strengths and weaknesses, what sold well where. She'd be a perfect choice. Except for one thing.

'Where would she find the money?' Even with Billy's salary as an inspector on the fire brigade together with her earnings, they'd never afford it in a hundred years. 'They're not going to have much stuffed away in the flour bin.'

'I've thought about that. She could give me a little week by week. Everything would stay in my name until she'd paid it all off, but she'd run it and take the profits. I'd keep the kitchen; she'd still buy her bread from me.'

It was a generous offer. Very generous. And keeping the kitchen was smart.

'Have you discussed it with her?'

'Not yet. I wanted your opinion first, Tom.'

He grinned. 'I think the idea's a bobby dazzler.'

Annabelle sighed with relief. 'I was worried you'd think it was silly.'

'No. It's perfect. And you need to do what you feel is right.'

'Do you mean that?'

'Every word.'

'I—' she began, then cocked her head towards Mary, before continuing in a whisper. 'She's fallen asleep. I'll put her to bed.' In the doorway she paused. 'It's funny, isn't it? The way life's different now.'

Funny, he thought? It was bloody wonderful.

FOUR

'We have a murdered man who was involved with George Archer,' Superintendent Kendall said grimly. He puffed on his pipe. 'What was the relationship between Tench and Archer?'

'I don't know yet,' Harper admitted. The super had waved him into his office as soon as he arrived. Ash had joined them a few minutes later. Not Detective Constable Wharton; they'd left him working at his desk. 'The only thing I have is Horseshoe Harry mentioning the pair of them together. That's all.'

'What about you, Sergeant?' Kendall asked. 'What have you discovered?'

'Last night I talked to a few men that Len and me both used to know, sir, to see if they'd kept in touch.' Ash sat erect, hands in his lap, his gaze serious. 'One of them used to see him around in the public houses. He always had a little money to flash, evidently.'

'I thought he lived in a lodging house in Sheepscar?' the superintendent said.

'He did,' Harper answered. 'Always prompt with his bills there.'

'There is one thing.' Ash spoke into the silence. 'The wife reminded me last night. We grew up on the same street, I've told you that, and she did, too, down the other end. She said that Len had an older sister as well as a brother. I'd forgotten that. She's going to ask around.' He grinned. 'One of the women will know where she is. Maybe she can tell us something.'

'It's a start,' Kendall told them. 'George Archer.' He pulled his pipe from his mouth and eyed it thoughtfully. 'It'll be a big feather in our cap if we can collar him. He's got away with too much.' He looked pointedly at Harper. 'I want to know the link between him and Tench. We've got the body, now let's get the man.'

As they started to rise, the superintendent gestured for Harper to stay. 'Close the door, Tom. I want to tell you something.' The inspector waited as Kendall put a match to his pipe and puffed it into life again. 'About ten years ago I was working on a murder. I was just a sergeant back then. We were certain Archer had done it but we never managed to prove a thing.'

'I don't understand, sir. What does this have to do with Tench's murder? We don't even know that Archer was involved with this.'

'He has to be,' Kendall said with certainty. 'It took organization to get that body out there, and in a boat. Archer could arrange that.' The superintendent paused. 'Do you know where he lives?'

'No.'

'In one of those big houses that looks out over the lake at Roundhay Park. He could have watched it all from his window.'

That was interesting. But it certainly wasn't proof. 'I still don't see how that connects to a murder ten years ago.'

Kendall pursed his lips. 'Back then, he always seemed to know what I was going to do. Every single move. I was certain he must have someone on the force letting him know what was happening.'

Harper was silent. There were bent coppers, plenty of them, men who let little things go in exchange for a small payment or a good time with a willing girl. But in his years on the force he'd never come across someone willing to sell information to a criminal that way.

'Do you know who it was?'

'I had my suspicions. But never enough to be able to do anything about it.'

Harper heard the frustration in the man's voice. 'Who was it?'

'Sergeant Deacon over at C Division. He's based out in Headingley now. Like I say, I could never prove it. I've kept a weather eye on him since. He does all right for himself. Nothing too fancy, perhaps a bit more than a sergeant should have. Always claimed his wife was left some money. But I'm as sure as I can be he's the man Archer has working on the force.' He waited for a heartbeat. 'One of them, anyway.'

'One of them?' The inspector raised an eyebrow.

'Archer's always been careful. He probably has someone in every division.'

Christ, Harper thought. He didn't know what to make of that.

'Anything that comes close to Archer, I want you to play your cards very near to your chest. Whatever information you find is shared between you, Ash, and myself. No one else.'

Harper nodded, too stunned to think clearly.

'I want you to keep all your files, everything you have on this, locked up when you're not in the office. Away from prying eyes.'

'Yes, sir.'

'Give me a verbal report every day.'

'What about Wharton?' Harper asked.

'Keep him out of this for now,' the superintendent ordered.

'You don't think—'

'No,' he answered. 'But the fewer who know, the better.'

'Yes, sir. Do you really believe Archer's got his fingers that deep into us?'

'I hope not. But I'm not going to take any chances.' Kendall sighed. 'Make sure the sergeant knows, too. But not a word to anyone about Deacon. That's strictly between you and me.'

The file on Archer was almost six inches thick, years of papers piled one on top of the other. Reading everything could take a week. Harper skimmed through, drawing out a few letters and notes, then passing them to the sergeant.

The rumour was that he'd committed his first murder when he was just ten; a shopkeeper who clipped him round the ear when he came in and demanded money. No one had ever appeared in court for the death.

He'd been arrested and questioned more often than Harper had enjoyed hot dinners. But try as the police might, nothing had ever stuck and Archer always walked out with a smirk on his face.

Archer was clever, with the instincts to turn crime into real money. He kept two men close, lads he'd grown up with, both of them utterly loyal, ready to keep him safe whatever the cost. They did what he ordered, no questions asked. But if the gossip that floated around was true, he still liked doing his own dirty work, took pleasure in it.

He'd become a rich man, living in Lakeside, one of the big mansions built inside Roundhay Park. He had married a girl from Somerset Street; they had a boy and two girls, all of them raised to enjoy the good life, not to follow in their father's footsteps.

The bodyguards lived in, always there, always ready.

George Archer was untouchable. Or so he believed.

'Sir?' Wharton asked as Harper closed the file.

'What is it?'

'I went and talked to the captain of that dredger first thing this morning. I asked him if it was possible that all the movement could have caused the body to shift somewhere else. With the current, I mean. It would explain why we haven't found the rest of her.'

His words came out tentatively, nervously. Inside, Harper smiled. He remembered being like that when he started in plain clothes. Full of ideas and eager to prove himself but scared of saying anything for fear of appearing stupid.

'What did he say?'

'He thought it could have happened like that. Probably not too far if she did, though. They have to go over the area under Leeds Bridge today, but tomorrow he's going to try along the canal.'

'It's worth exploring.' He saw Wharton beam and blush. 'Are you going to see the sister today? What's her name again?'

'Cordelia. Yes, sir, I am.'

The lad had good experience on the beat. Working as a detective was entirely different, though. It took more imagination, more doggedness. If he had the instincts, he'd learn.

'Talk to her without the mother around if you can. Don't try and push her. Make her feel comfortable, she'll say more that way.'

'Yes, sir.'

'What do you think happened?' the inspector asked.

'I don't believe we can say until we have a body, sir.'

The young man hadn't even hesitated before answering. Good, Harper decided. That meant he'd been thinking about it and looking at the possibilities. The way a detective should.

'You're right.' He put the Archer file into one of his desk drawers and locked it. 'Let me know what Cordelia says.'

'Do you think your missus will have any luck?'

'Like as not. The way they all gossip, she probably has chapter and verse by now.'

They were sitting in the café at the market. He could hear the traders calling their wares outside as they sat with their cups of tea – 'Come on, luv, twelve for a tanner, and you'll not find better than that.' 'Last of this year's rhubarb, lovely and sweet, cheap to you and you know you want a bargain, luv.' It was a good place to talk, away from the station, a change from the four grubby walls of the office.

'Let's start by talking to her, then.'

It could be a way in. No one who worked for Archer was

going to say much; they'd be too scared. He was about to rise
when a hand clapped him on the shoulder.

'Inspector Harper and Sergeant Ash.'

A familiar voice. Tom Maguire, the union organizer and one
of the men behind the new Independent Labour Party.

'Mr Maguire,' he acknowledged with a nod. Maybe it was all
the work, but the man didn't look well. His face was paler than
usual and he'd grown thinner, almost gaunt, his red hair starting
to recede. 'How are you?'

'Fair to middling.' He smiled, showing stained teeth. 'I just
wanted to say I think the Society made the right choice with
Annabelle.' He'd grown up just a street away from her on the
Bank.

'She's looking forward to it.'

'I just wish the party involved women more, but . . .' He looked
pained.

'But that's how it is?' Harper said.

'For now,' Maguire agreed sadly, then brightened. 'That will
change. You must be busy. A body in a lake? That's
something.'

'It is.' A sudden thought struck him. 'Do you know anyone
who works for George Archer?'

'I do not,' Maguire insisted, 'and I'd rather keep it that way.
Is he involved?'

'You know I can't say.' He stared at the man. 'And neither
can you.'

'Point taken, Inspector.' He began to cough, bringing out a
handkerchief and spitting into it. 'I'll leave you gentlemen to
work. Give Annabelle my best, please.'

'Does your wife have a new venture, sir?' Ash asked as they
walked past the Town Hall and out towards Burley Road. Shanks's
pony was quicker than waiting for an omnibus.

'They've asked her to be the secretary to the Suffrage Society.'

The sergeant raised his eyebrows. 'Isn't that a lot to take on,
what with your little one?'

'She'll manage. You've met her.'

Ash chuckled. 'Indeed she will, sir. She's a force of nature, if
you don't mind me saying so.'

He didn't mind at all; it was perfectly true.

'There's something I'd better tell you, about this Leonard Tench case . . .'

'What about Wharton, sir?' Ash asked when he'd finished his explanation. 'Do we trust him?'

They were approaching the house, one of a row of through terraces on a street rising up the hill. The front step gleamed, neatly donkeystoned, and the windows shone; as they passed he could still smell the vinegar used to clean them.

'No,' Harper answered. 'The super's orders.'

'Fair enough.' The sergeant nodded. 'Here we are, sir. This one.'

Inside they went straight through to the kitchen at the back. He could hear footsteps moving around upstairs.

'She'll be down in a moment. Cup of tea, sir?'

How many tables just like this had he sat around since he became a copper? How many sculleries had he seen? The familiar blacklead of the Yorkshire range, tin bath hanging on the wall, the flagstone yard outside the window.

A shelf with photographs. A wedding photograph, bride and groom looking awkward, another of a girl.

'Is that Martha?' Harper asked. Ash and his wife had adopted her three years before. How old would she be now? Eleven?

'It is.' He beamed with pride. 'She's in service, out in Horsforth. Comes home to see us every other Sunday when she's off. It was that or the mills, really.'

He knew. It was the fate of most girls. No chance and little future. All the things Annabelle was trying to change.

The door opened and Mrs Ash entered. She was a tiny woman, a good twelve inches shorter than her husband, shapely as an hourglass. Her hair was caught up in a bun, her face startlingly, surprisingly beautiful.

'What are you doing having company in here?' she chided, but there was warmth in her voice. 'I just cleaned the parlour.' She shooed them through. 'I'm sorry, Inspector. Half the time he doesn't know what he's doing. I'm Nancy. I don't suppose he's ever told you that.'

Eventually she had them settled, tea in the good china, a buttered scone apiece, still warm from the oven.

'Have you managed to find anything about Tench's sister, Nancy?' Harper asked.

'That I have.' She looked down at the floor. 'Her name's Christina. Turns out she's in the workhouse now. Her children, too, poor loves. Well, them as is young enough.'

'What happened?' Ash wondered. 'I thought she was married.'

'Oh, she was,' Nancy Ash told him. 'But he died and then they had no money coming in.'

It was the old story. Times so hard and desperate that there was nowhere else to turn except the workhouse. The last resort.

'She was older than Len,' Nancy Ash continued. 'Must have been what – seven years?' She looked at her husband.

'Thereabouts,' he agreed.

'So we never had much to do with her when we were growing up. There was Christina, another brother who's dead now, then Len and the parents, that was it. Old Mr and Mrs Tench passed on years back from all I've heard.'

'Who did she marry?'

'Someone called Palmer.' She shrugged. 'No idea who he was. She moved away, that's all I know, and they had five children. He died four years ago. Just fell down in the street and that was that.'

'I don't suppose you managed to find out what contact she and Len had?' Harper asked. It was a long shot, but there was no telling what a group of women could discover.

She gave him a look that seemed to question his intelligence. 'Well, it can't have been much, can it, or he'd have had her out of there. She was family.' Suddenly she blushed. 'I'm sorry.'

He smiled. 'It doesn't matter, honestly.'

'It's your wife who does the work for the suffragists, isn't it?'

'That's right,' he answered.

'Fred's spoken about it. If you ask me, we need more like her.'

'I'll tell her you said so.' From the corner of his eye he looked at Ash. He could never see the man as a Fred.

There was small talk while they finished eating and drinking. Quickly, she gathered up the crockery and saw them out of the door with a swift glance up and down the street.

'Now, don't you be a stranger here, Inspector. I've told Fred before that you'd always be welcome.'

'Thank you.'

*   *   *

From the outside the workhouse looked intimidating. But that
was the intention. It was a few yards up Beckett Street from the
Industrial Training School – the orphanage in everything but
name. The corporation cemetery stood across the road. The little
corner of the city where they dumped the unwanted.

Billy Reed and his wife lived just a few streets away. They'd
passed not far from Annabelle's Burmantofts bakery on the way
out here. Everywhere he went in Leeds, some strand of his life
was there, Harper thought.

The matron had a cold, imperious manner, wearing her uniform
like armour.

'Christina Palmer is here,' she admitted reluctantly.

'I'd like to talk to her alone if I might. It's police business.'
The woman didn't need to know any more than that. The poor
might not have much, but he could leave her a little privacy and
decency.

'I'll have her brought here for you.' She sniffed and pursed
her lips. 'Please don't take too long.'

'Not a pleasant woman, eh, sir?' Ash said into the silence
when they were alone.

Christina Palmer looked sixty but couldn't have been anywhere
near that old. She wore a plain workhouse dress and apron, a
threadbare shawl around her shoulders, strands of lank grey hair
escaping from a stained white cap. Her face seemed ground down,
all the hope vanished from her eyes. She walked with a stoop,
eyes looking meekly down at the ground.

'Please sit down, Mrs Palmer.' It cost nothing to offer a little
kindness. God knew he had nothing else to give her. He pulled a
chair over, on his left side so she'd be speaking into his good ear.

She perched awkwardly, as if she had no right to the comfort,
and gathered her callused hands in her lap. He said gently,
'I'm Detective Inspector Harper with Leeds City Police. This
is Sergeant Ash. I'm afraid we have some bad news about
your brother.'

'Len?' She looked up suddenly, her eyes wild. 'What's happened
to Len?'

'He's dead,' Harper told her. 'I'm very sorry.'

'He can't be. He can't be.'

'I'm afraid it's true.'

'But he's only young,' she protested. He could see it in her eyes, the unwillingness to believe him. If her brother was gone then so was all her hope. She was truly on her own.

'I'm sorry, Mrs Palmer, it's definitely him. But I need to ask you a few questions.'

She was crying soundlessly, the tears running down her cheeks. Harper took a handkerchief from his pocket and passed it to her.

'Not much I can tell you.' Her voice was empty as a husk. 'I haven't seen him in years.' She turned to look at Ash. 'You, I know you, don't I?'

'I was Len's friend when we were little. Alfred Ash. I grew up in Dufton Court.'

'That's right. You always had a dewdrop on your nose.'

'Like as not.' He laughed. 'Even in summer it was always cold down there.'

'It were.' She seemed to shudder at the memory. 'That's why I got married, the first offer I had. Just to get out of there. My Charlie took care of us, too, until he died.'

Harper gave a small nod; better to let Ash handle this.

'When did you last see Len?' the sergeant asked.

'Years.' She frowned. 'Five? He came by the house, drunk as a lord and left ten quid on the kitchen table.'

'That's a lot of money,' Ash said.

It was more than a lot; it was a fortune, more than a maid would earn in a year.

'He said he'd come into some and wanted to share.' She dabbed at her face again with the handkerchief. 'I never saw him again.'

'Did you have a falling-out?'

She was silent for so long that the inspector wondered if she was going to answer.

'No,' she said eventually. 'We were never that close in the first place. After us mam and dad died, I doubt we saw each other three times. Me and my Charlie, we tried to do things right and Len just went his own way. You'd know, being mates with him.'

'I hadn't seen him in years, either.' He thought he could hear a note of regret in Ash's voice.

'Aye, well.'

'Do you know what he was up to?'

'Can't have been anything decent if he had money like that

to throw around, can it? That's what my Charlie said. It's why I was happy to keep my distance.' She stared around the room, confronting her loss. 'Look where it got me.'

'Did you hear anything about Len?'

'No. I didn't want to, neither.' She turned to Harper. 'What about the funeral?'

'I don't know,' he answered. It would likely be in the cemetery across the road, an unmarked grave. 'I'll tell the matron when I find out.' But whether she'd be allowed to go was out of his hands.

'We've still got nothing,' Harper said as they rode on the omnibus back to Millgarth. The day had turned hot, and sweat stuck his shirt to his back. 'What do you think? Was Len Tench one of Archer's enemies or one of his friends?'

'Maybe he was a friend who'd become an enemy,' Ash suggested. A traitor. That was perfectly possible.

'What about that man you mentioned? Bradley. Have you found him?'

The sergeant frowned. 'Not yet, sir. He seems to have vanished into thin air.'

Back at Millgarth, no sooner had they walked through the door than Sergeant Tollman wanted Harper's attention.

'A message came in for you just a few minutes ago, sir. Could you go down to Park Row and have a word with Inspector Reed? He said it's urgent.'

Harper looked at Ash and raised his eyebrows. 'Keep digging. I want to know all about Tench. And see if you can turn up this Bradley.'

What could Billy want, he wondered as he strode out along the Headrow. Harper dodged between people, smelling all the thick summer fumes and soot of the city. In the distance, down the hill, the Town Hall stood proud, its stone a deep black. He could faintly remember a time when the building looked pale and new. But things changed. Everything changed.

Reed had a small office at the fire station. He was sitting behind the desk, his uniform jacket unbuttoned to show a collarless shirt underneath, trousers held up by a pair of wide braces. A cigarette burned in the ashtray and a faded brass spittoon stood in the corner.

'Hello, Billy,' he said.

'Tom.' He looked up. 'I've got something for you.'

Harper settled himself in a chair. 'Nothing much, I hope. I'm already up to my ears with that body from the lake.'

'I know.' He gave a small nod. 'But see what you think. We were called out last night to a warehouse fire on Wellington Street. The lads were there quick enough to stop it doing any serious damage. But there was someone inside. He was dead.'

'Go on.' He didn't see what this had to do with him.

'It was arson. I could smell the paraffin as soon as I walked in. The place was all dry goods, there shouldn't have been a drop of it in the place.'

Inspector Reed pursed his lips. The man had settled well into his new rank, Harper thought. Assured, thoughtful, professional.

'Anyway, the body wasn't badly burned. I sent him off to Dr King. I heard from him a couple of hours ago. The man was killed the same way as your bloke in the lake. Hit on the back of the skull. He thinks it's probably the exact same weapon. He's sent a copy of his report to Superintendent Kendall.'

'That's the last news I needed, Billy.' Harper gave a long sigh. 'I don't suppose you have a name for him?'

'No identification. Nothing at all, no wallet, no keys, no coins. Just a handkerchief in his pocket.'

'Who owns the warehouse?'

'Someone called Goldsmith rents it. I had a word with him earlier. He wasn't behind the fire, I'm sure of that.' Billy had been a good detective; he could trust the man's judgement. 'I'm still looking into who owns the building. I thought you ought to know. It might be something to help you.'

'Or make everything more complicated.' He rubbed his cheeks. 'Thank you, Billy. Can you let me know what you find out about the owner?'

A quick handshake and he was back out on Park Row. Pleasant enough but all the camaraderie of the past had vanished. Now it was professional. Well, there wasn't much he could do about that. Billy had made his decision.

But what he'd just passed on was the last thing Harper needed.

*   *   *

He took Ash with him, down into the harsh smell of carbolic under the police station in Hunslet. Today King was humming loudly, some melody Harper didn't recognize. As they came through the door he gave a small cough.

'I wondered how long before I'd see you.' The doctor reached into his waistcoat pocket and drew out a watch. 'You're quick. I didn't expect you for an hour yet. Inspector Reed must be efficient.'

'He said you think it was the same weapon.'

The doctor nodded, wisps of hair flying around his skull. 'If I were a betting man I'd put money on it. Does that satisfy you?'

'Definitely.' If King was that certain it had to be true.

'My guess is that it was a metal bar of some kind. Rounded. Just like the other killing. I imagine the fire was supposed to destroy the body, but the brigade extinguished it before it could do much.'

'Was he killed there?' Harper asked.

'Probably. It's never easy to move a corpse.' He walked over to the table. A human shape was evident under a stained sheet. King drew it back. 'That's your man, Inspector. Whoever he might be.'

He heard an intake of breath beside him.

'What is it?' Harper asked, turning to Ash.

'Christ, it's Ted Bradley,' the sergeant said with quiet horror.

'Tell me about him,' Harper said as they marched hurriedly back over Crown Point Bridge. The river stank, and the sun tried to burn through the haze of smoke that pushed down on the city.

'He was more Len's friend than mine. He must have already been at the chemical works when we started there. Ted was older than us, thought he knew everything. Nice enough, but he'd get the hump easily. Not too bright, if you get my drift, sir.'

The sergeant sounded stunned as he dragged out the memories.

'Were you close?'

'We knocked about a bit until I left. Len liked him more than I did. There was something about Ted . . . I kept my distance a bit. I never knew where I was with him. After I left the works I hadn't seen him again until just now.'

'It's starting to look as if he and Tench were in something together. Is there anything else you can think of?'

'Nothing really, sir. Like I said, I've been looking for the last day and couldn't find hide nor hair of him. Not a sniff.' He sighed. 'Bloody hell, sir, eh? Bloody hell.'

'Billy?'

Elizabeth was sitting at the kitchen table when he entered, a cup of tea sitting cold and undrunk in front of her. He could hear her two youngest playing upstairs.

'You look worried.' He kissed the top of her head and took the chair next to her. 'What's wrong?'

'Nothing.' She looked up in confusion, her eyes bright. 'Something's very right. I think it is, anyway. Annabelle came by for a natter today. She's decided to sell the shops.'

'What?' She'd only opened the most recent one a year or two before. 'Why?'

'She says she doesn't have time, what with the little one and the politics and the pub.' She raised her eyes, biting her lip. 'The thing is, she wants me to buy them.'

'You?' The idea stunned him 'How? We don't have the money for anything like that.' Annabelle Harper had to know it. He made a better wage now he'd been promoted, but nowhere near enough to afford to buy a business.

'I know. She had a suggestion. We'd agree an amount and I'd pay her a little every week until it was all done. She'd sort of keep control but I'd make all the decisions.'

At first he didn't know what to say. It was so generous that it made him suspicious. What if the bakeries were failing? Was that why she wanted to be rid of them?

'Don't be daft,' Elizabeth told him. 'I manage them all, I know they're little goldmines. I said I wanted to talk to you before we decided anything. What do you think? We'd have our own shops. Who'd have thought that?' He could hear the excitement in her voice, the hope.

He smiled. 'Have you started doing your sums yet?'

She smiled back and shook her head. 'I wanted to hear what you thought first.'

Reed put his hand over hers. 'If you want to do it, I'm happy.'

'I want to but it scares me, Billy. I don't know. I just don't know.'

Even before he opened the door, Harper could make out the murmur of voices in the parlour. Annabelle must have guests. He turned the knob and entered, seeing her on the far side of the table, bouncing Mary gently on her lap as she listened intently. Tom Maguire had one of the other chairs, next to Miss Ford, the head of the Suffrage Society, her hair in a severe bun on the back of her head, and beyond her a man he didn't know.

'Inspector,' Maguire said with a smile and a short cough, 'you've caught us red-handed, plotting the overthrow of society.'

'You remember Miss Ford,' Annabelle said, 'and this is Mr Marles.'

The stranger stood and extended a hand. He was tall, hair neatly pomaded and parted, with whiskers down to his jawline and eyes blinking behind thick glasses. Broad cheeks and a ready smile. He was wearing a Barran's suit that was slightly too tight, and a shirt with a fold-over celluloid collar.

'Call me Arthur,' he said as he extended his hand. 'Grand to meet you. We're just talking about the pamphlet.'

'Pamphlet?' He didn't have a clue what the man meant.

'It's Tommy Maguire's idea,' Annabelle explained. 'We're going to produce something about the conditions in Leeds. The way people really live.'

'It's for the Independent Labour Party,' Maguire said. 'To show what things are like for the people who live here.' He coughed again. 'Maybe we'll open a few eyes.'

'It sounds like a good idea,' Harper agreed. But that would depend on how many read it.

'Mr Marles is an experienced writer.' Miss Ford raised her eyes. 'He's very sympathetic, and we all thought he'd do a good job. The Suffrage Society is going to prepare everything for the section on prostitution.' The inspector glanced at his wife. She didn't know anything about the girls who sold themselves, did she? 'I thought Mrs Harper would be perfect to lead the section on the problems of drink.' Annabelle gave a smile, nervous, shy. Miss Ford lifted her teacup. Her eyes widened as an idea seemed to strike her. 'Perhaps you could help us too, Inspector.'

'Me?' What use could he be? He wasn't even sure he wanted to be involved. He was safer out of it.

'You know about crime. About gambling.'

'That's my job,' he agreed. 'But I'm not sure if I'd be allowed . . .'

'Would it help if I talked to the chief constable?' Miss Ford asked.

'I don't know.'

He moved around the table, picking up Mary, wanting to be out of the parlour and away from the conversation. 'I'll just take her out of here so you can continue.' He rested a hand on his wife's shoulder and gave it a small squeeze before walking off with their daughter.

He didn't hear her come into the kitchen. The guests had all left in a tramping of feet on the stair. Mary was back in the parlour, happily playing with her blocks. Harper filled the kettle and put it on the range before emptying the teapot and washing it out. When she touched him on the neck he started in surprise.

'I said your name when I came in,' Annabelle told him.

'I'm sorry. I . . .' He didn't need to explain. They both knew. Deaf in his right ear. Not completely, but close enough. There was nothing to be done about it. He'd seen the doctors; he knew the truth.

She kissed his temple.

'You're going to be a writer now?' he asked.

'No, I'm not,' she said with utter certainty. 'Mr Marles or one of his friends is going to do that. I just have to put everything together for them, thank God.'

'You can do that.'

'Maybe. They want facts and figures and tales. All the damage drink does to people every year. But the idea's good.' She put a hand on his arm. 'If people do read it and start to understand what it's like to be poor, maybe they'll listen to the Labour candidates. It could change things.'

'Maybe.' He didn't hold out much hope that many would want to know. People were too wrapped up in themselves.

'It's still going to be a big chance, Tom. We've got to do something. They really want you working on it, too.'

'God only knows why.' But perhaps there was some sense to it, he thought. He saw the way people lived. Survived. He knew better than most. Still, it would never happen. The chief wouldn't allow him to take part: far too political. And he was grateful for that. They might not want to hear some of the home truths he'd be likely to tell.

He changed the subject. 'Did you think Maguire looked poorly?'

'He says it's just a summer cold.' She shrugged and then her face brightened. 'I made the offer to Elizabeth today.'

'Really? What did she say?' Steam started to rise from the kettle's spout. He brought the pot over and poured in a dash of water to warm it. Empty it again before spooning in the tea leaves. Annabelle watched approvingly.

'She wants time to think about it. Wouldn't you?'

A little yell came from the parlour and she dashed out, returning with Mary in her arms. The girl was crying, but it was half-hearted, astonishment more than real pain. Harper bent and kissed her forehead where the skin looked a little red and the tears instantly stopped. Just a tumble. She'd had them before and there'd be plenty more to come.

'With a magic touch like that you ought to have a job as a governess.' Annabelle's eyes were full of mischief as she stepped back and assessed him. 'Mind you, I'm not sure how you'd look in a dress.' She bounced Mary gently in her arms. 'Would you like to see your Daddy like that?'

'Give over,' he told her with a laugh. Then, more seriously, 'Do you think Elizabeth will accept?'

'I hope she does. I spent a lot of time building those businesses up, I don't want to sell them to a stranger. She'll do a good job and it's a fair offer.'

'What if she doesn't want to do it?'

'Then I'll have to think again.' Annabelle gave a sigh. 'I'd keep them if I could. But honestly, Tom, if I'm going to be working with the suffragists, have this little one running me ragged and trying to keep the pub in order, something has to give.'

'We could always get a nurse,' he suggested. They'd discussed it quite a few times before.

'No,' she replied firmly, the start of a blaze in her eyes. It was always her answer. 'If all the women round here can raise their children without one, so can I.'

'It's up to you.' They could afford it quite easily; they already had Ellen, the cook-housekeeper. But it was a matter of pride for her to be able to do everything she could herself. Around here what she couldn't afford was to look as if she was getting above herself.

But it was strange: the more she took on, the more Annabelle seemed to blossom. During the day she moved from one thing to another with grace, always capable, always thinking, reading one of her political books whenever she had a spare minute. She was as much at home with a local councillor or some bigwig from this Independent Labour Party as she was with the crowd downstairs in the bar.

She didn't only think about the present; she kept her eyes on the future, too. Six months before, when Mary was suckling one evening, she had looked down at the baby and said with certainty, 'This one will have the vote.'

'Have you been reading the tea leaves again?' Harper teased her.

'I don't need to, Tom,' she replied seriously. 'It'll happen sooner or later; it's bound to. We might not be around to see it, but she will.'

He'd never forgotten that. It had sounded as if she'd seen something through the years. He wanted to believe her, but who really knew? And he had too many other things on his mind. Len Tench. Ted Bradley. George Archer.

FIVE

Harper wrote a note to Billy Reed. He was officially taking over the investigation of Bradley's death.

Bradley and Tench had been in something bad together; he could take that as read. Now the police needed to discover if anyone else had been with them, then keep whoever it was alive while they found the killer. And they needed to know exactly what they'd been up to.

He'd already sent Ash out to talk to people again, hunting for each tiny scrap of information. As soon as Harper finished his report he'd be back out there, too.

'Sir?'

Wharton had entered without him even noticing; he'd been too engrossed in his thoughts.

'Did you talk to the sister? Cordelia?'

'I did, sir.' The lad's face gave too much away, Harper thought. He could see the doubts behind his eyes. That would pass; he'd learn to keep it all hidden.

'You sound as if something's wrong.'

'It's just that some of the things she said don't chime with what the mother said.'

The inspector put down his pen and leaned back in his chair. 'You'd better sit down and tell me about it.'

According to Cordelia, Charlotte had enjoyed going out with young men. She'd hidden it from her parents, of course, knowing they'd never approve. But she'd confided in her sister. There was no particular young man, it seemed; the girl liked to flirt and tease before moving on to someone new.

'Was she able to give you any names?' Harper had been making a few notes.

'No, sir,' Wharton replied slowly. 'And that's not all. She told me that Charlotte was often quiet, too. Dark moods, she called them. She didn't come out and say it, but it was like she was hinting Charlotte wasn't quite right in the head.'

'And you had nothing about any of this from the mother? Nothing at all?'

'No.'

The inspector thought for a minute.

'Go back and have a word with the mother again. Don't tell her where you learned all this. Just say you've heard a couple of rumours. Ask her. Chances are she'll deny it all, but watch her, especially the eyes.'

'Yes, sir.' Now he had orders, Wharton looked relieved.

'See what you can find.'

Wharton left, and Harper had just locked the file on the Bradley killing away when the superintendent called him into his office.

'Two of them murdered the same way,' Kendall said. 'And they knew each other.'

'They both knew Ash, too. A long time ago.'

'Anything to connect them to Archer yet?'

Harper shook his head. 'Not a thing. All I ever had was that tip from Horseshoe Harry. No one else has mentioned Archer.' He shrugged helplessly. 'You couldn't fill a thimble with what we've learnt so far.'

'Any ideas?'

'Tench and Bradley met at the chemical works. I'm going out there to ask a few questions. What worries me is there could be someone else walking around with a death sentence over his head. Or already killed, for all we know. If he's out there and we find him, we can keep him safe and find out what's happening.'

'And if it was just the two of them?' the superintendent asked.

'Then we're back to the beginning.'

'Keep working on that connection to Archer.'

'There might not even *be* one,' Harper pointed out.

'It's there,' Kendall told him. 'I can feel it. It was sheer luck we ever found the first body. As soon as he's discovered, a second turns up dead. Same method, and a fire to try and cover it up. How many people in Leeds have the power to sort out something like that?'

'There's Charlie Gilmore, Tosh Walker . . .' Harper began.

'It's not Gilmore's style, you know that. And you put Tosh away three years ago. It's Archer.'

'I'll keep looking.' It was all he could say.

'Remember, Tom, that body in the lake was in the London papers.' His voice was grave. 'They'll expect us to find answers.'

'Yes, sir.' He hadn't forgotten. But he was going to be thorough.

'And not a word.' The super tapped the side of his nose. 'Just you, me, and Ash.'

'What if I need more men?'

'I'll help if you need me. It'd do me good to get out of here.'

Harper stepped out into the noise of the city. The rattle of carts, the squeak of wheels, the metallic groan of the omnibuses and trams, the clop of hooves on cobbles. Voices everywhere. At least his hearing muted it all; everything seemed to be at a remove, as if it was coming from a distance.

Without even thinking, he ended up at the café by the market, sipping a cup of tea. No one came near him. Even Tom Maguire simply looked, nodded and took another table.

He didn't know how long he'd been there when a chair scraped and someone sat across from him.

'I've been looking for you, sir,' Ash said with a smile.

'Anything?' He took another sip of the tea. Stone cold. He waved for two more cups.

'Maybe. I ran into one of the lads from the chemic. It seems that Len and Ted were often seen with a chap called Morley.'

'Did you know him, too?'

'He must have started there after I left.'

'Is he still at the works?'

'No, sir. It's *Eustace Morley*, sir.' He said it as if everyone should recognize the name.

'Who?'

'The boxer, sir. You must have heard of him.'

Of course. Now he remembered. He'd heard people talking and seen pieces in the newspaper a few times. Everyone seemed convinced that he was one of the best fighters in Leeds, a man with a future in the ring.

'Do you know where he lives?'

'Not yet, sir. I'm working on it. He's been gone from the chemic a year or more, same as the others. But he spent a lot of time with Len and Ted. Thick as thieves, someone said.' He grimaced and shook his head.

'We'd better find out, and see if he's still alive. It sounds like it all began at the works, doesn't it?'

'Whatever it was, sir.'

'Let's go back out there and talk to the managers.'

'That's what I was thinking, sir.'

'As soon as you've drunk up.'

As they walked through the gates of the chemical works the smell seemed to descend like a cloud. He felt it stinging in his throat and his lungs.

'How did you stand it?' he asked Ash.

'Like anything else, sir. You get used to it.'

'Go and talk to more of the men here. See if there's anything they can add.'

'Yes, sir.'

'Why don't we meet at the Victoria when we're done?' It was close, and perhaps he'd have a minute or two with Mary.

'Good enough, sir.'

The people in the office seemed to bounce him from pillar to post. First a clerk, who made him wait to see a senior clerk, then twiddling his thumbs until one of the managers had time to see him.

Mr Hardisty carried the prissiness of a man certain about everything in his life. Someone with destiny. His hands were spotless, the nails pared short, and his face was clean-shaven. He wore a modern three-button suit, his high wing collar the only concession to tradition.

'I understand you wish to learn about some of our former employees, Inspector.' The man perched on the edge of his chair, elbows on a desk where blotter and pens were carefully aligned.

'Three of them actually, sir. I gave your clerk their names. Leonard Tench, Edward Bradley and Eustace Morley.'

'Mr Morley was our most famous employee.' He said it with equal measures of pride and disdain. 'I have our information on all of them here.' Hardisty patted three thin folders and gave a quick smile. 'You understand that they haven't been employed here for a while.'

'Of course. I'd like to take those folders if I might, sir.'

'I'm not sure I'm happy with that.' Hardisty had thin lips; when he pursed them they seemed to disappear altogether.

'Two of those men have been murdered. The third might be in danger.' He watched the man blanch. He paused. 'I'm sure you understand.'

Hardisty pushed the files across the desk and gave a small cough. 'We'd like them back when you've finished with them, if that's possible.'

Harper was already picking them up as he stood. 'I'll see what I can do, sir.'

*   *   *

'She's out with the baby, Tom,' Dan the barman told him as he walked into the pub.

'Did she say where she was going?'

'Up to Burmantofts.' The man finished pouring the beer, took the money and turned back to him. 'She said she had some business there.'

Of course. With Elizabeth. Upstairs, Ellen shooed him out of the kitchen as he started to make tea. She'd just finished cleaning and she wasn't about to let any man make a mess in there.

Instead he pushed a pile of books aside, sat at the table and began going through the folders.

Ted Bradley first. Born in 1863, at nine years old he'd gone from school straight to work at the chemical plant. Disciplined three times over the years, all for minor things, and docked wages here and there for lateness. His first address had been out in Meanwood, then six years ago he'd moved to Roseville Terrace. Married? Into lodgings? He made a note of the address; they'd try there later. A year ago he'd handed in his notice at the works. And that was all there was.

He opened the next file: Eustace Morley. Started at the factory six years before. Fined regularly, everything from lateness to sloppy work. Several times for fighting. Sacked a year earlier after threatening a manager. An address close to the cavalry barracks.

And finally Leonard Tench, but the paperwork told him nothing they didn't already know. He'd left three years before, when he went to prison. A note said Do Not Rehire. Rarely late, but doubts about his honesty, suspected of having light fingers.

He was sitting thoughtfully when Ellen brought a pot of tea and a plate of sandwiches. She always cut the bread as thick as doorstops and slathered on the dripping.

'That'll feed you up,' she told him. 'Annabelle would kill me if I let you go hungry.'

'I don't think there's any danger of that.'

'You just make sure you eat it up.' It was part advice, part demand. He grinned.

'You're going to have to feed Sergeant Ash, too,' Harper said. 'He'll be here soon.'

'I'm sure we can manage,' she sniffed.

He felt the footsteps on the stairs before he heard them, then the door opened and Ash came in and sat across from him. A cup was already set, a full plate waiting, and he looked at it hungrily.

'Go on, it can wait until you've eaten.'

'Thank you, sir. Be good to get the taste of the plant out of my mouth.'

It was five minutes before he'd finished, washing the meal down with a long swig of tea.

'What did you manage to find out? The files have the basics, but nothing about who they were.'

'There are still plenty there who remember them. One or two who recall me, too,' he added ruefully. 'Most of them had time for Len and Ted. If they had something rum going on, no one seemed to know about it. They'd go out for a drink with the lads, just the usual, really.' He shrugged. 'People were sorry to see them go.'

'What about Morley?'

Ash sighed. 'Different kettle of fish altogether, sir. He wasn't too well-liked, although he got along fine with Len and Ted for some reason. People were scared of him, if you ask me. They still went to see him fight, mind.'

'I've never followed boxing.' Half his working life had been spent dealing with people who'd been beaten. Why would he want to see more of it?

'Morley's good,' the sergeant said. 'I watched him once, in '91. They held it in that old barn near the bottom of Lower Briggate. Packed the place. He was up against John Coyne. Beat him, too. No one expected that.'

'He was disciplined at the works a few times for brawling.'

'That sounds about right from all I heard. Most of them weren't sorry when he was sacked; wondered why it took so long, really.'

'We'd better go and find him. Leave the others for now. They're dead, he's still alive.'

'We hope he is, anyway, sir.'

Number five, Beaufort Place. Less than five minutes' walk from the Victoria. Bricks the colour of soot and smoke, the same as all the neighbours. The thin, dirty stream of Gipton Beck at the end of the street, where boys were playing; running, laughing, fishing hopefully.

The woman who answered the door looked weary, drained by the heat of the day, exhausted by life. Her hair hung lank over a faded cotton shawl, thin arms crossed over a small body, her face drawn, so pale she was almost grey.

'Eustace Morley? He's not lived here since they let him go from the works,' she told them. 'I said to him, no wage, no room. It was bad enough when he was earning, rolling in at all hours. Loud when he wanted, as well. But I had to put me foot down somewhere.'

'Do you know where he went?' Ash asked. He had the kindly tone that put women at ease and made them respond.

'I do not,' she insisted. 'I heard he'd gone up by Clay Pit Lane, but God only knows if he's still there.'

'What about his friends? Did you know any of them?'

'I only allow tenants on the premises,' the woman said with a loud sniff. 'It's a rule.' She looked at one of them, then the other. 'You know he was a boxer, don't you?'

'Yes,' Harper replied.

'He used to go down somewhere off Lovell Road for that.' She hesitated. 'But if you want to arrest him for summat, I'd be careful. He's even bigger than you,' the woman said, nodding at Ash, 'and he's good with them fists of his.'

'Which do you want?' the inspector asked as they walked back to Roundhay Road. 'To try and find where he trained or where he worked?'

'Trained, I think, if you don't mind, sir. Chances are he went to Tommy Dooley's gym. I'll try there first. If not, they'll know where to find him. I've not seen anyone box in a while. It might be an education.'

Harper pulled the old watch from his waistcoat pocket. 'Let's meet at Millgarth at five.'

'What if I find Morley, sir? What do you want me to do with him?'

'Bring him in. We need to talk to him properly. It's for his own safety.'

'And if he doesn't want to come?'

'Make him.'

A grim smile crossed Ash's face. 'Yes, sir. It can't be worse than when we had that Buffalo Bill Cody fellow here last year.'

The American had brought his Wild West circus to town the September before, performing down at Cardigan Fields. Harper had taken his family to the event. Mary was no more than a few months old. Plenty of excitement, riding and shooting. A proper spectacle with real cowboys and Indians. But the true excitement came later.

Harper had been off duty, but Ash had told the tale often enough. Cody and some of the cowboys had gone into the Three Legs on the Headrow for a drink. One whisky turned to several, then tempers began to unravel. The sergeant had been the one who'd waded in and ended things. Five arrested for affray, and Bill the cowboy left with a host of bruises and battered pride for his trouble. But not a mark on the policeman.

'Let's hope not, anyway.'

SIX

The quickest way to Wade Lane was on foot, up the hill west of Sheepscar. Faster than catching one tram into town and another going out the other way. But by the time he reached Carlton drill ground Harper was sweating in the July heat.

A pub was always a good place to begin. If Morley lived in the neighbourhood, people would know him. A boxer would be famous in all the streets around his home.

The Mason's Arms stood directly across the road. Inside it was all shadows, with the smell of stale beer and smoke that clung to the ceiling. A few customers were scattered in the corners, quiet drinkers keeping themselves to themselves with a glass or two teased out to see them through the day.

He bought lemonade from a suspicious barman, grateful for the tartness of the drink. He knew full well that the man had made him for a copper. That wasn't a problem; he was proud of the fact.

'Eustace Morley,' he said as he put the empty glass back on the bar.

'What about him?'

'I'd like to know where to find him.'

'Try over there.' He tilted his head towards the far corner where someone sat, half-hidden in the shade. 'If he wants to talk to you.'

Sometimes luck smiled, he thought. Just not often enough when you were on the force. But this saved him hours of trailing from address to address, following one empty lead after another. He walked across the bar, out of the sunlight, his eyes adjusting, until he was standing in front of a big man.

Morley had a shaved head, with something rubbed on his scalp to make it glisten. The only hair was a thick moustache over his upper lip. Massive, scarred hands held a newspaper.

'Hello, Eustace. I've been looking for you.'

Morley pursed his mouth and stared, eyes wary. 'You don't look like a sporting man.' He had a rasp of a voice, as if someone had taken a file to his throat.

'I'm with the police. Detective Inspector Harper.'

'So?' He didn't look worried or frightened.

Harper sat, his eyes on the man. 'Len Tench. Ted Bradley.'

Morley waited a few seconds, expecting more. Finally he said, 'Go on. What about them?'

'They're friends of yours, aren't they?'

'I know them.' It was as much as he'd admit.

'They're both dead. Someone murdered them.'

They hadn't released the names to the press. He watched Morley's face for a reaction. Nothing. It was like staring at a block of stone. Finally the man blinked once and pursed his mouth again.

'That's . . .' He sat back on the chair, head cocked to the side. 'Are you sure?'

'I'm certain,' the inspector told him.

'Why's that? Why would anyone want to kill them?' He didn't look stunned or shocked by the news. The only expression was the incomprehension in his voice.

'I was hoping you could tell me. After all, they're friends of yours.'

'I don't know.' He shook his head. 'I really don't know.'

'I hope you can work it out, Mr Morley. Because I think there's a good chance you'll be next.'

Those words seemed to hit him. 'Me?' he asked disbelievingly. 'Why?'

'For the same reason your friends were killed.'

'But . . .' Morley took a breath. 'Who killed them?'

'We don't know yet.'

'How did they die?'

'They were both hit with a metal bar that crushed their skulls.' He nodded at the newspaper on the table. 'Did you read about the body in the lake in Roundhay Park?'

The boxer nodded dumbly.

'That was Tench. And then someone tried to get rid of Ted Bradley's body in a fire. The brigade put it out.'

'God.' He'd turned pale. The man raised a hand to the barman for a drink and waited as he brought a glass of brandy. Morley downed it in a single gulp.

'I think you'd better tell me what the three of you have been up to.'

'Us? What makes you think we've done anything?' His colour was returning and there was a strain of defiance in his voice.

'They weren't murdered for nothing, Mr Morley.' Harper waited, sitting forward, elbows on his knees. Whatever Tench and Bradley had done, the boxer was part of it. He could feel it. 'Look, I don't care what it was. No charges.'

'I don't believe you,' Morley said flatly.

'I want whoever killed them,' Harper told him. 'The rest isn't important.'

The boxer lit a cigarette. He seemed in control of himself again, impassive, impervious.

'Do you know how many fights I've had, Inspector?'

'No.' It didn't matter and he didn't care.

'Sixteen. I won fourteen of them with knockouts, put Willie Morn down in three rounds. The two who stayed awake both threw in the towel.' He recited his achievements with pride. 'Do you really think I'd let anyone get close enough to kill me?'

Harper banged his fist down on the table, making the glass jump. 'Don't be so bloody stupid. An iron bar's not like a fist.'

He paused long enough to let the words sink in, hearing the urgency in his own words. 'It doesn't matter how tough you are. You wouldn't stand a chance. For God's sake, all I'm trying to do is keep you alive and find whoever murdered your friends.' The inspector exhaled slowly. 'I need to know what Tench and Bradley were doing. You too, if you're involved. And you're going to tell me.'

'What makes you think I'm involved?' Morley asked, but the way his gaze shifted around gave him away.

'You are. You knew them at the chemical plant. You were close. And no one makes a living as a boxer. Look at you. I can see the guilt in your eyes.'

The man slowly flexed his right hand, making it into a thick fist and saying nothing.

'I need you to come down to Millgarth with me,' Harper said.

'What if I refuse? You think you can make me?' His tone was lazy and mocking, the voice harsh as sandpaper.

This was it. From here it would either go easily or turn violent and bloody. The inspector kept his face empty, his tone straight-forward and casual.

'Me?' Harper smiled. 'No. I wouldn't even try. But I can go outside and blow this.' He drew the police whistle, on its chain, from his waistcoat pocket. 'In three minutes there'll be enough constables here to make you go. Believe me, if they took you down they wouldn't have to buy their own drinks for a month.'

Still Morley didn't move. He chewed his lip thoughtfully. 'What do I get from it?'

'If you're very lucky, maybe you'll stay alive.'

He came reluctantly, shambling along the street into town. He was a good four inches taller than the inspector, his shoulders far broader. He wore an old jacket, hands pushed into his trouser pockets, battered boots on his feet. People glanced cautiously as they passed.

Harper picked out the advertisements pasted over the gable ends of buildings as they passed – Nestlé's Milk, Whitelock's Ideal Pianos, Quaker Oats. A man shuffled by, hunched under a sandwich board with a sign for Crowther's Good Tailoring.

No more mention of Tench or Bradley. Not until they reached

the station. He wanted the boxer on his side, willing to trust him enough to talk.

'You've won all your fights?'

'Every single one,' Morley told him flatly. 'Taken a few punches, been knocked down once or twice. Queensberry rules. Gloves. But I've done some bare knuckle in my time.' He brought out one of his hands and spread it wide. 'You know how I toughen them?'

'How?'

'Soak them in piss.' His short laugh was like a bark. 'It works, too. I put vinegar on my face. It's supposed to stop the skin cutting so easily.'

'Does it help?'

'Mostly.' He shrugged.

'Why do you do it? Box, I mean.' Harper was genuinely curious.

'I'm good at it,' Morley answered simply. 'And I like to win.'

The Headrow was crowded, but people seemed to part in front of them, as if they were fearful of coming too close.

'You must get hurt, too.'

'Of course.' The man shrugged. 'You expect that, it's part of the game. But if they hurt me, I give them bloody hell in return, and they know it. Never been in anything as bad as Rothery and Asquith, though.'

Harper understood; everyone did, it had filled the papers for days. A bout at Temple Newsam. Rothery had died in the ring and his opponent had been found guilty of manslaughter.

Morley said it so matter-of-factly, as if it was obvious. That was chilling. And Harper began to wonder if the man could have killed his friends. An executioner, not another victim.

At Millgarth he sent a constable to fetch two cups of tea and settled Morley in an empty room, watching as he lit a cigarette and glanced around curiously.

'I need to know what the three of you were doing,' the inspector began.

'Who says we were doing anything?'

'You were.' No doubt in his voice. 'They weren't murdered for the fun of it.'

A knock on the door and the nervous recruit brought the tea. The silence grew until it filled the space.

'Do you know when I lost my first friend?' The boxer rested his elbows on the table. 'I was three. Three. Jem, his name was. We used to play together. I can still remember his face, clear as owt. One day he was there, next day he was poorly, the day after that he was dead. I've probably known as many who are in the ground as are still standing.' He paused, just for a heartbeat. 'Where did you grow up?'

'The Leylands.'

Morley nodded. 'And how bad did you think that was?'

'I never really considered it.'

'I was raised on Marsh Lane. We had an upstairs room. The walls were damp, we had rats. By the time I was six my younger brother and sister had both gone. I've had death all around me since the time I was born.'

'Plenty of people have. What are you trying to say?'

'We're all going to die. You, me, every one of us.' He shrugged.

'Instead of stating the obvious, why don't you tell me who'd want to kill Len and Ted? What were the three of you doing?'

Morley looked at him for a while, stubbed out his cigarette, pulled out the packet and lit another, watching the smoke rise.

'Give me one reason why I should trust you.'

'Because your friends are both dead and whoever did that is going to come after you, too.'

'Then I'll do for him first.' Morley's face was grim. 'I told you, I can look after myself.'

'You can try. I'll come to your funeral,' Harper said. 'What flowers do you want?'

'Why does it matter to you?'

'This is my job. I'm good at it. And I like to win, too.'

The echo of his own words brought a thin smile to the boxer's lips. 'You want to know what we did?'

'I've already told you that.'

'And you won't arrest me for it?'

'You have my word.'

The boxer considered the promise for a moment, then, 'It was threats and kidnap. For money.'

'What do you mean?'

'You asked what we did.' Morley shook his head in frustration. 'I'm telling you.'

'Who?' He hadn't heard of anyone being kidnapped; no one had reported anything.

'It's easy enough. You find someone with a little money. It doesn't have to be a lot. It's better if they don't have too much, really. A businessman, someone who's made a few bob but isn't too sure of himself.'

'Go on.' He listened attentively, turning his head to catch every word.

'It's simple. We got them on their own and told them that if they didn't give us money, bad things would happen to their family. If they told the rozzers, we'd know and they'd wish they'd never been born. Get someone scared enough and you walk away with a few quid.'

There was nothing new in the racket; it was as old as the hills. As long as there were strong men and weak ones it would carry on. But . . .

'Who do you have on the force?' Harper asked sharply.

'No one.' Morley threw his head back and laughed. 'We wouldn't even have known how to start. But say it to someone who's already scared and it works like a bloody charm.' He picked a shred of tobacco from his bottom lip.

'You said kidnap.'

'Aye. Just a few times, mind.' Morley shrugged. 'It was only if they didn't want to hand over any money. We'd grab a child or the wife. That would really terrify them. They knew we meant business then. The usual warning: not a word to you lot or the next thing they'll find is a corpse. It always worked. Always,' he emphasized.

'How often did you do it?'

'The threats? Every couple of months. Fifty pounds can stretch, even split three ways.'

A few of those a year and they should be able to live like kings, not in lodgings.

'And the kidnaps?'

'Only three times. We'd take one of the children. Never hurt any of them, mind. But if it had to go that far, we charged them more.'

Another shrug, as if none of it mattered. Perhaps it didn't; perhaps to him it was no more than another job.

'Who were you working for?'

'No one,' Morley answered in surprise. 'It was Len's idea. Him and Ted would scout out the people, then the three of us would have a word with them. Decent little money spinner. They always paid up the next day. Never failed. Easy as you like.' He wore a satisfied smile.

'When was the last one?'

The boxer thought for a moment. 'A month ago, I suppose. Give or take, anyway.'

'Who was the victim?'

'Some draper. I didn't even know his name.'

He didn't seem to care, either.

'How could you do it if you didn't know his name?'

'Me? I'm only there as a frightener. You don't need a name for that.' He balled one of his hands into a large, scarred fist as an illustration. 'You understand?'

'Where was his shop?'

'Oxford Place, by the Town Hall.'

Time for the big question. 'Do you know George Archer?' It took the man by surprise. For a second his eyes looked worried.

'Why? What does he have to do with it?'

'Do you know him?'

'Course I do.' Morley snorted. His expression was composed again. 'He comes to all my fights. Likes to be seen there. He looks after a couple of fighters. I talked to him a few times.'

'But he doesn't look after you?'

The boxer shook his head. 'He asked if I was interested but I told him no. I'm doing fine on my own.' He gave a quick shrug. 'He's never made a fuss about it.'

'You know his business, don't you?'

'Do I look like I was born yesterday? Everyone knows.'

Thoughts ran through Harper's mind. 'Does he know what the three of you did?'

Morley shook his head. 'No.' His voice was firm. 'We all knew enough to keep quiet. Safer that way.'

'I think you'd better tell me all about this draper,' Harper said. 'And the other kidnappings.'

The tale took an hour, but there was nothing in it that connected to Archer. Morley didn't know the names of most of the victims, only the streets where they had their businesses. He didn't seem to care. It was a job, nothing more or less.

'Going to arrest me now, Inspector?' A smile twitched across the man's face as he finished. 'You've already got my confession.'

'I gave you my word. I'm interested in solving the killings. Nothing else. Whatever it is,' he added darkly.

Morley nodded. 'Then I'm free to go?'

'You'd be safer here,' Harper told him. 'Your friends are both dead.'

He stood. 'I'll trust you more when I walk out of here.'

Harper hesitated. 'I can't protect you outside.'

'You don't need to. I told you, I can look after myself.'

'No,' the inspector insisted, 'you can't.' He banged his hand down on the table. 'I don't give a monkey's what you think, your fists won't save you this time.'

The boxer spoke with slow deliberation, his rasp clear in the room. 'I've got a fight coming up soon. Johnny McGowan from Bradford. It's going to be a right scrap. I can't train if I'm in a cell.'

'And if you don't stay here you might not be around to put on your gloves.' He watched Morley's face. There was no sense of fear or danger.

'Then you'd better arrest me. If you don't, I'm leaving.'

Harper held up his hands. 'I'm not going to stop you. Just think first. Please.'

'I already have. Good day, Inspector. I hope you find your murderer. For Len and Ted. They were good lads, they deserve that.'

SEVEN

He was still writing up the interview when Ash arrived.

'I hear you found him, sir.'

'For all it helped.' He shook his head in frustration and explained. 'Tomorrow we'll start talking to the victims. Maybe one of them took revenge.'

'Or knows someone,' the sergeant suggested.

'That's possible.' They'd assumed that the deaths were linked to Archer. More fool them. Now it seemed like he wasn't involved. 'Damn it.' He looked up hopefully. 'Did you find anything worthwhile?'

'Perhaps we should have a word in the superintendent's office, sir,' Ash said quietly.

'Tom. Sergeant.' Kendall lowered his pen as they entered and closed the door and looked at their faces. 'Well?'

Harper went through what he'd discovered.

'You let him walk out?' the superintendent asked in astonishment.

'He thinks he can take whatever happens.'

'For God's sake, you should have arrested him. You had enough.'

'I'd given my word.'

'And he confessed to a list of crimes,' Kendall pointed out. 'I'd have put him in the cells. At least he'd have been safe.' He ran a hand through his pomaded hair. 'What the hell were you thinking?'

'I did what I thought was best.' He held his head up.

'And we still don't have anything on Archer, do we?'

'No.'

'Do you believe Morley could have killed Tench and Bradley himself?'

'It occurred to me,' Harper admitted. 'It's easy enough to set a fire. But the business up at the lake? A cart, a weight for the body? I don't see it. And he seemed genuinely shocked when I told him they were dead. It passed soon enough but it was real.'

After a moment Kendall nodded his agreement and turned to Ash. 'What about you?'

'I went looking for Morley at Dooley's gym, sir,' Ash began slowly. 'I started talking to the chap who runs the place. He was telling me about someone who's been around there a few times in the last couple of days. Not interested in learning to fight, just watching.'

'Go on.'

'From the description it sounds a lot like Dusty Watson.'

'I thought he was doing four years,' Harper said. 'Is he out?'

'I checked, sir. He was released a fortnight back,' Ash continued. Watson was bad news. He'd been a thug since he was fourteen. He'd worked for half the gangs in Leeds, large and small, making sure people did what they were told and punishing them when they stepped out of line. His last conviction had been for grievous bodily harm. 'I asked in a couple of the pubs.' He paused, making sure he had their attention. 'Watson's been seen drinking with Charlie Gilmore.'

The room fell silent.

'Are you certain?' the superintendent asked finally.

'The landlord recognized him, sir. Not a doubt about it.'

Gilmore led the Boys of Erin, an Irish gang based on the Bank. For years they'd had a feud with Archer and his men.

Kendall stayed quiet for a long time, pulling out his pipe, filling and lighting it, then puffing for a while.

'Do either of you have any idea what's going on here?' he said.

Harper shook his head. The Irish battling against Archer was nothing new. But killing Tench and Bradley? How did that fit with anything? And what about Morley?

No answers. Just a hail of questions. The three of them sat, trying to make sense of it all.

'Tom,' the superintendent said, 'did you believe Morley when he said they weren't working for Archer?'

He was in no rush to answer, weighing everything. The man's words, his expression, the way he held himself.

'Yes,' he replied eventually, 'I did.' The words had felt like the truth. 'I'm positive.'

'Then we'd better start untangling all this. And we're still going to keep it quiet as long as we can, just in case.' Kendall looked at them. 'Only the three of us. Get to it in the morning.'

Back in the detectives' office Wharton was waiting, pacing around the room with an eager look on his face.

'You look like you've found something,' Harper said with a smile.

'Yes, sir.' He stopped for a moment. 'Well, the dredger did. It's Miss Brooker.'

'All of her?' He hadn't expected they'd ever recover the body.

'Yes, sir. She'd drifted into that bit of the canal, after it splits from the river.'

'Sounds like your suggestion was a good one.' The young man blushed at the praise. 'What have you done with her?'

'The body's gone to Dr King.'

'Good.' He nodded. 'The parents?'

'I told them as soon as she was found, sir,' Wharton replied. 'They should be over there now.'

At least they had the rest of their daughter, the inspector thought. They could bury her whole. Then he remembered:

'Weren't you going to talk to the mother again?'

'Yes, sir. I went there first thing. She stood by everything she'd said before. Charlotte was happy enough, no melancholy, and she was certain she wasn't stepping out with anyone. There was one odd thing, though.'

'What's that?' Harper asked.

'According to her, Charlotte and her sister didn't get along. They hadn't since they were young.'

'So one of them could be lying.'

'Or mistaken, sir.'

The inspector smiled. It was the polite reply, especially with a grieving family. He glanced at the clock on the wall. After six.

'We'll go over to Hunslet in the morning and see what the doctor has to say about the cause of death. You're learning well.'

'Thank you, sir.' Wharton blushed again.

'You look all in,' Annabelle told him. She was sitting at the table, patiently feeding Mary with a spoon. As soon as the little girl saw her father she began to wave her hands, grinning and gurgling. And once again his heart melted. He kissed her forehead, trying to avoid the sticky fingers, then put his lips against his wife's cheek, inhaling the scent of her.

'I am. Any more tea in that pot?'

'There should be.'

He took off his suit jacket and folded it over the back of a chair. 'I stopped in with Ash at dinnertime.'

'Ellen told me. Like feeding a pair of shire horses, she said. Come on, poppet, last mouthful. That's good.' She turned back to him and sighed. 'If she keeps on eating this way she's going to be as bad as you when she grows up. I swear she has hollow legs. That's the second helping already.'

Mary laughed as if she understood every word.

'Dan said you'd gone to Burmantofts.'

'It was just a visit. Give them a chance to make a fuss over this one.'

'Has Elizabeth made her decision yet?'

Annabelle shook her head. 'Give the lass some time. She's not going to rush it. I'd do exactly the same. If someone offered me a gift horse I'd want to count all its teeth, too.' She wiped Mary's face, examined her work, then carried on until she was satisfied. 'That's better, now you don't look like half of it ended up all over your mouth.'

Finally she let the squirming girl down on to the floor, and they watched her walk directly to play with a pile of wooden blocks.

'How long before she makes up her mind, do you think?' he asked.

'As long as it takes.' She stroked the back of his hand. 'It's not like there's a huge rush. A few weeks longer won't make any difference. Whatever she wants to do, it'll be easier than going through these bye-laws for the Labour Party.' Annabelle shook her head and pointed at a small pile of books on top of the piano. 'I've never seen hairs split so many ways.' She raised her head. 'Oh, I meant to tell you, I'll be out Saturday evening. They've asked me to speak at a suffragist meeting. Will you be at home?'

'I'll try. The way this new case is growing I can't promise.'

'I can always ask Ellen to look after Mary.'

He was proud of all his wife had become. Speaking for the suffragists, the new secretary of the Society, working with the young political party that would stand for the workers . . . it was such a big leap. One he couldn't have predicted when they met. But life changed; it took some odd turns.

'Why's your case growing, anyway?' she asked. Suddenly Annabelle raised her hand to her mouth and her eyes widened. 'Oh God, there hasn't been someone else killed, has there?'

'No,' he told her, 'and I'm hoping it stays that way. But now it's starting to look like Charlie Gilmore might be involved somehow.'

Annabelle's expression turned to a sneer. 'He was always evil. I remember him when he was young.' She'd grown up on the Bank, where the Boys of Erin held sway. 'I'll tell you who once knew his little brother well.'

'Declan?' His reputation was even more violent than Charlie's. 'Who?'

'Tom Maguire.'

'Really?' He found that hard to credit. The union man was fiery, but not with his fists.

'Oh aye, thick as thieves for a while. That was a long time ago, though. Back when they were just nippers.'

But it might be a way in, Harper thought. In the morning he'd go over to the union office and have a word with the man.

'Did you have a think about it last night?' he asked Ash.

The sergeant nodded glumly. 'If Gilmore's and Archer's gangs are going up against each other it's going to be bloody, sir.'

'I know.' He'd had exactly the same thought. The last thing any of them wanted was a gang war in Leeds. 'I still don't see how Tench and his friends fit into the puzzle.'

'Maybe they've done something to upset Gilmore, not Archer,' Ash suggested.

Harper shook his head. 'It's not Charlie's style. He'd want to send a message, not try to hide the bodies.'

They sat quietly until the sergeant asked, 'What are we going to do about Morley, sir?'

'He's not going to give us the chance to help him. He seems to think he can handle anything.'

'We're going to end up looking for his murderer too, aren't we?'

'Very likely,' Harper answered with a sigh. 'I think today we'd better go and beard the lions.'

'Sir?'

He stood and clapped the sergeant on the shoulder. 'We're going to talk to Archer and Gilmore.'

'Does the super know, sir?'

Harper grinned. 'I thought I'd better tell him, in case we don't come back.'

First things first, though. Harper trod the familiar path over to Hunslet Lane, Wharton keeping pace beside him, full of questions about the job. His eagerness was refreshing. But tiring, too. No sooner had he given one answer than there was more the lad wanted to know.

He was relieved when they went down the stairs at the station and through the door into King's Kingdom.

'It's not quite Cinderella and the shoe,' the doctor told them, smiling at his own humour, 'but the leg fits the rest of the body. Same stockings, same boots. In case there was any doubt,' he added with a twist of his mouth.

'How did she die?' Harper asked.

'She drowned,' King said. 'That much is certain. Tell me, do you know if she could swim?'

The inspector looked at Wharton.

'The mother said she couldn't,' he stammered.

'I see.' The doctor reached into his waistcoat pocket, drew out a cigar and enjoyed the ritual of lighting it. 'For whatever it's worth, in my experience, people who can't swim rarely choose to die by water. Don't ask me why, I've no idea. There are cuts on her hands and face as if she'd been scrambling and trying to get out. If you want my opinion, she simply fell in by accident and couldn't get out again. Slipped, perhaps. There are injuries from the dredger, but those all happened after she was dead.'

'Anything to indicate she'd been hit?' the inspector asked. 'Killed that way?'

'No,' King replied. 'Not that I've found. But it's always possible someone could have pushed her in. Someone who knew she couldn't swim.' He shrugged. 'Sorting out the truth of it is your job.' He smiled. 'The chances are it was nothing more than a terrible circumstance, poor girl.'

'What now, sir?' Wharton asked as they marched back to Millgarth.

'You work out what the truth is,' Harper told him. 'That's what the job is all about.'

He needed to see the kidnap victims, to see what they could give him. If any of them could find the courage to speak, anyway. But first he needed to visit Horseshoe Harry again, he decided. It was time to find out more about this link between Tench and Archer, and it had better not have come out of his imagination.

He marched up George Street, cutting through the small, sunless courts that led to Briggate, then along behind the music hall and into the Swan. No sign of the man.

Down the Headrow to Rockley Hall Yard where Harry had his business. But the gate to the forge was locked, a small sign scrawled on cardboard and nailed to the wood: *Closed due to bereavement.*

Dead? Harry had inherited the farrier's from his father and now he ran it with his two sons. Harper began to feel the sickness at the pit of his stomach.

There was one other business in the yard, the office and storage for Townend and Sons, painters and decorators. He banged on the door, and was taken by surprise when it was pulled back swiftly by a woman.

'What?' Her eyes were blazing. 'You're hammering the place down.'

'I'm looking for Harry,' the inspector told her.

Her expression changed, softening a little. 'Then you'll be looking a long time, luv. He died yesterday, God rest him.' For a moment she looked down at the ground.

'What happened?' He needed to know, but at the same time, part of him didn't want to hear the answer.

'He was in the Swan last night having a drink, and he keeled over. That's what one of his lads told me this morning when he came to put up the sign.' She glanced over at the gate. 'I'll miss the old bugger. We had a few laughs together when things were slow.'

'I'm sorry to hear the news,' was all he could say.

'Did you know him?' the woman asked. She was curious now, assessing him with her eyes. She looked to be in her late forties, dark hair caught back in a tight bun.

'A little. I'm Detective Inspector Harper.'

'I'm Alice Townend.' She pointed at the sign above her head. 'I run this, since my husband passed on, anyway. Needs must.' The woman sighed. 'What did you want with Harry, anyway? You don't look like you need a horse shoed.'

'I hadn't seen him in a while, that's all.' It was better to be vague.

'I daresay you'll have a chance at his funeral.' She took a

handkerchief from her sleeve and dabbed at her eyes. 'Look at me, eh, getting all upset.' Mrs Townend gave a wan little smile. 'I'm sorry I can't help you.'

It could be a coincidence, he thought as he walked back along the Headrow. And this time perhaps it was. The death sounded innocent enough.

At the Swan no one seemed to know much. The place had been full the night before. The first anyone knew was when Harry toppled over on to the floor. By then it was too late. Nobody recalled seeing anyone with him, but they'd all been run off their feet . . .

He was never going to know what happened. He might have his suspicions but they wouldn't help now. The only person who'd connected Leonard Tench and George Archer had gone. Another dead end.

What he needed was some inspiration. Or a stroke of luck. And he knew the chances of that happening.

Oxford Place ran next to the Town Hall, a short street of pleasant, unassuming houses almost hidden by the big building: solicitors, and businesses that wanted to cater to the better sort of client.

There was only one draper's shop, the sign as modest as the place itself, just *A. Peters* over the door. There was a selection of cloth and patterned scarves in the window. He entered, hearing the bell tinkle lightly.

It was an airless place, too warm. Inside, items were neatly displayed, most of the stock out of view. A dapper man hurried from the back room.

'Yes, sir,' he said with a nervous smile. 'How can I help you?'

'I'd like to see that scarf in the window. The pale yellow one.'

'Of course, sir.'

The man eyed him doubtfully for a moment, then eased it out of the display, draping it tenderly over both hands.

'It's silk,' he said in a clipped, prissy voice. 'From China. Beautifully made. The fringes make a wonderful contrast.'

They did, Harper thought. Deeper, the colour of buttercups. He ran his fingertips over the material, feeling the smoothness. It would be perfect for Annabelle.

'I'll take it.'

'Yes, sir.' There was pleasure in the man's smile as he moved behind the counter. Deftly he wrapped the scarf in brown paper, tying it with string.

'You're Mr Peters?' the inspector asked as he paid.

'I am.'

'I'm Detective Inspector Harper from Leeds City Police. I'd like to talk to you.'

Peters seemed to stop for just a second, his fingers still and his head down, then started again.

'What about, sir?' As he raised his gaze his eyes were filled with fear and pleading.

'You know exactly what, Mr Peters.'

'I'm sorry, sir, but I don't have any idea what you're talking about. Is something wrong?'

'Two of the men who kidnapped your daughter are dead,' Harper said. 'It was the third who told me about it. Don't worry, you're safe. *All* of you.'

'I honestly don't understand, sir.' Peters looked at him, trying to keep his expression empty. But the tremor in his voice gave him away. 'Kidnapping?'

He wanted to shake the man. Yet part of him, the father, understood. If someone took Mary . . .

'Yes, Mr Peters. I know they told you never to say a word to the police, but they can't hurt you again.'

Then the man muttered something too low for his hearing to catch.

'Pardon?'

'I said I'm sorry, sir. You must have the wrong person.'

'Perhaps I do,' Harper said tightly. He picked up the package with a nod and slid it into his jacket pocket. 'Good day, Mr Peters. If you should remember something, please get in touch.'

Fear, he thought. The most powerful enemy of all.

In the sunshine he sighed with frustration. He doubted if Peters would ever say a word. He'd always be too frightened to talk. He couldn't blame the man. At least it hadn't been a complete waste; he'd come away with a gift for Annabelle.

Harper took his watch from his pocket. The other victims would need to wait. He had appointments to keep.

EIGHT

Everyone knew where Gilmore held court: the Sword, just on the far side of Marsh Lane. It was right on the boundary of his territory, next to Quarry Hill, where Archer had made his start, and facing out towards Leeds with a challenge. It was the only pub in Leeds with a Fenian Brotherhood flag hanging behind the bar, right next to a picture of William Gladstone, the man who supported home rule for Ireland.

From the outside it looked shabby, as rickety and empty of hope as the rest of the Bank. A big man leaned against the door jamb, picking at his teeth with a sliver of wood.

'Ready?' Harper asked.

'As I'll ever be, sir,' Ash answered. 'I made out my will a few months ago.'

They'd made one more stop on the way, at the union office on Kirkgate. Tom Maguire was working, writing furiously, scratching out words almost as soon as they came, then carrying on. He glanced up at the footsteps.

'Make yourselves comfortable,' he told them. 'I need to get this thought down before I lose it forever.'

He looked no better than he had a few days before, the inspector thought. His pale skin was almost translucent, and every few seconds he gave a small cough.

Finally he finished, blotted the sheet, and sat back.

'How's the little one, Mr Harper? Still blooming with health?'

'Of course.'

'Good, good.' He nodded. 'Well, I know I've done nothing, so the pair of you must be here for information.'

'It's just something Annabelle mentioned last night. She told me you used to be close to Declan Gilmore.'

'I did,' he admitted, his face serious. 'But that was another world and time, back when there was some innocence in his soul. Before he decided he wanted to follow in Charlie's footsteps.

Poor man's turned out as bad as his brother.' He coughed again and covered his mouth.

'But you knew the family.'

'I knew Declan and I knew his parents,' Maguire answered cautiously. 'Not his brother. Charlie was always the wild one, a law unto himself.' He might have grown up in Leeds, yet there was still the faintest hint of an Irish accent that touched his words. 'Why do you want to know?'

'Because I'm off to see Charlie in a minute.'

'Then may God go with you, Mr Harper. Part of the way, at least. I hear He refuses to pass through the man's door.'

'What can you tell me about him?' He'd read everything in the thick police file about the Boys of Erin. So far they'd kept their activities to the Bank and Cross Green, preying on the poor and the weak. But maybe Gilmore had greater ambitions and he'd simply been biding his time.

'I'll put it to you like this,' Maguire answered after a little thought. 'Everything you've heard is probably true, and I don't doubt that's only the half of it. People are too scared to say much. And,' he added pointedly, 'the police haven't done anything to stop him.'

'That might change.'

'You'll hear no argument from me if it does. Just be careful, Inspector. Not only around Charlie. Declan's probably more dangerous than he is these days. I don't want to see Annabelle a widow. Not when you've got that grand little girl.' The cough came again, longer and harsher.

'You should see a doctor,' Harper told him.

'It's nothing,' he said when he'd caught his breath. 'Just a summer cold. Another few days and I'll be fine.'

The man outside the Sword nodded: permission to pass. Harper pushed open the door and walked in. Inside, it looked much like any other public house, with a polished wooden bar and gleaming brass. The green and yellow stars and stripes of the Fenian flag took pride of place, there for all to see. Men stood around drinking, small groups playing dominoes, the quiet clack of the tiles in place of conversation. It was as hushed as a church.

The only thing to mark the place out as different was a single large, round table that dominated one side of the room. There, sitting by himself, a newspaper spread out in front of him, was Charlie Gilmore.

Other than the thatch of red curly hair and abundant whiskers that crept along his jaw, there was nothing to mark him as special. He wasn't tall or broadly built; he looked ordinary, dressed in a suit from Barran's when he could afford better. No outward sign of wealth.

The inspector had tried to arrest him once before and failed. The evidence and witnesses vanished. Gilmore and Archer were the mirrors of each other, both ruthless, and the pair of them wealthy on the back of other people's pain.

'Inspector Harper and Sergeant Ash.' He didn't look up. Someone would have warned him of their approach.

He could wait to be invited or he could take the initiative. Harper pulled out a chair and sat down, nodding for the sergeant to do the same.

Gilmore took his time, finishing the article before he folded the paper and set it aside.

'What'll you have to drink, gentlemen? It's my shout.'

'We're on duty.'

'Up to you.' He shrugged. 'You don't want my hospitality. Why are you here then, Inspector?'

'Leonard Tench. Ted Bradley.'

Gilmore's face showed nothing. 'Am I supposed to know who they are?'

'You tell me.'

'The names don't mean a thing to me.'

'George Archer.'

The man gave a thin smile. 'Now that's someone I do know.'

'What's going on between the two of you?'

'I have no idea what you mean, Mr Harper.' He raised a hand and within a few seconds a waiter brought him a glass of beer.

'I've got two bodies. Someone killed them. My guess is it's you or Archer.'

'Then you'd better ask him.' Gilmore gazed steadily. 'It's nothing to do with me.'

'Do you know Eustace Morley?'

The man blinked, surprised by the change of subject. 'I do. Why?'

Harper smiled. 'I just wondered. Do you think he's a good boxer?'

'Very good. He might even be great one day. Have you ever seen him in the ring?'

'Not my sport.'

'You should. It's real treat to watch him fight, Inspector. He has the makings of a champion.'

'Not interested in looking after him?' Harper asked. It was worth a shot; Morley could be the cause of it all if his future was that golden. But Gilmore simply shook his head.

'I hadn't even thought about it. I'm a spectator at fights, nothing more.'

'George Archer's talked to him once or twice.' Harper stared at the man as he spoke. There was still no expression on Gilmore's face. 'And you've had someone going to that club where he trains.'

The man roared with laughter. 'Is that all? Morley has a big bout with Johnny McGowan coming up. I just want to make sure he hasn't gone soft before I put my money on him. I daresay George thinks the same.'

'There are other ways to make sure your man wins, too.'

'True enough,' Gilmore acknowledged lazily. 'But I like to see the skill in the ring. An honest bout. That's the pleasure of it.' He took a sip of the beer. 'Why are you so interested in Morley, Inspector?'

'Let's just say I don't want anything to happen to him.'

'Might it?' He frowned.

'I hope not. After all, you'll be putting good money on him.' He stood. 'I'm sure we'll be talking again.'

'Look after yourself, Inspector.'

That was the second time he'd been told that today, Harper thought. Were people sending him a message?

'Are we going to see Archer now, sir?' Ash asked.

'Not just yet,' he replied. He wanted to digest everything Gilmore had told him first. Not so much the words themselves as the meaning behind them. 'What did you make of him? Do you think he was telling the truth?'

The sergeant smiled under his moustache. 'I doubt Charlie Gilmore's come within shouting distance of the truth since he learned how to talk. But there might have been a few places where he wasn't lying too much.'

'Where?'

'When he was talking about boxing.'

'Yes.' He nodded. There'd been passion and belief in his words then.

'I still wouldn't trust him as far as I could throw him, mind, sir.'

Harper grinned. 'That makes two of us.' He pulled the watch from his pocket. 'Come on, I'll buy you something to eat. After that we can go out and brace Archer.'

'You know me, sir. Never turn down a meal.'

'Just as well, I don't offer too often.'

'I always worry about the reason for it, though.' Ash raised his eyebrows and started to walk alongside the inspector.

At least on the open top of the tram a breeze blew to cut the heat of the day. Not a cloud in the sky, the sun bright; the full, brilliant summer of July.

They alighted at the terminus by the entrance to Roundhay Park, and walked through the arch and on to the fields. If the weather held, the place would be packed on Sunday, young couples doing their courting, families queueing to spend tuppence for a trip around Waterloo Lake on the *Maid of Athens*.

'That must be Archer's house over there.' He pointed to a pair of stone pillars in the distance. 'Hidden down the drive.'

'And they say crime doesn't pay.' Ash coughed. 'I know it sounds strange, sir, but before we go there would you mind showing me where they found Len's body?'

Interest? Harper wondered. Or did he want to pay his last respects to an old friend?

'Of course.' He changed direction, leading the way down Park Avenue, then along the dusty path by Waterloo Lake. It was impossible to judge the exact spot; the best he could do was guess from the position of the small copse on the hill. 'Close to here,' the inspector said finally. 'He was about halfway out. Probably twenty yards.' He pointed. A few stray pieces of floating debris from the sunken boat still bobbed around on the water.

'I see, sir.' Ash gazed over the water as if he might see below the surface. 'That rope around his waist . . .'

'It must have been attached to something heavy to keep the body down.'

'Yes,' the sergeant agreed slowly. 'What kind of knot was it, do you know, sir?'

One of the men who brought the body ashore had told him; he just needed to recall the name.

'A bowline,' he answered after a few moments.

'Thank you, sir. That's how a waterman would tie something, isn't it?'

'Yes.' He remembered what he'd been told: a sailor's knot.

'I just wonder if it might be worth asking around on the wharves by the river.'

'That's a thought,' Harper said as they walked away. He glanced up at the houses dotting the top of the far hill. One of those belonged to Archer. Crime definitely paid.

The drive curved neatly in front of the house. The building was new and designed to impress, three storeys of heavy stone blocks and tall windows. The broad wooden door was studded with iron nails, hoping to appear ancient and solid.

But the man who answered the knock didn't look like a servant. A luxuriant waxed moustache, bushy whiskers that extended along his jawline, pomaded hair, and an expensive suit. A broad body and cold eyes. One of Archer's bodyguards.

'Hello, Roger,' Harper said. He'd arrested Roger Harrison twice over the years, once for grievous bodily harm, once for murder. In both cases the witnesses had changed their testimony and he'd walked free. 'I want to see George.'

The man didn't move.

'Mr Archer doesn't see callers.' He had a rough Leeds accent, the bark of his words at odds with his sleek appearance.

'He sees the police,' the inspector told him. It wasn't a request.

'Wait.' The door closed again, leaving them standing. A few seconds became one minute, then two.

Finally he'd had enough. He twisted the knob and stepped into the hall.

Large black and white tiles covered the floor. The wainscoting was polished dark wood, as high as a man's chest. Paintings lined the walls, hunting scenes, portraits, still lifes, a mish-mash that seemed as if they'd come in a job lot from the auctioneer.

He heard a ring of footsteps then Archer appeared, Harrison by his side.

'Roger didn't say he'd invited you in.'

'I took advantage of your hospitality,' Harper replied with a smile. 'After all, we know each other, don't we, George?'

He used the Christian name deliberately. Archer's face darkened for a moment, then he covered it with a smile.

'Of course. Welcome, Inspector. What can I do for you?'

Archer was dressed in the new style, a lounge suit, beautifully cut, with a fold-over collar on his shirt and his tie in a small knot. His hair was cut short and he was clean-shaven. A thoroughly modern man. He wasn't physically imposing – Harrison made him seem small – but he had presence; eyes were irresistibly drawn to him. And always there was a sense that just below the skin lay a deep current of violence.

He was violent, a criminal. A killer. That was how he'd come up, that was his reputation, and all of it was justified. These days, though, he was reinventing himself as a businessman. He invested in property, in factories and ideas now. He attended the right charity balls. He still had a few of his dirty enterprises but he was turning respectable. Maybe that was how it worked, Harper thought: acquire enough wealth, keep it, and people stopped asking where it had come from. Another generation and no one would even remember.

Unless Archer went down for murder, of course.

'I'm sure you heard about the incident on the lake.'

'The torpedoes? I watched it from the window.' He pulled out a packet of Army Club cigarettes and lit one. 'Before you ask, I heard about the body, too.'

'The dead man was called Leonard Tench,' the inspector told him.

'So someone said.' It was a casual remark, but very telling. That information hadn't been made public.

'He was a friend of yours, wasn't he, George? That's what I've been told.'

Archer smiled and shook his head. 'You need better informants, then. The name doesn't mean a thing to me.'

'What about Ted Bradley?'

'No. Should I know who he is, Inspector?'

'Bradley's dead, too. The same way, an iron bar to the head. Someone tried to get rid of that corpse, too.'

'Nothing to do with me.'

'Eustace Morley. Do you know him?'

'The boxer? Of course I do.' He answered without even thinking. 'I've seen every one of his fights.'

'He was a friend of Tench and Bradley.'

'So?' He shrugged. 'If you're trying to say something, spit it out.'

'He's got a big fight coming up, hasn't he?'

Archer nodded. 'Johnny McGowan. It'll be a good match. I've already put ten pounds on him to win.'

'Then you'd better hope he doesn't end up like his friends, George.'

The man laughed. At his side Harrison remained still, glaring at the policemen.

'Is that the best you can do, Inspector? I've had worse threats from a six-year-old.'

'I'm just putting you on notice. The same way I did with Charlie Gilmore. He has a man watching Morley.' Harper gave a thin smile. 'I'll bid you good day.'

They'd reached the door when Archer called out, 'I'll have my carriage take you back to town if you like. Save your shoe leather. I know you coppers don't make much.'

The Inspector turned and saw the man's mocking look. 'The tram will be fine. Thank you, anyway.'

'Trying to put the cat among the pigeons, sir?'

Harper shrugged. 'They can all watch each other now. Archer will put his own man on the boxer. Between them, maybe they can keep him alive.' If the man wouldn't take police protection maybe someone else could do the job more effectively.

'There's only one problem that I see.' Ash pursed his mouth. 'If something happens to Morley, then there's bound to be a war of some kind.'

'Let's cross that bridge if we reach it. Right now George Archer's going to be wondering why his police contact didn't warn him we were coming. Someone's going to have hell to pay for that,' he said with dark satisfaction.

'Do you have a plan, sir?'

'No,' he admitted. 'About all we can do for now is stir things up and be ready when something happens.'

The electric tram ran to the Sheepscar terminus, just outside the Victoria, then they took another to Vicar Lane. Harper checked his pocket watch. Four o'clock. Still plenty of time to for the sergeant to make more enquiries.

'You said something about asking around on the wharves,' he reminded Ash.

'That's right, sir. I think it's worth a try.'

'So do I. You might as well go home to your Nancy afterwards unless you turn up anything worthwhile.'

The doors at Park Row Fire Station were open, letting in the afternoon sun. The brass of the engine gleamed, polished within an inch of its life. The hoses lay neatly coiled, everything laid out with precision.

Harper tapped on a door and heard a grunt from inside.

'Hello, Billy.'

'Tom.'

'I was wondering if you'd managed to discover who owns that warehouse where you found the body.'

'I thought I'd already sent you the information.' He opened a drawer, pulled out a file and riffled through the papers. 'Here. Someone called Worthington. It doesn't mean anything to me.' He passed the sheet across the desk. 'I'm sorry. They've come out with all this new paperwork. I've been up to my ears in that.'

'It doesn't matter.' He folded the information. 'Still enjoying the job?'

'When I have the chance to do it.' Reed shook his head. 'I seem to spend most of my time sitting here.'

Harper chuckled. 'Wait until you make superintendent. You'll never see the light of day again.' He rose to leave.

'Do you have a minute to spare, Tom?'

'Of course.' The inspector sat down again. Billy's voice had been serious, concerned.

'It's about these shops.'

'You know that's Annabelle's business—'

'I realize that, but . . .' Reed groped for the words. 'I want to be sure there isn't a problem with them, that's all.'

Harper shook his head. 'Everything's fine, as far as I know. She's never said anything to me. Honestly, Billy, I'd tell you if it wasn't. The Suffrage Society has asked her to be secretary and she doesn't have time to do it all. That's the whole reason.'

Reed sighed. 'It's a big decision for us. A risk. I'm sure you understand that.'

'Of course.'

'I don't want Elizabeth to lose everything.'

'We don't either, believe me. It's a good, going concern. That's all I can tell you.'

'Yes,' he agreed. But his voice had more resignation than pleasure.

'Nothing wrong, is there?'

'No,' Reed replied. 'Plenty of sleepless nights and sitting at the table doing sums, that's all. Whatever she wants, I'll back her, she knows that.' He lit a cigarette. 'Anyway, how's your case moving along?'

Harper snorted. 'Going nowhere fast. So far it looks like it might involve George Archer *and* Charlie Gilmore. Does that tell you anything?'

Reed shook his head. 'It says I made the right choice moving to the fire brigade.'

Harper stood again and extended his hand. Reed shook it. 'You're doing a good job here, Billy.'

'I'm trying. Good luck with the case.'

'To you and Elizabeth as well. Whatever she decides.'

NINE

'You shouldn't have asked him, Billy.'

Elizabeth was curled up against his shoulder, one warm arm stretched across his chest. The bed was comfortable; he'd been on the verge of sleep when she spoke.

'Why not? He was there, it was a fair question.'

'It's just not right, that's all.'

'I needed to find out.'

'I'd already told you.' She shifted position, raising herself on one elbow to look at him. 'I see the books. I'm in all the shops every day. They're good earners. I'd know if there was a problem.'

'I wanted to be certain. Maybe there's something they haven't said.'

'Even if there was, do you think he'd tell you?'

'Yes.' They might not be as close these days, but he knew Harper would give him the truth.

'I'm scared,' Elizabeth said. 'It's so big. And once I say yes . . .'

'I know.' He pulled her close again. 'But you can do it.'

'What did they say down on the wharves?' Harper asked.

'That there are probably thousands of men in Leeds who know how to tie a bowline, sir,' Ash replied as he raised an eyebrow. 'Anyone worth his salt would be able to do it.'

'So we're no further along.'

'Not really. I'm sorry, sir.'

'Never mind. It was worth a try.' The inspector took out the paper Billy Reed had given him. 'This is the owner of the building where Ted Bradley was killed. See what you can find out about him.'

'Yes, sir.'

Most likely it would be another dead end. But sooner or later they'd find a way through. Patience and persistence, that was half the job. He turned to the detective constable.

'What about you, Mr Wharton? What else have you managed to discover about Miss Brooker?'

'Very little, sir,' he admitted. 'I had the names of two of her friends. They both said Charlotte was always cheerful and helpful. That fits with what her mother said. But they also said she could be low at times, which goes along with what the sister told me.'

'That's not particularly helpful,' Harper agreed. 'What about a young man?'

'Here's where it becomes complicated, sir.' Wharton frowned. 'Charlotte had hinted to her friends that there might be someone, but she wouldn't tell them who it was, just a man her parents wouldn't approve of. But they're not sure if she was telling the truth, whether there really was anyone or if it was just a tale. Sort of take your pick. I'm not sure how to find out.'

The inspector tried to recall the details. 'She liked to walk, isn't that right?'

'Yes, sir.'

'On her own?'

'Sometimes, or with her friends.' Wharton scrambled back, checking his notebook. 'Occasionally her sister, but that seemed to be rare from what I could find out.'

'That would be a perfect opportunity to meet someone, don't you think?'

For the first time, Wharton seemed to smile. 'Yes, sir. Of course.'

'Find out where she liked to go and when. Between them the friends and the mother should be able to tell you. Then get out there and talk to people. Someone must have seen her. Ask if she was on her own.'

'Won't that take a long time, sir?'

'It might. Or you could be lucky with the first person. That's what detective work is like, Mr Wharton.'

And sometimes the answers never appeared. Better not to say that, he thought. Sooner or later the lad would discover it for himself.

'Yes, sir,' the constable said doubtfully. 'Sir?'

'What, Mr Wharton?'

'The investigation you and the sergeant are working on,' he began. 'Will you be needing me for it? I'd be interested, I could learn a lot.' His eyes were full of hope.

Harper stared at him. 'I'd prefer you to keep on with Charlotte Brooker,' he said kindly. 'You're doing an excellent job and you're taking a great deal of weight off my shoulders.' And it was good experience in how to conduct an investigation with all its frustrations and triumphs.

'Yes, sir.' He could see the disappointment on Wharton's face; he was still too young, too new, to disguise his feelings.

'There's one thing you'll never need to worry about in this job,' the inspector advised. 'There'll always be another case, and you'll learn from every one of them.'

*   *   *

'I talked to a few of my old informants yesterday,' Kendall said with a wry smile. They were in his office, the door firmly closed, voices low. 'Half of them are gone. It's been too long. I'm rusty.'

'Did anyone tell you much?'

'Nothing we don't already know. Everyone's scared of Archer. None of them had even heard of Tench and Bradley.'

'That supports what Morley said, that they'd never talked about their crimes,' Harper said. 'Maybe Horseshoe Harry was wrong. We could be sniffing at the wrong tree. He's the only one who's mentioned it and he's dead now.'

'Who killed them, then?' Kendall asked. 'It leaves us with no one in the frame. And look at the ways they tried to dispose of the bodies. No, Tom, there's planning and manpower there.'

They kept returning to that, how everything was arranged, the sheer luck of even finding Tench's body, then the timing of Bradley's death, so soon after his friend had been discovered.

'I like your idea of having Gilmore and Archer watching each other with that boxer,' the superintendent said. 'That ought to keep him safe. Have you seen him fight?'

'No.'

'You should. He's wonderful to watch in the ring.' He started to fill his pipe, tamping down the tobacco with a fingertip, then striking a match and puffing until the air around his head was thick with smoke. 'We're still scratching around the outside of all this, aren't we?'

'It feels that way,' Harper agreed. 'I've got Ash out chasing leads that'll probably come to nothing and I don't have a clue where to turn.'

·'I told you, Archer's canny. Remember that the newspapers are watching. Very soon they'll start demanding results from us.'

'We just need a way in.' The inspector raised his eyes. 'Even if it's just a single thread. But honestly, I'm not sure Archer's involved.'

'We'll see,' the superintendent said. 'I'll go looking for more of my informants today.'

'Thank you, sir.'

Kendall gave a small laugh. 'I'll tell you, Tom, it felt strange to be doing real police work again.'

'Good, though?'

He nodded. 'It made me wonder why I'd stopped. Then I came back here and saw this.' He gestured helplessly at all the paper on his desk.

The warmth of the day washed over Harper as he left Millgarth, all the stink and soot and noise of the city. He stood on the pavement, hearing the shouts from the market as people cried their wares. People flowed around him and the traffic passed. Where now, he wondered.

TEN

Harper went to visit the other men who'd had family snatched by Tench and his men: a chemist with premises on Kirkgate and a bible seller on Cookridge Street. Both of them were nervous, well-dressed, carefully groomed. But neither would say a word, no matter how much he assured or cajoled them. Exactly the same as Peters the draper.

They were lying. He could see the anxiety in their eyes. But nothing he did made them even acknowledge it. They must have had the fear of God put in them.

Ignorance wasn't bliss, Harper thought. Anything but.

By five he was back in Millgarth. He'd gone round his narks once more, pressing them. Again he'd gained nothing apart from more frustration and men shaking their heads. With Horseshoe Harry dead he needed someone else to connect Archer to the murders. And no one was doing that.

Ash had already returned, looking down in the mouth.

'Mr Worthington, the man who owns the building where they found Ted, he looks clean enough, sir. He's lost money on the fire – didn't have insurance.'

'Any connection with Archer or Gilmore?' the inspector asked.

'Not that anyone found. The place came to him in his father's will. Everything seems above board. Nothing dubious.'

'It doesn't matter; I hadn't expected much. Go and spend the evening with your wife.' Ash brightened. 'All this will still be here in the morning.'

There was no sign of Wharton as he finished writing out his report. Harper was blotting the ink, ready to lock the paper away when the superintendent appeared, nodding towards his office.

Kendall didn't look pleased, Harper thought as he closed the door behind them. His face was flushed and worried.

'Did you have any luck?' His voice was sharp.

'No, sir.'

'Well, I have something to tell you.' Kendall ran his tongue around the inside of his mouth. 'I ran into someone who used to pass me a few tips.' He put his pipe down and picked it up again. The inspector waited, trying to hide his impatience. 'He likes to go fishing. Gets up in the middle of the night so he can be on the spot before dawn. That's when they start biting, he says. He was up at Waterloo Lake a few days ago.'

Suddenly Harper was very attentive indeed. 'When was this, sir?'

'Two nights before the torpedo demonstration.'

For a moment he could hardly breathe. He could feel the pulse beating hard in his neck. 'What did he see?'

'Three men with a horse and cart going away from the lake. There was a rowing boat up against the bank. He thought that was odd since they're usually tied by the café. The air was still, and he could hear them go out along the carriage drive to the Wetherby Road.' Come on, Harper thought. He needed more than that. 'And there was enough of a moon that he could make out the faces.'

'Who?'

The superintendent stood and began to pace, hands pushed deep in his pockets. Come on, the inspector thought, spit it out.

'Tim O'Shea,' he said finally. He looked stunned.

'But—' Harper began.

'I know. Before you ask, he says he'd swear on it,' he said dully, no expression in his voice.

Tim O'Shea was one of Charlie Gilmore's men. Harper's mind was racing, questions spinning and skittering around. This changed it all.

'There's one more thing,' Kendall continued. 'He thinks one

of the others was Declan Gilmore.' He held up his hand. 'He didn't get enough of a glimpse to be absolutely certain.'

They stared at each other.

'I'd like to talk to your friend.' It was all Harper could think to say. He needed to hear it for himself, to be *sure*.

Kendall shook his head. 'He only told me because we've known each other for donkey's years. I'm not even going to tell you his name, Tom.'

If he couldn't speak to the source, there was one question he had to ask. 'Do you believe him, sir?' When the man didn't reply immediately, he continued, 'Gut feeling?'

'I do.' The super nodded and sighed. 'Believe me, Tom, I've thought about nothing else since he told me. But he didn't come looking for me, I found him. He couldn't even have known I'd be asking.'

The silence was like a weight on them.

'I had myself convinced it was Archer,' Kendall said quietly, a dazed expression on his face. He chuckled and shook his head. 'What did I teach you when you were starting out as a detective?'

'Always keep an open mind.'

'Shows how well I remembered my own lessons, didn't it?'

But Harper was already trying to look ahead. 'Your nark, did anyone spot him?'

'He's sure they didn't,' the superintendent replied slowly. 'It was still dark and he was on the other side of the lake, back among the trees. As soon as he saw them he hid.'

'But he can't be certain he wasn't seen.'

'He says it's fine, and he's not a hothead.'

'What if we need evidence in court?' the inspector asked.

'Let's cross that bridge when we come to it, shall we? We've got O'Shea's name, that's a start.'

'Yes.' Harper turned things over in his mind. 'We still have the same question, though, don't we? Why did someone kill Tench and Bradley?'

Gilmore must have been behind both murders. For the life of him he still couldn't see a reason.

'We'd better get O'Shea in,' Kendall ordered. 'See what he has to say.'

'There's one good thing – Tim was never much of a liar. We'll get some truth from him.' He'd been convicted and in prison at least three times that Harper could recall; probably more than that. 'As soon as we grab him Charlie Gilmore's going to know.' He'd hear from anyone who witnessed it.

'Can't be helped.'

'If Declan Gilmore's involved . . .'

He was a hard man, brutal, vicious. He revelled in pain and violence. Declan made his brother seem mild.

'Worry about him later.'

'Yes, sir.'

'Tom,' Kendall added, so softly that his hearing could barely catch the words. 'We're still keeping this between the three of us. Even if Archer's not directly involved I don't want him getting word. Not yet.'

'Are you going to be working on Sunday?' Annabelle asked.

The question took him by surprise. His mind had been elsewhere, trying to make sense of the information from the superintendent. He'd only picked at the meal, no appetite for the lamb chops and mash. Harper put down his knife and fork and pushed the plate away.

'I don't know,' he answered, and ran a hand through his hair. 'Did you have something in mind?'

She smiled at him.

'You know I start that job for the Suffragist Society on Monday. I thought we could go up to the park if the weather stays warm. All three of us. Make an afternoon of it. Concert at the bandstand, take a picnic.'

He glanced at his daughter. As soon as she'd finished her food she'd wriggled down to the floor. Now she was back with the wooden blocks, her favourite toy, at least for today.

'That sounds perfect.' He put his hand over hers and grinned. A chance to promenade with his family.

It was a gentle, quiet evening. No tantrum from Mary during her bath or as they settled her down to sleep. She didn't try to fight it, but closed her eyes as Annabelle told her a story. Harper stood in the doorway, watching, feeling content in a way he'd never imagined.

'Are you ready for it all?' he asked when they sat together later.

'The job? As much as I'll ever be.' She chuckled. 'I've been reading so much my eyes are going square.'

'You'll be fine.'

'I'll do my best,' she said with a sigh. 'That's all I can do.'

'Has Elizabeth said anything more about the bakeries?'

'Not yet.'

'When I saw Billy yesterday he was asking me about them. He wanted to know if there was something you hadn't told Elizabeth.'

'Cheek.' For a moment the colour rose on her cheeks but it passed as quickly as it arrived. 'Still, I suppose I can't blame him. She'll set him straight, anyway.'

Downstairs in the pub people were singing.

'Someone must be celebrating,' she said and listened a little longer. 'God, I'd better have the piano tuner in. That thing sounds like a cats' chorus.'

They pushed the man down on a chair in the interview room.

'I'll kill you.' His gaze moved from one to the other. 'This is a free country. You can't just come and take me like that.'

'Maybe you'd rather we dropped you in a lake,' Harper said softly.

For long seconds O'Shea went silent, enough for the inspector to know he was guilty.

'What are you talking about? What do you mean?' But it was only bluster and hot air; he'd given it all away.

Ash closed the door. Just the three of them in here, and O'Shea looked worried.

Harper took his time, sitting, watching, in no rush to speak as O'Shea fidgeted. He was a small man with ragged dark hair and a scrubby beard, old clothes and battered boots. Dirt was ingrained on his hands and face, as if he never saw a proper wash from one week to the next. His gaze fluttered nervously, not settling on anything.

Time, the inspector thought. Let his worry build into fear.

Tim O'Shea wasn't a captain in the Boys of Erin. He didn't even rank as a lieutenant or a sergeant. Men like him were simply

cannon fodder, muscle and bone to be used. Not bright, but loyal.
Snatching him had been the easiest thing in the world. He was
a creature of habit: a drink at the Sword to start his day and
steady his hand. Then into town, looking for titbits of work to
put a few pennies in his pocket. At dinnertime he'd return to the
pub and spend his afternoon there, one of so many fawning
around Gilmore, hoping for some job, any job.

All they had to do was wait and watch as he began his wander-
ings. On Kirkgate, O'Shea was one of many people on the street,
with no one to protect him and nowhere to run. The policemen
came up from behind, Harper on one side, Ash on the other,
each grabbing a wrist. The man hadn't even tried to run. He
already knew he didn't have a chance. But Tim O'Shea had been
born without hope. He sat there now, left eye twitching with a
nervous tic.

'I'm going to tell you a story.' The inspector broke the silence.
'Maybe you've already heard it.' He waited but O'Shea said
nothing, not even glancing at him. 'Once upon a time there was
a man. You'd never call him a good man, but there were far
worse in the world. For one reason or another, though, he was
killed. Murdered. Are you listening to me, Tim?' He watched
the man give a quick, nervous nod. 'Now tell me, what do you
think would be a good way to get rid of the body? How about
tie him to something heavy and dump the corpse in the water
where no one would ever find him? Who'd ever know?' He kept
his eyes on O'Shea. 'Do you know the problem with the best-
laid plans, Tim? They don't always work, do they?' The man
didn't reply. He tried to keep his face blank. 'That's not all,
though,' Harper went on. 'The fellow who was killed had a
friend. A very good friend, they'd been close for years. Perhaps
he knew too much about things. So he had to die, too, especially
after the man in the lake turned up. A well-set fire doesn't leave
much behind. Nothing more than ashes. It was just good fortune
that the brigade arrived in time to put out the blaze before the
corpse really burned.' He paused. 'How do you like the story
so far, Tim?'

'I don't know what you're talking about,' O'Shea muttered.

'But you do, Tim. You do.' Harper spoke lazily, as if he already
knew everything. 'After all, you were in the cart that took Leonard

Tench out to the lake. You probably rowed the boat.' For a second
he thought about bringing up Declan Gilmore's name. Not yet;
it wasn't time to play that card. 'Turn your hands over, Tim. Let
me take a look at your palms.'

Between the grime and the calluses there was little to see.

'I told you, I don't know.' O'Shea grinned in triumph.

'Tim.' He kept staring until O'Shea was forced to lower his
gaze. 'Two dead and so far yours the only name I have. That's
something to think about when they put the noose around your
neck for murder.'

'Prove it.' The man stared at him.

'I have someone who saw you at the park. Someone who put
a name to your face. Be very careful, Tim. That noose is getting
tighter every minute.'

'It weren't me.' But the defiance had vanished from his
voice. The words sounded hollow, as if he didn't even believe
them himself.

'Come on, we both know it was. I think it's time to stop
playing games. What did you use to kill them, Tim? Was it a
metal bar?'

'I didn't kill no one,' he answered, his voice a mix of desperation and hopelessness.

'No jury's going to believe that. Especially since you were
there and you put the body in the water.' He sat back. 'Or do
you want to tell me a better story?'

At times like this, silence was a friend. It could rise and
press down on O'Shea as he considered how short his time
might be.

Harper glanced across at Ash, standing at attention by the
door. He was staring at O'Shea with an expression the inspector
hadn't seen before – pure hatred. Hardly surprising, he thought,
given what the man had done to Tench. But maybe he could
use that.

The room was hot; summer sunlight streamed in through
closed windows. He could see the sheen of sweat on O'Shea's
face, could almost read everything going through his mind.

'I helped move the body but I didn't kill him.'

ELEVEN

'Is that really the best you can do?' Harper asked, shaking his head.

'It's the truth.' The tic had grown worse. O'Shea's voice was frantic. 'I helped load him on the cart and sank him in the lake, but that's all.'

'Perhaps it's time you told me a story, Tim.' Harper waved a hand and sat back in his chair. 'Go ahead. We have all the time in the world.'

It came out haltingly, bits and pieces that fitted together awkwardly. O'Shea had received a message: be at the waste ground near Beckett Street cemetery at one in the morning. Two other men were already there, the cart standing close by, and Leonard Tench was lying dead in the dirt. They'd loaded the body, driven out to Roundhay Park, over the grass and halfway round the big lake, far out of sight.

O'Shea had done as he was ordered, stripped the corpse and brought one of the boats while the carter knotted a rope around the dead man's waist. Between them they hauled Tench on board, along with a heavy iron weight. Over the deep water the rope had been fastened to the weight and everything tipped overboard.

'That was all,' he said, as if it was no more than an ordinary day's work.

Harper chewed the inside of his lip. He'd let the man tell his tale. For the most part he was willing to believe it. But there were a few things he wasn't ready to buy just yet.

'Tell me, do you always answer messages ordering you to be somewhere in the middle of the night?'

'I were promised a guinea.'

Very likely true, the inspector thought. A lot of money to a man like him.

'That was very generous of Charlie Gilmore.'

'What? Charlie?' O'Shea looked at him, confused. 'It weren't Charlie.'

Harper chuckled. 'You're his man, Tim. He snaps his fingers and you come running.'

O'Shea was leaning forward, almost pleading. 'This weren't Charlie.' He blinked and shook his head, greasy hair flying around. 'He dun't work like that. Never has.'

The inspector sat back, not satisfied. 'If it wasn't Charlie, why was Declan Gilmore with you?'

'Declan?' There was genuine confusion on O'Shea's face. 'Declan weren't there. I en't seen him in weeks.'

Harper said nothing. He believed the man, no shadow of a doubt about that. Tim O'Shea couldn't lie his way out of a paper bag and this was the truth. Not Declan, not Charlie. Then who was behind it?

'Who sent you the message, Tim?'

'I don't know.' He looked up, almost in tears. 'Honest, I don't. I was in the Bull and Mouth and a man came up to me.'

'What man?'

O'Shea shook his head. 'I'd never seen him before.'

'Tim,' Harper said softly, 'you know every crook in Leeds.'

'Not this one.' His look was haunted, beseeching. He was telling the truth. 'He told me where to be, said I'd get a guinea. That's all, Mr Harper. You know Charlie, he wouldn't have to do that.'

'It wasn't Charlie, but you still went? At one in the morning.'

O'Shea dipped his head. 'I needed the money.'

'Tell me about the other two men waiting for you.'

'I didn't know them. But the other man called the carter Jeb.'

The sweat glowed brightly on O'Shea's face and he wiped his forehead with the back of a dirty hand.

'How did you know the dead man was Tench?'

'They said his name.'

'And did they say why he'd been killed?'

Tim swallowed hard before answering. 'I didn't ask.'

He was willing to believe that. In O'Shea's world people didn't ask questions; not knowing could keep you alive.

'You didn't even wonder?' Harper asked. He kept up the hail of questions, too fast for O'Shea to think and try to lie.

'Wan't my business. I just wanted me guinea.' The man shrugged.

'Why did you go all the way out to Waterloo Lake?'

'I don't know. I was just there.' He looked down at the ground.

'What you don't know could fill a book, Tim.'

'They were paying me.'

'Ted Bradley.' He changed the subject, seeing a startled frown cross O'Shea's face. 'Tell me about him.'

Another midnight message, another corpse to move. Breaking into the warehouse then setting the blaze.

'Who was with you that time?'

'The same two men.'

'And you still didn't know who they were.' Harper shook his head in disbelief. 'You should have been good pals by then.'

'The carter was called Jeb, I told you that.' His hands were moving, fingers lacing together nervously.

'What did they look like?'

'The carter was skinny,' O'Shea answered slowly. 'Dark hair. He had a twist to his mouth.'

'What about the other man? The one in charge.'

'Ah, he was tall. Reddish hair. That dark red, like copper. Short.' He traced the shape with a finger. 'I don't know who he were. I really dun't. But God's truth, it weren't Declan.'

'No?'

'It was me and this Jeb and that other one—'

Harper watched O'Shea run his tongue around his lips to wet them. Now was the time to make sure of the truth.

'You want to know about those men, Tim?' he began. 'You see Sergeant Ash over there?' The inspector gestured with his thumb. 'He grew up with Len Tench and the two of them used to work with Ted Bradley.'

'I didn't know that.' He turned to look at the sergeant. 'I'm sorry, I truly am.'

'I have to do a few things before we send you down to the cells. I need to send people out looking for carter Jeb, for a start. Mr Ash will stay with you. Tim will be safe, won't he?'

'As houses, sir.' He made the words sound ominous.

The inspector passed the word to Sergeant Tollman about Jeb, the carter with a twisted mouth. The beat bobbies would have it soon enough; one of them might know the man. The errand only took two minutes, but he lingered in the office, letting time pass.

Finally he pulled the watch from his waistcoat pocket. A quarter of an hour. Perfect.

O'Shea was still in his seat, not a mark on him. Ash stood by the door, looking as if he'd never moved. As soon as he opened the door, Harper could sense a shift in the atmosphere.

'Have you thought of something else, Tim?'

'Why don't you tell the inspector what you told me?' Ash said. His voice was quiet and calm, somehow all the more worrying for its even tone.

'It was the one with the red hair who killed them.' He was eager to talk now, the words rushing out of his mouth. 'When I arrived at the second one he still had the metal bar in his hand.'

Harper waited. 'Is that it?'

'He looked like he'd enjoyed it. He was smiling. His eyes . . .' O'Shea's voice tailed away.

'Put him in the cells,' the inspector ordered.

Ash took the man by the arm and guided him to the door. Outside, a constable would be waiting to escort him down. O'Shea halted by the door.

'It weren't Charlie. Really, it weren't.'

Then he was gone, just Harper and the sergeant in the room.

'What did you do to him while I was gone?'

'Just a quiet word, sir.'

The inspector raised an eyebrow in disbelief.

'Sometimes that's more effective than a fist, sir. I learned that a long time ago.'

'This carter, Jeb,' Kendall said. 'Find him.'

'I've put the word out.'

'Begging your pardon, sir,' Ash said, 'but we need to look down on the wharves again.'

'You checked down there once,' Harper reminded him.

'But now we know who we're looking for, sir. It was a sailor's knot on the rope around Len's body, we know that. And O'Shea said it was the carter who tied it.' His face was grim.

'Go and find him.' Dammit. He should have connected the two things himself.

'Charlie Gilmore,' Kendall said after the door closed. He filled his pipe and lit it, puffing thoughtfully.

'Tim swore up and down that Charlie Gilmore wasn't involved and that the red-haired man wasn't Declan.' He sighed. 'He was telling the truth.'

'Maybe he's just a better liar these days.'

'He isn't,' Harper said with certainty.

The superintendent stayed quiet for a long time, breathing slowly as he weighed everything. He shook his head.

'First I was certain Archer was behind it all and I was wrong. Then it looked like Gilmore had to be involved and I was wrong again. Am I getting old, Tom?' Kendall asked. 'But if it wasn't either of them, who's behind this?'

'I don't know.' Everyone had their obsessions, he thought. God knew he'd had enough of his own, the ghosts that wouldn't leave. 'I'll tell you one thing, sir. Whoever's doing this must be laughing his bloody head off now. He's leading us round by the nose, first one direction, then another.'

'Then who is it? Who could handle something like this? And why, for God's sake?'

'I don't know,' Harper admitted in frustration. 'I haven't a clue.'

'It has to be someone who knows the city,' Kendall pointed out. 'About the lake, the warehouse, the gangs.'

The inspector nodded. That made perfect sense. 'He's clever, he's organized.' He picked up the line of thought. 'Probably has some money to pay people.'

'And yet we have no idea who he is. Do you know what all that sounds like to me?'

'Like someone wants to take over the crime in Leeds.'

'Exactly,' Kendall agreed bleakly. 'But if there's a man with plans like that, why haven't we heard anything about it?'

'It's not just us, sir. I don't think Archer or Gilmore have either.'

'Red hair,' the superintendent mused. 'Does that mean anything to you? Anyone you can think of?'

'Not beyond the Gilmores.' He'd been poking at that question in his mind. 'Maybe this Jeb can tell us.'

'You need to find him first.'

'We will.' He sat back. 'Do you know what's so strange in all this, sir? Killing Tench and Bradley. They were nothing. No one had even heard of them.'

'Morley could have been lying.'

Harper grimaced. 'No. He's odd, but he was telling the truth. I went to see the shopkeepers who'd had family taken. They wouldn't talk. They were petrified. He didn't lie.'

'Someone's making us look like fools. And it's only a matter of time before the press finds out. We can't afford that, Tom.'

Not when Leeds had just become a city. The police had to show they were capable, that the place was worthy of its new status.

'I know.'

They turned at a sharp tap on the door. Sergeant Tollman entered, his face pale.

'You'd better come, sir. There's a body. They say it's Declan Gilmore.'

TWELVE

'Where?' the inspector asked as he dashed out of the office.

'Bread Street,' Tollman told him. Up on the Bank. Boys of Erin turf. 'The word from the constable is that Charlie Gilmore's already there.'

'I need as many bobbies as you can send.'

'Yes, sir,' They didn't even need to discuss the danger. Charlie would want his revenge. He wasn't going to worry about how he found his brother's killer, and he'd take pleasure in what happened once he had him.

Harper ran. Through the cramped courts and yards, the hobnails on his boots sending sparks off the cobbles. Out along the street, dodging between carts and omnibuses, breathing hard. By the time he reached York Road his lungs were burning as if a fire raged through them. He forced himself to keep going, gasping, legs like lead as the hill rose. At the corner of Bread Street he stopped to catch his breath, one hand resting against the dirty bricks.

A crowd had gathered, a thick circle of the curious and the angry. Harper forced his way through them. In the middle, everyone keeping their distance from him, stood Charlie Gilmore, staring down at the body on the cobbles. Declan was dead. No doubt about that.

The inspector moved closer, kneeling to examine the corpse.

'Leave him be,' Gilmore ordered quietly.

Harper rounded on him. 'You don't tell me how to do my job.' He spotted a nervous constable in a doorway and motioned to him.

'And you don't give me orders. Not here,' Gilmore told him. 'Not when my brother's lying there.'

The inspector stood slowly, coming close enough to smell the man's sour breath and see the fury deep in his eyes. 'We're going to get this straight right now.' His voice was firm but even. 'I'm sorry for your loss, but I'm the police, and we take care of the law, not you. Even round here. I don't care who the hell you think you are. Do you understand that?'

Gilmore kept his gaze steady. 'I've got six men here who could kill you just like that.'

He knew he should be scared, but all Harper felt was anger.

'You didn't say that,' he said quietly. 'Not unless you want me to march you off to jail.'

'You wouldn't dare. People would tear you apart.'

'Do you want to put money on that? How much do you really want to bet?' Gilmore didn't answer, hatred glittering in his eyes. 'You've got your gang, you've got everyone round here cowed. I've got the whole bloody city behind me. Do you still like those odds?'

They were inches apart. He could see the sweat on Gilmore's face and the first streaks of grey on the red whiskers. Then the man turned away suddenly.

'Come on,' he said loudly as he walked away, 'we'll find the fucking murderer ourselves.' Half a dozen men followed him, brushing through the throng.

Harper watched them leave, jamming his hands into his trouser pockets to stop them shaking.

'That was brave, sir.' The constable had finally found enough courage to come forward. Already the crowd was starting to thin. The show was over.

The inspector shook his head. 'No, that was the law.' He took a few deep breaths. 'What's your name?'

'Constable Thompson, sir.' He was in his forties, with a thick face and the bright veins of a drinker.

'You'd better tell me what happened.' He looked at Gilmore's body. It was face down, turned away from York Road. The arms were splayed, and three knife wounds pierced the back of his jacket. Blood had leaked on to the cobbles, flies already feeding in the pools.

'I was two streets away when I heard people shouting, sir. I came as fast as I could. He was like that, already dead. About five minutes later Charlie and his lads showed up.'

'Why would Declan be here?'

Thompson gave a small cough. 'He has someone at number twenty-seven, sir. In a manner of speaking, anyway. A woman named Maggie Dawson. She's the mother of his child. Sean, the lad's called. He's five.'

'Go on.' The sooner he knew, the sooner he could get to work.

'They're not together any more but he wouldn't let her leave the area. He wanted to keep the boy close.'

Thompson turned his head. Harper listened but couldn't hear anything; then six coppers came marching round the corner.

'Two of you look after the corpse,' the inspector told them as they approached. 'The rest of you house-to-house along the street and back on York Road. I want to know everything people saw.' He pointed at the youngest of the uniforms. 'You— find something to cover Gilmore and arrange for the van to take him to Dr King.' He turned back to Thompson. 'The child. Who knew about it?'

'Everyone, sir.' The man smiled. 'It's not a secret. He comes here twice a week, every Tuesday and Thursday.'

'This boy Sean, does he go to school?'

'No, sir. Declan wouldn't allow it.'

There was no point even asking who'd want Declan dead; the list would never end.

'Who should I talk to?' This was Thompson's beat; he'd know.

The constable scratched his chin. 'Maggie Dawson's landlady.' He pointed toward the house. 'And Maggie herself. Though I daresay all she'll feel is happiness, poor lass.'

'You look after things here,' the inspector told him. 'Once the body's gone, start talking to people. I need witnesses.'

'A lot of people will have been going round with their eyes closed this morning, sir. You know what I mean.'

He did. Being deaf, dumb and blind meant being safe.

'Remember, Charlie's going to be looking. I want the killer first.'

'Yes, sir.'

Number twenty-seven was exactly the same as every other house on Bread Street: soiled bricks, front door opening on to the pavement. He glanced over his shoulder. The only people left were Thompson and another policeman standing over the corpse. Everyone else had melted away. Around him he felt the heat of the day building and pushing against his face.

The woman who answered the door had a hawk face and hard eyes, her thin mouth frowning at him. As she glanced out and caught a glimpse of Declan's body she crossed herself quickly.

'You'll be the police.' There was no pleasure in her voice.

'Detective Inspector Harper. You know Declan Gilmore?'

'Of course.'

'What kind of arrangement do you have with him, Mrs . . .?'

'Riley,' she told him. 'My man was Ben Riley.'

He remembered the name. A violent little man, one of Gilmore's Boys of Erin, he'd died in a knife fight. So this was his widow's reward, the inspector thought.

'What do you do for Declan?'

'I give Maggie and her boy a place to live. He pays her rent.'

'What else?'

'He wanted me to keep an eye on her.' Her own eyes were defiant, but he wasn't going to rise to that challenge.

'Did you see anything this morning?'

'Nothing until I heard everyone outside. He was lying in the street.'

'No one running away?'

She shook her head. 'Not a thing.'

'I'd like to talk to Miss Dawson.'

'Upstairs, the door straight ahead.'

He climbed the stairs to a cramped landing with bare boards, feeling her eyes on him. The bannister wobbled under his hand. Maggie Dawson answered at the first knock. Her window looked down at the street, Gilmore's body displayed in front of her. A small boy sat on the bed, knees gathered up. He and his mother both had the gaunt look of people who'd never had enough to eat, and the pale colour of people who didn't see the sun.

'Miss Dawson, I'm Detective Inspector—'

'Is he dead?' She was in her middle twenties, a thin shawl tied like a scarf around her dark hair.

'Yes.'

She gave a deep sigh of relief. 'Good.'

'Do you know who did it?' he asked. 'Did you see it happen?'

'No,' Dawson replied. 'But if I did I'd give him a kiss.' She reached across and ruffled her son's hair. The boy looked up at her hopefully. 'We're free now, Sean.'

'Free?' He didn't know the word. But how many on the Bank would?

She was happy to talk, as if it had been too long since she could speak her mind. Maggie had been Declan's girl when she was younger. He'd been dangerous, attractive, and she'd been proud to be seen with him. Never mind what her parents thought; Gilmore was an important man and some of that rubbed off on her when she was at his side.

It lasted until she became pregnant. He stopped calling on her then, but still kept a watchful, controlling eye. Any man who showed an interest was warned off. Gilmore wouldn't marry her but he wouldn't let her go. Her parents forced her out of the house, refusing to be shamed by their daughter.

Maggie had nothing. With her belly growing, no one would give her a job. Declan made the offer of a room. She had no choice; she grabbed it. When Sean was born he wanted to take the child and have him raised. But with nothing else in the world she wasn't going to give up her baby.

'I told him he'd have the bairn over my dead body,' she said with a sad, wry laugh. 'For a while I thought he would.'

She was kept to the house under Mrs Riley's eye, never allowed out alone. No callers, no friends. Declan came on Tuesday and Thursdays to see the lad, an attentive father but not generous. He refused to let Sean go to school. He'd never gone himself, he said, and it had done him no harm.

Harper stared out of the window. The mortuary cart had arrived, the horse standing placidly as Gilmore's body was loaded in the back. All that remained was a smeared pool of blood on the cobbles.

'Did you arrange for someone to kill him?'

'Me? How would I do that?' She turned, eyes wide. 'That bitch doesn't let me talk to anyone. She worshipped the ground he walked on, the bastard. You know what I did when I saw him down there? I thanked God.'

He wasn't going to learn anything more here. Gilmore would already have his men out, asking questions. In his mind the inspector could hear the clock ticking.

'If you hear anything, Miss Dawson, please tell me.'

She nodded and he turned away towards the door.

'You never said your name.'

'Detective Inspector Harper.'

'Is your missus called Annabelle?'

'Yes.' Her question surprised him. 'Why?'

'Tell her Jenny Dawson's sister said hello, will you?'

Nothing yet from the house-to-house but the inspector didn't expect much. This was the Bank, where no one liked the police. Gilmore would hear far more from these people. They were scared of him.

Millgarth was quiet, the bobbies out on their beats. Superintendent Kendall waved him in as he tapped on the door.

'Well?'

He summed up the little he knew, and finished: 'It's going to be a race between us and Charlie Gilmore.'

Kendall rubbed a hand across his mouth. 'Any ideas who's responsible?'

'Not a clue. It must have happened on York Road or right at the corner of Bread Street. It's busy there, especially in the morning. Someone saw it. Whether they'll talk to us is another matter.'

'Could it be our mystery man? The same one who killed Tench and Bradley. Upping the stakes?'

'It's possible.' He'd tried to puzzle it on the way back to the station. There were plenty who'd love Declan dead, but few with the courage to try. George Archer would never be so stupid. His men would stand out round there. And why would he want to start a war when he was trying to become respectable? There was nothing in it for him.

'I'm going to need more men, sir,' he said.

'Do you think Wharton's up to the job?' He could sense the superintendent's reluctance.

'He's good. Real potential.' Harper hesitated. 'But I thought you didn't want him around anything that might involve Archer.'

'We don't have much choice.'

A noise made them stir, loud shouts that lasted so long even Harper heard it clearly. He dashed through to see Ash forcing a man up against Tollman's desk.

'What have you got?' the desk sergeant asked.

'Resisting arrest, assaulting a police officer, suspicion of murder.'

'I'll get him down in the cells for you, Fred.' Tollman grabbed the prisoner's shirt with a large fist and pulled him close. 'You'd best do as you're told if you know what's good for you.'

'That's the carter I was looking for. Jeb,' Ash explained, brushing dirt off his suit. 'He didn't seem to think he needed to help us.'

'Let him stew for a while. Tollman will make him feel welcome. We have something else.'

'It's not Archer, is it, sir?'

They were back up on Bread Street, Ash at his side. Only the blood dried on the road was a reminder of the death. Women were out, donkeystoning their steps and gossiping, eyeing them warily as they passed.

'No. He's got more sense than this.'

'Declan,' the sergeant mused, 'where do we start?' He glanced back and nodded. 'Sir.'

It was Wharton, rushing to join them. He hadn't heard the slap of shoe leather on pavement. Bloody hearing.

'The superintendent said you wanted me, sir.' The young man's eyes were wide with excitement, eager to work on his first big case.

'I need everyone I can get,' Harper told him.

'What do you want me to do, sir?'

The inspector remembered how he felt the first time he'd been involved in a murder. Wharton would learn it was nothing special. Just the grind of police work, knocking on doors and asking questions, then hoping people had told you something close to the truth.

But what did he want them all to do? All the house-to-house had yielded was people who might as well have been in another county for the help they'd given.

'Sergeant, go and talk to Archer. I really don't believe this has anything to do with him, but I don't want him poking his nose in.'

'Yes, sir. About this time he should be at the Bull and Mouth for his dinner.'

'And if he has any ideas about who killed Declan . . .'

'He might decide to dob someone in for the fun of it.'

'Use your head.' He watched Ash stride away and turned. 'Right, Mr Wharton, you're with me. I hope you're feeling brave.'

The Sword was alive with men. A crowd had gathered on the pavement, spilling over on to the road. Men in their shirt-sleeves, trousers held up with braces, caps on their heads. Young and older, and not a woman to be seen.

Harper pushed his way through, sensing Wharton close behind. Two large men blocked the door.

'You'd better move,' the inspector told them. 'I'm going inside.'

'Mr Gilmore gave his orders—' one began.

'We're the police,' he stated. 'You can let me in or I can arrest you. It's your choice.'

'You and whose army?' the larger one laughed. He was heavily muscled, bushy red mutton-chop whiskers obscuring his cheeks.

Harper didn't bother to reply. He brought his knee up fast and hard between the man's legs then watched him gasp and topple.

'Do you want the same?' he asked the other guard.

Gilmore was sitting at the large table, a glass of Irish whiskey in front of him, giving orders to waiting men.

The babble of voices faded away as people turned to stare.

'Get out, Inspector.' Gilmore kept his voice even. 'You're not welcome here.'

'You and I are going to have a talk.'

'We don't have anything to say to each other.' He made the words sound final.

'Then I'll do the talking, and you're going to listen.' Harper glanced around the faces in the room, all of them hard as stone. 'I'm going after Declan's killer, not you. Make sure you remember that, because if you get in my way, you'll end up in a cell.' His gaze moved slowly across the room. 'Any of you.'

'Have you finished?' Gilmore's voice was a rumble.

'You've been warned.'

'You've said your piece, Inspector. I did you the courtesy of listening. Now get out of here.'

Harper barged his way past sullen faces out on the pavement and through to fresh air, riding the anger inside. It had probably been a waste of breath. But he'd needed to do it, to tell Charlie Gilmore publicly that he was in charge.

'Will you do it, sir?'

He'd forgotten that Wharton was there. The lad was pale and scared.

'Arrest them?' the inspector asked in surprise. 'Of course I will. Charlie knows it, too. I don't make empty threats. But it won't stop him.'

'Then why bother, sir?' He kept looking around.

'Because if we hadn't gone in there, he'd think he was in command. I needed to remind him that he's not.' He looked at Wharton's face. 'We were safe enough. Even Charlie Gilmore isn't stupid enough to attack a copper.'

'What are we going to do now?'

'Back to Millgarth.'

'The people round there are only going to talk to Gilmore,' Harper said. They were in the office; Kendall leaned against a desk, smoking and listening intently. 'We won't hear a word.'

The superintendent turned to Ash. 'You spoke to Archer. What did he have to say?'

'He'd already heard by the time I found him, sir, but he looked shocked,' the sergeant said. 'Like he couldn't believe it.'

'Couldn't believe his luck?'

Ash shook his head. 'Stunned more like, sir,' he answered after a moment. 'But he did tell me he'd pass on anything he learned to Gilmore.'

Kendall raised an eyebrow. 'What did you say to that?'

'I suggested he might like to speak to us instead.'

The super ran a hand through his hair. 'Any ideas?'

'Have you talked to the carter you arrested yet?' Harper asked Ash.

'It's the next thing I'm going to do, sir.'

'I want a name for this red-headed man. A better description. Anything we can use.'

'Do you think he could be involved in Gilmore's death, sir?'

Harper sighed. 'Right now I don't know a damned thing.'

'I want men out there. Talk to your informants. I'll go and see the ones I know.' Kendall took a watch from his waistcoat pocket. 'Meet back here at six.'

They all looked dispirited. The window in the office was wide open but the air still felt heavy and stifling. The clock ticked loudly on the wall. Five past six.

'Anything?' Kendall asked and they all shook their heads. Wherever they went, Gilmore's men had been there first. He was offering good money for information about his brother's murder; the police couldn't compete with that.

Only Ash had news.

'Jeb the carter admitted everything in the end.'

'Who hired him?'

'It's just the same as O'Shea, sir. Received a message to be somewhere at such-and-such a time. Two guineas for his trouble. No names.'

'What about this red-haired man?'

'Claimed he'd never seen him before, doesn't know his name. He had his face hidden most of the time.'

'Do you believe him?' Kendall asked.

'I do, sir.' He hesitated. 'I might have pushed him a little to be sure . . .'

'Anything that shows?'

'No, sir.'

'Then don't worry about it.' Harper could see the concern on the super's face. 'Go home, let's think about it again in the morning. We'll have plenty of uniforms out tonight to stop any trouble.'

THIRTEEN

'Tom?'

'What?' He looked up from his food. White's Chop House was crowded and noisy. Too many voices, too much sound confusing his ear.

Annabelle smiled. 'I just asked if you were enjoying it.'

He'd barely noticed the food. The lamb was juicy, with a strong mint sauce to set off the taste, roasted potatoes, and a large helping of cabbage. But it was simply something to put in his mouth.

She'd been waiting when he came home from Millgarth, wearing her best frock and the pale yellow scarf he'd bought her, her hair artfully arranged and a bonnet in her hands.

He'd pushed open the door to the parlour, glad to be back. It crashed into something, leaving a space just wide enough for him to squeeze through.

A wooden tea chest, crammed with books and folders, blocked the way.

A ledger with *Bye-Laws of the Society* written in flowing script on the cover. Another marked *Minutes of Meetings*. Everything she'd need for her new role as secretary.

'I've been waiting for you.' Mary was in her arms, reaching out for her father. He took one of the tiny, pudgy hands and squeezed it lightly. Annabelle nodded towards the chest. 'There's another like that arriving tomorrow.' She shook her head. 'God only knows where we'll put them all.'

'Starting to regret it?'

'Not a chance.' She grinned and kissed him. 'Someone's going to be coming to help out with the accounts, anyway. I'll be able to focus on other things.'

'Your research on drink?'

'That, arranging the meetings, and about a hundred and one other bits and bobs. Now Miss Ford's working with the Independent Labour Party so much I'll be a Jill-of-all-trades.'

She paused. 'Anyway, it made me decide something. We're going out tonight, you and me. It's about time we stepped out on our own. And the way you look right now it'll do you the power of good.'

She was right. It had been too long – too far back to remember. But tonight? He was dog-tired, his brain swirling and numb from the day.

'Before you say a word, I heard all about Declan Gilmore,' she continued. 'You know the world's a better place without someone like that. Come on, Tom, it'll take you out of yourself.'

'What about—?'

'Ellen's going to look after her ladyship. She'll spoil her rotten.' Annabelle took his arm. 'Hurry up, I'm famished.'

The hackney had dropped them on Boar Lane, all the hubbub of a summer evening around them. People paraded, stopping to stare at the extravagant displays in the windows at the Grand Pygmalion. A young couple, their heads together, stared at rings in the jeweller's window. Somewhere in the distance a group of men was shouting and laughing.

'I told you,' she said, smiling at all the life around them. 'Now, where are we going to eat?'

'I thought we might go on to the music hall afterwards,' Annabelle suggested as they ate their pudding. She wiped a trace of the jam roly-poly from her mouth. 'Do you fancy that?'

He knew what the question meant: she already had the rest of the evening planned.

'Who's playing?'

'There's Vesta Tilley at the City Varieties.' She glanced at him from under here eyelashes. 'We could have a good singalong. Burlington Bertie.'

He wasn't keen. All he wanted was his bed. But she had that look in her eyes, and he couldn't deny her. Tomorrow was Saturday and she had a meeting of women to address in the evening. Monday she'd start as secretary to the Suffragist Society.

'I can manage that.'

She beamed. 'Good. We'll have a laugh. The other acts don't look bad, either.' She seemed so eager that it was impossible to gainsay her. Like a little girl given a treat. Would their daughter be like that in ten years or so? She could do a lot worse than take after her mother. Annabelle played with the fringe of the scarf. 'I love this. The colours are beautiful. I don't know what possessed you to buy it, though.'

'I just saw it,' he told her. No need to mention that he tried to question the draper selling it.

'Well, it's beautiful. Thank you.'

As soon as they'd finished she was on her feet as he paid the waiter, adjusting her hat, ready to leave. They strolled up Briggate, the evening still warm. Omnibuses and trams trundled by, but the carts had all gone for the night. The air was still heavy, filled with the stink of industry.

All the pubs were doing good business, bustling and loud, gin palaces glittering with lights while the old inns remained darker and more sombre, and the cheap beershops littered with sadness and regret.

There was a queue for tickets at the Varieties. He started to ask for two in the circle but Annabelle nudged his elbow.

'Give over. You can't enjoy yourself properly up there,' she said to him.

'Stalls,' he told the young woman behind the desk.

A glass of gin for her, a beer for him and they took their seats. The theatre was splendid, lamps glowing, plush red velvet and gold paint. A place to forget all their cares, to laugh at the old jokes and sing the songs they all knew.

Glancing around, he picked out a few familiar faces. Crooks, pickpockets, thieves, all of them enjoying a night off from crime. As soon as the compère announced Vesta everyone began to roar and shout and Annabelle grinned and grabbed his hand.

'That was lovely,' she whispered as she removed her dress, taking time to hang it properly.

'I enjoyed myself,' he answered, bending over the cot to watch Mary sleeping. So innocent, so wonderful, he thought. He recalled something. 'I met someone who asked to be remembered to you.'

'Oh?'

Annabelle sat on the bed and began to roll down her stocking. His eyes followed her hands carefully.

'She said she was Jenny Dawson's sister.'

Suddenly she was attentive. 'Jenny? She helped me out of a lot of scrapes when we were young. We started at Bank Mills together when we were eight. Which sister was it?'

'Maggie.'

Then she wanted to know everything and he told her, seeing the determination growing on her face.

'What's she going to do now?' Annabelle asked as he finished.

'I don't know.' He'd been thinking about Declan's killer, not the woman.

'Number twenty-seven, you said?'

'That's right.' He didn't ask why she wanted to know. She looked as if she had her plans. Then her expression softened.

'I don't suppose you'd like to help me get this corset off, would you?'

It was half-request, half-invitation. How could he refuse?

'Sir?'

Harper was reading the brief reports from the night constables. There'd been no real trouble after Declan's death, but violence simmered close to the surface. He glanced up at Wharton, standing to attention in front of him.

'Easy, you're not on parade.'

'Yes, sir.' He appeared even less comfortable as he tried to relax. 'It's this thing with Miss Brooker, the girl in the river.'

'I know there's plenty going on but I remember who she is,' the inspector told him with a smile.

'I can't put it out of my head. I thought I'd take a walk again last night and see if I could find anyone who remembered her.'

'Did you have any luck?'

'I came across two women who claimed they'd seen her, sir. Sometimes by herself, and with a young man on a couple of occasions.' He smiled.

'What about the night she vanished?'

'They're not sure, sir. Don't really remember.'

The chance of ever discovering the truth behind Charlotte Brooker's death was tiny; there'd probably always be some small question over it. Still, the investigation was giving Wharton a good taste of the job – frustration, as much as anything else. That was an important part of being a detective, though. It wasn't like being on the beat, where most things were resolved in minutes.

'What about this young man she was supposed to have? Did anyone give you a description?'

'Not a good one, sir.' The lad frowned. 'About the only thing everyone can agree on is that he had red hair.'

Red hair? No; he dismissed it, it had to be coincidence. There had to be hundreds of red-headed men in Leeds.

'Anything more?'

'Not really sir.'

Harper sat back, stroking the bristles on his chin. 'What does your gut tell you about all this?' Wharton had experience in uniform, he'd been picked for his potential.

'Honestly, sir, if I had to say, I'd call it an accident,' he replied hesitantly. 'I'm not sure I believe the sister that Charlotte was sometimes low.'

'Do you want to make that your decision?'

'Not quite yet, sir,' he answered after a little thought. 'I'd like to go out once or twice more and see if I can find anything else.'

'So you're not convinced?'

'Just something niggling, that's all.'

Harper grinned. It was the kind of attitude he liked. Someone too sure about everything was no good to him.

'Then carry on a little while longer, until you're satisfied. But it'll have to be on your own time. At least until we find who killed Declan Gilmore.'

'Do you think we will, sir?'

'That's why they pay us, Mr Wharton.'

'Yes, sir.' He didn't move. 'Do you mind if I ask?'

The inspector cocked his head. 'What?'

'Is it true what they say about your hearing?'

'Yes, it is.' He tried to hide it but everybody knew; you didn't keep secrets like that on the force. At least the lad had the grace to look embarrassed by his question.

'Only you'd never know, sir, really,' Wharton said, trying to recover.

'Thank you.' He smiled. It might be a lie but it was a comfort. The inspector spent the day hunting his informants. By afternoon he'd seen most of them, but he might as well have stayed at Millgarth. All of them stayed tight-lipped. Even the offer of money didn't help.

If any of them knew who'd killed Declan they weren't going to admit it. Not one of them had heard a whisper about it. But why would they, when Charlie Gilmore would be offering more for information? And if that didn't work he'd use threats.

From the faces in the office when he returned, it was clear that none of the others had learned anything either. King's post-mortem report lay on his desk. Declan had died from three stab wounds to his back. He'd probably staggered up to fifty yards before collapsing and dying. No facts they didn't already know.

Wharton brought in the only snippet. He'd talked to someone who claimed to have seen a man running up York Road, away from Bread Street. But there was no description and no one else seemed to have noticed.

Harper's feet ached; he was tired and not in the mood when Tollman motioned him over as he was leaving the station.

'I thought you'd better know before you went home, sir,' he said quietly.

'What?' He could feel the pulse beating in his neck. 'Has something happened?'

The sergeant's lips twitched into a smile. 'In a matter of speaking, sir. Evidently your missus was up on the Bank today. Went to visit that lass of Declan Gilmore's and brought her out of there.'

So that was what she'd started planning last night, he thought.

'Thank you for telling me.'

Tollman's smile became a broad grin. 'That's not the half of it, sir. Someone must have told Charlie Gilmore. According to Constable Thompson, he wasn't too happy when he heard and went haring up there. He and your wife had words and she slapped him.' He beamed. 'Thank her for me, will you, sir?'

Harper laughed. It was easy to believe. Annabelle wouldn't let any man cow her.

'Did she leave with Miss Dawson?'

'That's what I was told, sir.'

She'd won. He'd have loved to see it. It was rare that anyone got the better of Gilmore, especially in public. He'd never forget that humiliation.

The tea chest of books had been moved and another stood next to it. In the bedroom Mary was playing on the floor, toddling quickly towards him when she heard the footsteps and wrapping her arms around his leg until he picked her up. Annabelle was examining herself in the mirror, making an adjustment to the ribbon around her neck. Her saw her smile reflected at him, disappearing as swiftly as it came.

'Ready to speak tonight?'

'As I'll ever be.' It was always the same. She'd been a speaker at suffrage meetings for two years now, but she was always nervous, scared of failing.

'I heard about your exploits,' he said.

She sighed. Her face held an air of sadness and regret.

'I couldn't leave Maggie there like that. I found her a room with Mrs Hardisty and offered her a job making bread. The timing's good, Caroline's given in her notice, anyway.'

'And you slapped Charlie Gilmore.'

'He had it coming. He thought she shouldn't go. I just reminded him that the Gilmores don't own her.' She shrugged and tugged lightly at the ribbon again then nodded with satisfaction.

He leaned close and kissed her lips, smelling the faint perfume she wore. 'I'm proud of you.'

'You don't think it was stupid?'

'Not at all. About time someone reminded him he's just a man.' He paused. 'Talking about the bakeries, has Elizabeth made her decision yet?'

She gave a tight shake of her head. He could see the cloud in her eyes; something was troubling her and it wasn't the encounter that morning.

'What is it?' Harper asked. 'What's wrong?'

Her took her hands and led her to the settee.

'It's nothing really.' Annabelle's voice was dull and empty as she raised her face to his. 'I saw someone I once knew this afternoon. He looked so terrible. I just know he's dying.'

The story came out: she'd taken Mary down to the city art

gallery on the Headrow. They'd strolled around the galleries and stopped to look at some of the new work on display.

'Have you heard of someone called Atkinson Grimshaw?'

'Of course,' he replied in surprise. Everyone in Leeds knew who he was. He was famous. The painter of moonlight, that was what the newspapers called him. 'Why?'

'They had two of his new pieces there. He was looking at them.'

'You know him?' He was confused. 'You never said.'

'It was a long time ago. Before any of this.' She shook her head and gazed around the room. 'Years back, when the warehousemen went on strike. I'd been turned off from my position and I was on my way back to the Bank feeling sorry for myself. He was out sketching.' Annabelle gave a brief, sad smile. 'The whole place must have looked dead, I suppose. No boats, the river empty.' She shook her head, clearing the memory. 'Anyway, he made me stand there with my bundle of clothes, and put me in his picture. Paid me two guineas for doing it, too. It just . . .' The words faltered for a moment. 'Someone being kind, it meant a lot.'

He didn't know what to say. She'd never told him that someone had painted her. But there was so much Annabelle had never said about the murky country that was her past. He'd never asked; it was her choice to talk about it or not.

'Did he remember you?'

'He gave me one of those looks. You know: I-know-you-but-I-don't-remember-where-from. I had to tell him.'

'What did he say?'

'Laughed a little and asked what I thought of his work.' She paused. 'He looked as if something had hollowed him out, Tom. Like he was just a shell. Trying to keep a brave face, but you could see it. I don't know why, but it hurt me. In my mind he was still the same person who'd put me in his picture. Not older and wasting away.'

He squeezed her hand then held her close as she began to cry. As the tears flowed he knew they weren't really for Grimshaw but for all those she'd cared about who'd gone.

Finally it passed, and she dabbed at her eyes with a handkerchief.

'Daft, I know.' Her eyes moved to the clock. 'I'd better get a move on. The hackney will be waiting downstairs.' She cuddled Mary. 'Are you sure you'll be all right on your own? I can ask Ellen to look in before she goes out with her fella.'

'We won't have a problem,' he assured her. But she still insisted on going through the routine.

'Go,' he told her finally and hugged her close.

'If you need anything . . .' she began and he shooed her out.

'Well,' he said to Mary once they were alone, 'it looks as if it's you and me tonight. What do you think? Should we have some fun?'

FOURTEEN

'**B**illy?'

He stirred, half-hearing her, not opening his eyes. He was comfortable in the bed, the pillow soft under his head. It had been a long day, investigating a fire in a yard that had killed a child and left three others in hospital.

'Billy Reed,' Elizabeth hissed and he turned slowly.

'What is it?' His voice was a mumble smothered by the sheets.

'I'm going to do it.' She sounded wide awake. 'I'm going to buy them.'

'Are you sure?' He turned, blinking in the darkness, pushing himself up on one elbow.

'I'm positive. We're never going to have a chance like this again, are we?'

No, he knew they wouldn't. Owning the shops could be the making of them. It would change everything in their lives. But it would be her name on the signs, she'd be the one running them; it had to be her decision. He wanted her to do it but he dared not come out and say so. Elizabeth had to be the one to make the choice.

'I'll tell Annabelle on Monday,' she continued, rolling on to her back and staring up at the ceiling. 'Billy, am I doing the right thing?'

'You'll be wonderful at it,' he said, pressing his hand over hers. 'It'll be fine.'

She fell asleep, soft snores coming from her mouth. He lay awake, staring up at the ceiling. Life took strange turns. Five years before he could never have imagined being here. Being happy. For so long after fighting in Afghanistan, he'd pushed away his devils with evenings of drinking. Now he didn't care if he touched another drop. Elizabeth had changed him and she hadn't even needed to try. This business of the shops scared him; they could lose all they had. But after what she'd given him, he wanted everything for her. That wasn't a debt. It was love.

Harper left his wife and daughter asleep in the bedroom, dressing silently then closing the door with a quiet click. In the afternoon the three of them would go up to Roundhay Park. Before that, though, he needed to work.

No tram on a Sunday morning and only the sound of his own boots for company as he walked into town. It was so early that dawn was still dull, just the promise of sun and more heat out on the horizon, close enough to leave him sweating by the time he reached Millgarth.

The city seemed eerily silent. No smoke rose from the chimneys. No rumble of carts and omnibuses on the streets. Good men and bad would still be in their beds. The day of rest, he thought wryly. For some, perhaps.

A pile of reports sat on his desk. Even as he began to leaf through them the inspector knew they'd contain nothing. Charlie Gilmore's money and men had silenced everyone. If not that, Declan's killer was clever enough to be invisible.

Was it linked to the murders of Tench and Bradley? He didn't know how but something told him that was right. Trying to connect them had plagued him all through the evening as he played with Mary, bathed her, then read from *The Princess and the Goblin* as she lay in her bed, eyes slowly closing.

The thoughts were still with him when Annabelle returned, her face flushed with joy. The worries and fears of her day had been banished. But his wouldn't leave.

He'd gone through everything by the time Ash arrived, followed closely by Wharton and Superintendent Kendall.

'Any suggestions?' the super asked. He looked as dapper as ever, but the strain showed on his face. His eyes looked tired. More than that: exhausted.

'We can lean on people more, sir,' Ash suggested. 'I'm not sure it'll work, though. Not against Charlie Gilmore.'

'Nor am I,' Kendall agreed slowly.

'We're not going to get anything on Declan's murder,' Harper said. 'The best we'll manage is the dregs after Charlie's got the rest. This happened on his turf.'

'We're the police—' the superintendent began.

'I know. Honestly, I don't think he'll find much of any use, either. Whoever did this was thinking far ahead. What we need is to go back and find out why Tench and Bradley were killed.'

'Why, sir?' the sergeant asked.

'There's no shortage of people who wanted Declan dead. We're agreed on that?' He looked at the others, seeing them nod. 'But who'd do it there, right on the Bank? No one in their right mind. You'd wait until he was elsewhere and more vulnerable.'

'It could be someone desperate,' Wharton said.

'I don't believe that,' Harper answered. 'Look, Tench was never meant to be found. That's why he was thrown in the lake with a weight around him.'

'Yes, sir.' Ash's voice was grim as he remembered his friend.

'It was pure luck that we discovered his body. As soon as we had, though, Bradley ended up dead as well.'

The superintendent pulled out his pipe and started to fill it. 'We know that. But I still don't see how it leads to Gilmore.'

'It's a feeling,' Harper admitted. 'There's nothing I can point to. But the timing . . .'

'Someone coming in and trying to take over. Is that what you mean? Find me some evidence to connect them, Tom. That's what we don't have. In the meantime let's keep our minds open. All of us,' he added before vanishing into his office.

'You're with me this morning,' Harper told the sergeant.

'What about me, sir?' Wharton wondered.

'Back to routine for you, I'm afraid.' He picked three thin folders off his desk. 'Burglaries. Other crimes don't end just because someone's killed Declan Gilmore. We still have to deal with them.'

'Yes, sir.' The lad looked crestfallen, as if someone had told him off.

'You need the experience and I'm trusting you to do a thorough job.'

'Where are we going, sir?' Ash asked as they walked out along Woodhouse Lane. In the distance church bells were ringing. How many would answer the call, he wondered? He hadn't grown up with church; his parents never went. When you worked six long days a week, the chance to sleep longer on a Sunday meant more than a hymn and a sermon.

'We're going to have another word with Eustace Morley.'

'That idea of yours, sir. That someone's trying to take over.'

'Do you think I'm mad?' the inspector asked with a smile.

'Not all all, sir. But there are two questions, aren't there?'

'I know. Who could arrange all that without anyone knowing, and why didn't they kill Morley, too?'

Ash's moustache twitched in a grin. 'That's more or less what I was going to say.'

Claypit Lane was nothing special, but it was far enough from the factories for the air to smell a little sweeter and cleaner. Number two stood at the end of the terrace, a garden barely larger than a postage stamp in front, a small yard at the back, hidden from the ginnel by a wall. Two men stood, one on either side of the street: the guards sent by Gilmore and Archer to watch the boxer and each other.

The landlady let them in grudgingly, pointing them up the stairs and to the bedroom at the back.

'He'll not be up yet,' she warned. 'He likes his sleep on a Sunday.'

Harper banged on the door for a full minute before Morley answered, bleary-eyed and angry.

'What?' was all the boxer said when he saw them.

'I don't think you've been telling me the truth,' the inspector told him.

Morley shrugged and turned back into the room. A half-light came through the closed curtains, and the air was stuffy, catching in the throat. There was a smell of sweat, a very male musk.

'What do you mean?' The boxer sat on the bed, yawning and rubbing the sleep away from his face.

'Tell me something, Eustace. Why are you still alive and your friends dead?' Harper wanted to catch the man before his mind was awake and see what escaped. 'Here you are, sleeping well all night while they're under the ground.'

The boxer shook his head. 'You make it sound like my fault.'

'Is it?'

Slowly, Morley stood, flexing his fists, until he was looming over Harper.

'Don't start accusing me,' he said through gritted teeth. 'Not if you want to get out of here in one piece.'

The inspector stood his ground, Ash ready behind him.

'Don't threaten me,' Harper told him. 'Unless you prefer a cell to your own bed.'

'Give over.' He poured some water from a jug into the basin on a chest of drawers and splashed his checks, wiping a hand over his bald skull before reaching for a towel.

'Who's the red-haired man?'

'Eh?' Morley turned. 'You what?'

'Who do you know with red hair?'

'The Gilmores,' he answered after a pause. 'And Declan's dead, that's what they say.'

'That's right. He was spread out on the cobbles with stab wounds in his back.'

'I never really knew him.' His face hardened. 'And in case you're going to ask, how could I do anything with two men following me everywhere?'

'Why did Tench and Bradley have to die, Mr Morley?'

'How the hell would I know?' he snapped, on the edge of shouting.

Good, Harper thought; he was rattled. Maybe he'd reveal something. 'No ideas?'

'No.' He drew back the curtains, light pouring into the room.

'You haven't even thought about it?'

'Of course I bloody have.'

'They died and you didn't. Is that what you thought about?' The man didn't answer. 'Feeling guilty, perhaps?' Harper was prodding, provoking.

'Go on. Get yourselves gone.'

'Why, Mr Morley? A bit too close to the truth?'

He saw the boxer tense his muscles then breathe deeply. 'I said go.'

For a moment he weighed the decision. The man had control of himself once more. He wasn't going tell them a damn thing. If they stayed he'd be throwing his questions against a wall.

'Good day to you, Mr Morley.'

'Was it a waste of time, sir?' Ash asked as they walked away. Harper tipped his hat to the men keeping watch on Claypit Lane.

'No. I'm sure he knows something. The problem is discovering what it is.'

'I'm don't know we ever will. Not from him, anyway. Did you see it, though, the way he managed to close down? It was as if he shut a gate.'

'Yes.' Maybe it was a technique boxers learned, a way to keep the pain at a distance. He sighed. 'We're back to square one.'

'If we keep digging happen we'll turn up something, sir.'

The inspector snorted. 'With our luck we'll just find more bloody holes.'

At noon he left. There was nothing more on Declan. All they were doing was covering barren ground. Kendall had been seeking out his snouts once more, but he came back shaking his head.

Tench and Gilmore, Harper thought. Somehow it all began there. They needed to find the copper-haired man.

'Talk to Jeb the carter again,' he ordered Ash. 'And O'Shea. Get everything else you can on this mystery man.'

'Yes, sir.'

'Tom,' the superintendent said wearily, 'go. Enjoy your family. I think you've earned it.'

By one he was strolling up Roundhay Road with Annabelle and Mary, past the businesses and the factories and the endless streets that fanned away like fingers. Harper was dressed in his best suit, the one she'd given him as a Christmas present. She wore a pale grey gown with a wide-brimmed hat, tied under the chin with a silk ribbon the colour of sunset, a parasol over her shoulder.

Mary sat up in the baby carriage as her mother pushed her along, eyes wide with wonder at all the new things before her. Past

St Aidan's Church and through Harehills, then out beyond Gipton Woods before reaching the arch that led them into Roundhay Park.

It felt like a dusty, high summer day. Out here the clouds weren't so thick. There was blue sky, the sun shining down on their shoulders.

The band was already playing, brass notes ringing out over the grass. A large crowd was gathered around the stand. Ladies sat primly on rugs. Young men and their belles stopped to listen. One old woman in a bath chair smiled, nodding in time with the music as she was pushed by a bored nurse.

They stayed for the whole concert, right through to the national anthem at the end.

'That was grand,' Annabelle said when it was done. 'Can't beat music on a Sunday. Where do you want to go for our picnic?'

In the end they settled on the Upper Lake, spreading a rug on the slope and watching Mary as she ran around, tumbling and exploring. They had food in a basket, bread and dripping, and a bottle of beer to share. Rowing boats moved across the water, while ducks clamoured for crusts that children threw from the path.

'This'll set me up nicely for tomorrow. I've been looking forward to it all week.' Annabelle's voice was lazy. She stretched, keeping an eye on their daughter. 'And you need it, too.'

'I need a piece of luck even more.' Talking about it did no good. He changed the subject. 'Have you been to see Maggie Dawson today?'

'I popped over this morning. She seems to be settling in.' She shook her head. 'Kept thanking me like I'd done something special.'

'You did.'

'Not really.' She was on her feet, scurrying to stop Mary as the girl tried to speed away down the hill to the water. 'She's like greased lightning. What's it going to be like once she really starts, eh? We're going to need eyes in the back of our heads.'

'Especially if she's as lovely as her mother.'

'Go on. You could charm the birds off the trees, Tom Harper.' But she was grinning. 'I'll tell you one thing. It won't be the mills or service for her. Not if I have anything to do with it. She's going to get an education and do something with it. She's the real reason I'm doing all this, you know.'

'With the suffrage people, you mean?'

'Yes. To see she has something better. Her and the other little lasses, like that one over there.' She nodded towards a girl playing with a stick and a hoop. 'All of them.' Annabelle smiled and laughed at herself. 'Sounds daft, doesn't it? Me with my big ideas.'

In the distance he heard the steam whistle from the *Maid of Athens* as it glided around Waterloo Lake. 'Good ones, though.'

'Maybe.' She was silent for a long time, staring off into the distance. 'I said I was in service before I started at the Victoria. I never really told you much about that, did I?'

'No, you didn't.' She'd only mentioned it for the first time the night before. But there was so much about her past that she'd never revealed.

'I'd had it up to here with the mill, I wanted something different. Ended up at a big house. Turned into the old story.' She sighed. 'I was young and stupid enough to believe he really fancied me. I thought I'd end up as Lady Muck or something. As soon as they discovered I was up the spout I was out of there with no reference. Course, my family didn't want anything to do with me.' She was quiet for a long time. 'I lost the baby long before it was born. Who can tell, happen it was for the best. Then the Atkinsons took me on at the pub. The wife wasn't well by then and they needed the help.' Annabelle shrugged. 'You know the rest.'

'That's why you helped Maggie.'

'Maybe it was one reason,' she admitted. 'Anyway, now you know my big secret.' She turned and stared at him. 'Are you shocked? Wish you'd never married me?'

'Of course not,' he told her and squeezed her hand. 'But I wish I could get my hands on whoever did that to you.'

'I'm never going to tell you his name, Tom. It's all history now. But our lass isn't going to have anything like that. Nor any other girl, if I can do something about it.' She stood, gathered Mary up and put her in the baby carriage, then folded the rug and packed the basket in quick movements. 'Come on, we should probably start moving. It's a long walk home.'

Annabelle was quiet as they strolled. Mary fell asleep; all that exercise playing in the fresh air had tired her. He'd been honest, her admission made no difference to his feelings for her. He just hated that she'd been used that way. Like so many others before her.

'And tomorrow everything changes.' It was just words to break the long silence.

'Secretary of the Leeds Women's Suffrage Society.' She said it with wonder and pride, shaking her head. 'Who'd have thought it, eh?'

'You'll be wonderful.'

'I'll try. I'll give it my best. This pamphlet we're going to do could really change things. I'm sick of hearing people talk about the poor as if they're animals. Maybe they'll read it and learn something.'

He understood. He saw it every day. The line between hope and hopelessness. They were walking along it now. After the crisp green of the grass in the park, Sheepscar seemed dirty and shabby, the bricks covered with soot, every breath filled with smoke and dirt. It was home, though. There was nowhere else he'd rather be.

They left the perambulator in the hallway and he carried Mary tenderly up the stairs, her breath soft and warm against his neck. She didn't stir as he laid her in the crib and slipped off her tiny shoes. Harper stood for a moment, watching his daughter, enjoying the peace and the utter lack of worry on her face.

'Tom,' Annabelle called quietly from the parlour, 'someone slipped a note under the door for you.'

Sir, Please come to Millgarth as soon as you receive this. You're needed urgently.

He looked at her. 'I have to go.'

She nodded; by now she was used to this.

'At least we had a good afternoon,' she said.

FIFTEEN

'I'm sorry to drag you back in, Tom.' An empty plate stood on Kendall's desk, next to a cup and saucer. Even with the window wide open, the air felt baked, ripe.

'What's happened?'

The superintendent took a breath. 'One of George Archer's bodyguards has been killed.'

Christ. This could start a wildfire.

'Which one?' Archer kept four men around him.

'Bob Hill.'

The inspector tried to picture him. He had the faint image of a strong, tall man in an expensive suit and pomaded hair.

'What happened?'

'One of the constables was called to an empty house on Somerset Street. He found the body there.'

'Somerset Street?' It was where Archer had made his start. So close to where Tench and Ash grew up.

'Right on the corner with Dufton Court,' Kendall's voice was as weary as the ages. 'If that's not a message, nothing is. Ash and Wharton are out on the house-to-house. The word is that Archer's on his way.' His eyes flickered towards the clock. 'He's probably there by now.'

'How long ago did it happen?'

'The report came in just after four.'

When he was sitting on the grass and enjoying a picnic with his wife and daughter, all the cares banished from his mind. This certainly brought them all rushing back. He glanced at the clock. Almost seven.

'Do we know how he died?'

'The body's gone to Dr King but it looked like he'd been garrotted. I went over and saw the corpse.'

'Two bludgeoned, one stabbed, one garrotted.' Harper shook his head. 'I don't understand it.'

'At first I thought it must be Charlie Gilmore. Revenge for his brother. Then this arrived an hour ago.' He slid a piece of paper across the desk. The writing was shaky, only half-formed.

None of my men did this and not on my orders. CG.

'Will Archer believe that, though?'

'It seems like you were right,' the superintendent said darkly. 'Someone's trying to move in.'

Harper was trying to think, to find pieces that might fit together.

'I'm going over there.'

*   *   *

It took less than three minutes to reach Somerset Street. He didn't need to ask which house; a constable standing in the doorway of a building missing some of the slates from its roof told him everything.

The bobby saluted and moved aside to let him enter. Pieces of rubble littered the floor where part of the ceiling had caved in. Half the stairs were missing.

'Who found the body?' he asked.

'I did, sir.'

'What's your name?'

'Tollman, sir.' He paused for a heartbeat. 'The sergeant's my dad. This is my beat.'

He should have guessed: the lad had the same grave voice and mischievous eyes. All that was missing was the paunch and the moustache.

'Who reported it?'

'A lad and a lass, sir. I think they were trying to find some-where they wouldn't be disturbed, if you know what I mean.' He gave a smile. 'It scared them out of their wits.'

'How often do you go past here?'

'Every hour or so, sir. I wasn't that far away when I heard the shouting.'

'Where was the body?'

'Scullery, sir. He was face down. I recognized him as soon as I turned him over. George Archer likes to come round here regular and he brings his men with him.'

The inspector gazed up and down the street. Only a few people remained now there was nothing to see.

'I heard Archer was here.'

Constable Tollman pointed. 'Over at number twenty, sir. Him and the other bodyguard went inside half an hour ago. He came over but I wouldn't let him in. Had a face like thunder.'

'Who's on the house-to-house besides Wharton and Sergeant Ash?'

'Two constables, sir. I know they've done Somerset Street. They're fanning out from there.'

'Good,' Harper said approvingly. 'Keep your eye on this place for now. I'll go and have a word with Archer.'

There was nothing to distinguish number twenty; it was just

another house in the terrace, weighed down by years. There were cobwebs in the corners of the window frames, and the doorstep was dirty.

The tiny woman who answered his knock glared at him then moved aside. He followed the voices through to the parlour. The men filled the room. Archer had the only chair, his three body-guards standing. Roger Harrison looked away, keeping watch over Somerset Street. He moved forward as Harper entered.

Archer was impeccably dressed, the tie knotted just right, not a hair out of place, his face looking as if it had been shaved no more than an hour before. A businessman in the slums.

'Come to gloat, Inspector?' Acid dripped through the words. He gave a crooked smile. 'Do you need me to speak up so you can hear me?'

Everyone knew now, he thought. Water off a duck's back, Harper told himself. All Archer wanted to do was rile.

'I'm here to find out who killed him,' the inspector said.

'That's hardly difficult. We both know who did it.'

'And who's that?' He knew the reply but he wanted to hear the man say it.

'Charlie Gilmore.' Archer spat the name. 'He reckons I killed his brother so he's murdered one of my men.'

'Did you stab Declan? Or have it done?'

'Of course I didn't.' He gave Harper a withering look. 'I told your sergeant. Why would I do that?'

'I've got some news for you, then.'

The man looked at him with interest. 'Go on.'

'Charlie sent us a note. He says he's not responsible for this. For what it's worth, I believe him.'

'He's hardly going to admit it, is he?' Archer lit a cigarette.

Harper put his palms on the table, leaning forward until he was close enough to smell the bay rum on the other man's skin. 'Someone wants the two of you battling each other.'

'What would they gain from that?'

'You're a clever man, George.' Harper pushed himself upright. 'Work it out for yourself.'

He could see Archer thinking, chewing on his bottom lip.

'If it's not Charlie, who's doing it?' Archer asked after a minute.

'I don't know. But you can bet he's rubbing his hands

together with glee right now, waiting for the two of you to destroy each other.'

'Maybe Gilmore's lying.'

'He's not.'

'What are you going to do, then?' Archer was quieter and calmer now, his mind working.

'I told you: I'll find out who's doing this and put him in jail.' He paused for a moment. 'When did you last see Hill?'

'Yesterday afternoon. He said he was going out on the town. When he didn't turn up this morning I thought he was probably under the weather. You know, hungover. Then I got the message. When I find . . .'

He left the threat hanging in the air.

'I'm going to do my job, George,' Harper said quietly. 'And both you and Charlie are going to help.'

'Help the police?' He sneered.

What he needed was the pair of them sitting together, talking to each other. But that was never going to happen. Not with a copper in the room, anyway.

'By not attacking each other and staying out of my way.'

'You tell him that.'

'I'm going to,' Harper said. 'But right now I'm telling you.'

Archer stayed silent for almost a minute.

'How certain are you that Charlie's telling the truth?' he said finally.

'I'm positive.'

'I'm willing to admit that what you say makes sense. I know I had nothing to do with Declan.' He took a breath. 'Tell him I'll not go after him if he leaves my men alone. But,' he added, and the inspector knew exactly what he was going to say, 'I'll be hunting the bastard who killed Bob Hill.'

Of course. Anything less would look weak and vulnerable. Harper understood that; he knew he'd have to accept it as part of the deal. He just had to make certain he found the killer first.

'Good enough.'

'And if Charlie doesn't agree, it's no deal.'

'He will.'

It was less than a quarter of a mile from Somerset Street to the Sword, but it felt like crossing an entire country, over a boundary where the accents changed, filled with the lilt of Ireland. He walked past the guard on the door with a nod, then pulled out a chair across from Gilmore.

'I've got a proposition for you, Charlie.'

'You did well, Tom,' Kendall said approvingly. 'You stopped things turning bloody.'

The air had grown closer over the last hour, dark clouds massing to the west. There was going to be a thunderstorm tonight.

'For now.' Harper smiled wanly. 'It's a very fragile peace. They'll still be looking, but not at each other. But it buys us a little time.' He turned to the sergeant. 'What did you find?'

'If I had to guess, sir, I'd say it happened during the night. People over there know it's safer not to check if something wakes them up. One or two thought they might have heard something.' He shrugged. 'I doubt we'll get anything better than that, sir.'

'What about you?' the inspector asked Wharton. 'Did you find anything?'

'Nothing more than the sergeant told you,' he answered. 'I'm sorry, sir.'

If there was anything worthwhile, the people on Somerset Street would be saving it for George Archer. He'd grown up there, they were his people, the way those on the Bank belonged to Charlie Gilmore.

Harper looked at the superintendent. Each day he seemed a little more worn, the strain telling on his face. The man had to be under pressure from above, no question of that, but so far he'd shielded them from it. This killing would only add to it all.

'Wharton, Ash, I want you in the pubs tonight,' Kendall ordered. 'Have a listen to the gossip. It'll probably be nothing but there might be some little nugget.'

'What about me?' the inspector asked after they'd left. 'Where do you want me?'

'Go and see Dr King in the morning. He might be able to tell us something. Take a look at the body.' He sighed. 'Do you have any idea who's behind all this?'

'This man with the copper hair. He shows up and all this starts happening.' One question still niggled at him. 'I still don't understand why it began with Tench and Bradley.'

'I don't either.' Kendall ran a hand through his hair.

'If we can find the reason, maybe we can find the man.'

The superintendent snorted. 'Listen to us: ifs and maybes. Ideas, not answers.'

'What else do we have?'

'I know.' His voice was tired. Finally he nodded. 'Go ahead.'

He beat the storm. Walking through Sheepscar he heard the thunder off to the west and began moving faster. The bar in the Victoria was busy, people drinking beer to dampen the cloying heat. Dan the barman waved as he moved from customer to customer, sleeves rolled up, a wide grin on his face.

Upstairs, Mary was asleep, a thin sheet tucked around her in the cot, a few heat bumps standing out red on her skin. All the windows were open, the noise from the pub drifting up. Annabelle was sitting at the table, books and ledgers spread out in front of her.

'I thought the job didn't start until tomorrow,' Harper said, and kissed the nape of her neck.

'I want to see what I'm letting myself in for.' She smiled and purred, leaning back against him. 'Probably just as well, too. Miss Frobisher's a lovely old dear, but from the look of these books she should have retired long ago. It's a mess. It's going to take us a week just to put it in order. I'm glad they're giving me someone to help.'

The thunder crashed again, close enough to rattle the panes of glass. She put down the pen and capped the inkwell.

'We'd better get those closed before it starts pouring.'

The rain lasted more than half an hour. Even with the curtains drawn, the flashes of lightning were vivid in the sky. Rain hammered against the windows, bouncing off the ground and turning into rivers that flowed along the road. And Mary slept through it all with barely a whimper.

Finally it was over, rumbling away towards Selby and the coast. He cracked open the sash. The stuffiness had vanished and for once the air in Leeds smelled clean and fresh.

'Good sleeping weather,' Harper said as they lay in bed.

'Not bad for something else, either,' Annabelle told him. 'Is it?'

SIXTEEN

Harper woke with a start. Half past four and already the half-light of dawn. He shaved in cold water, the cut-throat razor cold against his skin, then dashed out of the pub. There was just enough of a chill in the air to make the morning beautiful, the sketch of blue, clear skies. But already smoke was rising from a few chimneys. Soon there'd be grime and dirt all the way to the horizon and the week would have begun.

Bobbies were coming in from the night shift, ready to go off duty with all the usual talking and moaning. Soon enough Ash and Wharton would arrive to write their reports.

He needed to go back to the beginning. To the kidnaps that Tench, Bradley and Morley had done. The draper, the chemist and the bible seller.

Six o'clock. At least two hours before any of those places would be open. His face grim, the inspector walked through the market to the café. He needed food, he needed tea. And he needed to calm his mind.

'You don't look like a happy man, Inspector. Nothing wrong with your daughter, I hope.'

He glanced up and saw Tom Maguire watching him, a cup of tea in his hands.

'She's fine. This is work.'

The union man sat with a smile. 'Work, the undoing of us all, eh?'

'All the deaths. I'm sure you've heard.'

'I have.' Maguire's voice was serious. He was still pale, but his face wasn't quite as hollow and the suit didn't hang so loosely on him now. Maybe he'd been right and his illness was no more than a summer cold. 'Four of them and hopefully no more.' He sat back in his chair. 'Tell me, Inspector: the ones who died, were they good people?'

'Not really.'

'Would you say that Leeds is a lesser place without them?'
Maguire asked.

He weighed the question. 'No.'

'They chose their lives.'

'I know, but . . .'

'I won't mourn them. Speaking as a Leeds man, I doubt many
will.'

'Perhaps you're right,' Harper admitted.

'Drink your tea before it goes cold,' Maguire said gently.
'That's what my ma always used to tell me.'

The inspector smiled. The words had been a litany of his
childhood, too. He raised the cup in a toast.

'I heard what Annabelle did on Bread Street,' Maguire grinned.
'Slapping Charlie Gilmore.'

He hadn't forgotten. Nor had Gilmore. The man had reminded
him the day before. Not with a threat, but with quiet words before
he left the Sword: 'You need to keep your wife under control.'

Harper had simply shaken his head and said: 'And you need
to learn that people aren't property.' In the end he'd walked away
with a truce between Archer's gang and the Boys of Erin. Brittle
but still holding.

'You know what she's like.'

'Oh, I do.' He chuckled and coughed again. 'Once she starts,
God help anyone who gets in her way.' He paused. 'Just like
you, Inspector. Maybe that's why you're such a good match.'

'Me?' Harper asked in astonishment.

'Think about it when you have the time.' He stood, placing a
hat on his head. 'Good day to you.'

The man had given him something to chew on. But not now;
it could wait till he had a moment to consider it.

Rossiter the chemist was surprisingly young, only in his thirties,
with clean, delicate hands and an early streak of grey hair. He'd
barely unlocked the door of his shop when Harper entered.

'I-I-Inspector.' He coughed himself out of a stammer. 'I hadn't
expected to see you again.'

'I was just wondering if you'd perhaps remembered anything
about a kidnapping, sir.'

Rossiter tried to laugh, but the sound was hollow. 'I told you before.' The smile was as false as the words. 'Someone must have been lying to you.'

'I don't believe so. I need some help, sir, if you can.' He waited for a reply, seeing fear and relief cross the man's face as he relived it all. 'Why don't you tell me what happened?'

'I told you last time – nothing happened,' Rossiter snapped. 'I don't know who gave you the information, but it's just ludicrous. Now, I have a business to run.'

It was the same when he returned to the draper's on Oxford Place. A quieter denial, but just as insistent.

Finally he made his way back to the bible shop. The young man who hurried from the back room couldn't be the owner. He was barely eighteen, the down of a young moustache on his upper lip as he tried to appear older.

'Can I help you, sir?'

'I'm looking for Mr Cookson.'

'He's tied up at the moment, sir. I'd be glad to help however I can.'

'If you could tell him that Detective Inspector Harper from Leeds Police is here . . .'

Less than a minute later Robert Cookson was standing in front of him.

'What can I do for you, Inspector?' He tried a weak smile. 'I thought we covered everything last time. Or perhaps you've come for a bible?'

'I was hoping you had some truth in stock, Mr Cookson.'

'I told you the truth when you asked me before.'

'No, Mr Cookson, you didn't.' Harper kept his voice soft, easy. 'Please, I need to know what happened. No one can hurt you now, believe me.'

It took a long time for the sigh to come. But when it arrived, the inspector knew Cookson would tell everything.

'I'd prefer not to talk here,' he said quietly. 'Jeremy, look after the shop for a few minutes, please.'

Outside, Cookson led the way down to Victoria Square by the Town Hall and stood watching the traffic.

'How long ago did it happen?' Harper asked.

'Three months. Almost four now.' The man pulled a cheroot from his jacket and lit it, watching the smoke spiral. A cart drove by, its axle grinding and shrieking as it moved. He recounted it all slowly, something he'd chosen to put away, to try and forget.

It had all gone exactly the way Morley said. Demands for money. When Cookson had refused to pay they snatched his son. Within a day the ransom was paid and the boy had been returned unharmed, even spoilt with toys and food.

'They said if I ever told anyone they'd come back.'

'They won't,' Harper assured him again and the man nodded slowly, tapping ash on to the pavement. 'I need to know. Did you tell anyone?'

'No,' he answered. 'I was too scared. But Sarah, my wife, did.'

'After your son was at home again?' the inspector guessed.

Cookson nodded. 'Neither of us would take the risk before.'

'Who did she tell?' He stared at the passing traffic, the omnibuses and trams. A driver whipped his horse along. A hackney dodged in and out between vehicles as it tried to make time. Everyone was in a rush.

'Her sister-in-law. It was just . . . relief, I don't know.' He glanced down at the cigar as if he was surprised to be holding it. 'I was terrified they'd find out and come looking for revenge.'

'Why would they?' Harper asked.

'They said they had people in the police, they'd know if we reported it.'

'They don't. They wanted to scare you.'

The man drew himself up straight. There was no pride in his expression. 'Then they succeeded, sir.'

After a few seconds of silence, the inspector nodded and asked, 'Who's your sister-in-law, Mr Cookson?'

'Her name is Susan Keeble.'

'Is she married?'

'No. She's a housekeeper.'

'For whom?'

Cookson turned to stare at him. 'I'm sure you'll have heard of the man, Inspector. George Archer.'

He walked back to Millgarth. Everything had moved back to Archer. But now it made absolutely no sense at all.

Kendall listened to the story, frowning hard.

'Could Archer be responsible for everything?' he asked when Harper finished. 'Has he been fooling us?'

'I don't know.' He shook his head. 'I really don't know, sir.' He'd believed all Archer's denials, and they'd been honest and heartfelt. The man was no actor. He was hard but he'd never have murdered one of his own. And he knew full well that nobody gained in a war with the Boys of Erin.

'It all points to him again,' the superintendent said.

'I know. But . . .'

'Follow it, Tom.' It was an order. Kendall still ached to see Archer in the dock; he made no bones about that.

Where could he go? He wasn't ready to face Archer once more. Not until he could go back with information, more ammunition.

He needed to talk to Susan Keeble.

Instead he sat at his desk, writing all the names on a piece of paper and trying to establish connections between them. Dinner time arrived, but still no ideas that stood up to scrutiny.

At the Old George he ate a chop. For once he was glad of his poor hearing; the conversation around him was nothing more than a buzz of sound. Every few minutes even that was drowned out as a railway train passed on the viaduct outside, rattling the building and making the tables shake a little.

Somerset Street baked in the heat of the early afternoon. There was no copper standing outside the murder house. There was nothing to keep safe. A man had been killed here, but what was there to see? No blood, no gore. It was just another empty building.

He walked through to the scullery. It was a barren room with a flagstone floor, half the plaster gone from the walls, the lath showing underneath.

How had it happened, he wondered? Bob Hill was a big, powerful man. How had someone managed to take him?

Harper searched the floor on his hands and knees, groping for the wire that had been the murder weapon. He was concentrating so hard that he never heard the footsteps. Until a man cleared his throat he had no idea anyone was watching. Bloody hearing, he thought.

'Saying your prayers?' George Archer asked. 'You'll need them if I find whoever did it first.'

Harper pushed himself upright and dusted off his clothes. 'What brings you here?'

Harrison the bodyguard stood in the other room, tense and ready. Archer was staring at the ground.

'I had business in town. Is this where it happened?'

'Right here,' the inspector told him. 'I don't know for certain, but I was told he was garrotted.'

He saw Archer's face harden. 'Bastard. Couldn't face him man to man. Bob would have taken him.'

Harper moved past him. As he slid by he said quietly, 'I'll find him. Me.'

But Archer just shook his head. 'You're in a race against me and another against Gilmore. You're on a hiding to nothing.'

'We'll see.'

Pushing his way out of the house he bumped against Roger Harrison, forcing the man out of the way.

A hackney carriage dropped him at the park entrance and he walked quickly across the wide expanse of grass and down the drive at Lakeside. With Archer busy in town, this was the perfect time to question the housekeeper. Word would come out later, but by then he'd have his answers. For once he'd be a step ahead.

The front of the house was imposing. The back, for tradesmen and staff, was plain. The entry was undecorated, almost an after-thought. A maid answered the bell and led him through to the kitchen.

Pots bubbled and steamed on the large range. A long oak table ran down the centre of the room, covered here and there with large smudges of flour. And keeping an eye on it all was the housekeeper.

She was a thin woman with sharp eyes, her hair tucked up under a cap, a white apron over a plain brown dress.

'What do you want?'

'You, if you're Miss Keeble.'

'What if I am?' She turned to the girl beside her. 'Be careful with that dish. Break it and it comes out of your wages.' Her eyes returned to him. 'Who are you?'

'Detective Inspector Harper.' He paused long enough for her to take it in. 'I think you know what it's about.'

'If it's Bob Hill, you're wasting your time. Everyone here liked him. We're cooking for the wake.'

'No. Something else. You know.'

At first he thought she wasn't going to move. Then she spun on her heel.

'Follow me,' she instructed.

The room lay at the end of a short tiled hallway, the window looking down the hill towards the big lake in Roundhay Park. The fireplace was swept and empty, an old rag rug in front of the hearth. She sat in a rocking chair. Harper stood; there was nowhere else to sit. None of the luxury of the rooms above stairs.

'Now, Miss . . .' he began.

'It's Mrs,' she corrected him. 'Mr Keeble's dead. And I know why you're here.' She snorted. 'He couldn't keep his mouth shut, eh?'

'Two of the men who took your nephew are dead.' He nodded towards the lake. 'One of them was the man we pulled out of there.'

'Oh?' She cocked her head. 'That still doesn't tell me what you want here.'

'What did you do after your sister-in-law told you about the kidnapping?'

'Made sure they were all well,' she said disdainfully. 'What would you have done?'

'And who did you tell?'

'No one, of course.' She gave him a withering look. 'The silly cow shouldn't even have mentioned it to me.'

'You live in a house of criminals . . .'

'It doesn't mean that I'm one.' Her voice took on a raw edge. 'Is that what you're suggesting?'

'No,' Harper replied slowly. 'All I meant was that if you were angry or upset at what she'd told you, you might have mentioned it to someone. Mr Archer, possibly.'

'No.' Her voice was firm. She stared at him.

'You didn't tell anyone?'

'Sarah said they'd warned her. A word to anyone and they'd come back. Do you really think I'd do that to my nephew?'

'I needed to ask.'

'I daresay you did. And now you've had an answer.'

'Then I thank you, Mrs Keeble.' He stood and gazed out of the window, towards the lake. The water had the hard grey colour of iron. No working men and their families parading during the working week. A few governesses and children, an older couple strolling arm in arm. 'How is it, working out here?'

'Mr Archer's a fair employer.'

Something in her tone made him wonder. It was no more than a note in the words but it felt like damning with faint praise.

'Do you know much about what he does?'

'I know. But don't ask me to tell you.' She offered a thin smile. 'I won't.'

Susan Keeble seemed like a cold, distant woman, he thought. But that didn't mean much, it could just be her way.

'It must be a sad time here with Mr Hill's murder.'

'That's hardly a surprise, is it? He'd been with Mr Archer for years. Since the old days.'

'Did you get along with him?'

'Well enough.'

She gave up very little; it was like drawing blood from a stone.

'Do you have any idea who killed him?'

Mrs Keeble raised her eyes to the ceiling. 'That's their world up there. Mine's down here.'

Harper nodded. 'Then I thank you for your help.'

At the back door he tipped his hat to her and set off down the drive. By the stone gateposts he turned to gaze back at the house. It wanted to look solid and permanent, built for the ages. A testament of wealth. New money trying to look old. He was happier at the Victoria. At least that was built on honest labour.

The late afternoon was sultry; the city smelled of sweat, smoke, and metal. All the clean air after the storm was a faint memory. In the bar the windows were open, dark patches of welcoming shade in the corners.

'She's out,' Dan told him. 'Left about an hour ago with the little one.'

'Did she say where?'

'Burmantofts.' The barman paused. 'Tom, do you know that new lass who started today? Doing the baking.'

He had to think for a moment. Maggie Dawson; he'd forgotten about her.

'Maggie, yes.'
'Is she spoken for, do you know?'
Harper grinned. 'No, Dan, I'm sure she isn't. Not any more.'

SEVENTEEN

A quarter of an hour saw him in Burmantofts and at the shop. The writing over the door was still new enough to gleam, the windows freshly cleaned with vinegar and newspaper. A *Closed* sign hung in the door, but through the glass he could see Annabelle with Mary cuddled close, talking earnestly with Elizabeth.

He tapped on the wood and she waved him in.

'She's going to buy the bakeries!' Annabelle announced before he could even speak. She twirled around the floor, spinning her daughter in her arms and laughing. 'Isn't it perfect news, Tom?'

'It is,' he agreed. Elizabeth looked flushed and nervous, her face beet red. 'Congratulations. Really. Billy must be happy for you.'

'He is.' She smiled. 'But all this talk about lawyers and agreements, it scares me.'

'Don't you worry,' Annabelle told her. 'Everything's simple enough.' She was beaming with pleasure. 'I'm so glad you want them. You were meant to have them.'

'I've done the sums so often I can probably see them in my sleep.' Elizabeth took a worried breath then said, 'There's not many who'd give someone a chance like this. Are you positive you want to sell?'

'I am.' Annabelle looked like a weight had been lifted from her shoulders. Her face seemed smoother, younger, happier. 'They're all yours now.'

'Bar the contract,' Elizabeth said.

'Now,' Annabelle insisted. 'I just hope you'll want to keep buying my bread.'

'As long as the quality's good.' The both began to giggle at some joke he didn't understand. He felt superfluous, a cloud at the edge of the celebration. But the pleasure was infectious.

It was a giant opportunity for Elizabeth and Billy. The shops might not make them rich but they'd be comfortable. Life changed.

Annabelle seemed to radiate happiness as they strolled home. 'I'm so glad she said yes. I thought she would, but . . .'

'There was always the chance she'd refuse.' He paused. 'That's one thing done, anyway.'

'The big one.' She gave a contented sigh.

'How was your first day on the new job?'

'Like untangling a skein of yarn after a kitten's been at it,' she replied with a sigh. 'But I think I've started to tease the knots out now. The lass they sent to help me is a godsend, too. It'll get easier once we're on top of things.'

'They've found a treasure in you.'

Annabelle snorted. 'Fool's gold, more like. But I'm enjoying it,' she admitted as they walked. 'It's something different. Mind you, I could live without doing the books.'

'You'll feel strange, not having the shops.'

'I feel better already. Not like you.' From the corner of his eye he saw Annabelle assessing him. 'Bad news today?'

He shook his head. 'Strange, more like. I know it means something, but I'm not sure what.'

'That's about as mysterious as you've ever been, Tom Harper.'

'It's been a curious day.' He took her arm.

'We have four killings, two of them done by someone with red hair. The other pair might as well have been carried out by an invisible man for all the witnesses we have,' Harper said. He looked at Ash and Wharton. The pair of them were staring at the floor. 'Any suggestions?'

In the freshness of the morning he'd taken the first tram into town and walked down George Street to Millgarth. No reports of violence waiting on his desk; the peace between Archer and Gilmore had held for another night.

Half an hour later Ash had arrived. None of his questions the day before had brought answers. The same for Wharton. No one would admit to seeing a thing. Was the killer very clever, the inspector wondered, or just luckier than any man deserved?

Four dead. Two separate killers who just happened to be active around the same time? Possible, but it would be one hell of a coincidence. And he didn't believe in those.

'Right,' he said eventually. 'Back out there. We need something. I don't care how small it is, just *something*. Look back over Declan's murder again, too. See if anyone can recall our mystery copper-haired man anywhere. I'm off to see Dr King.'

At least it was cool in King's Kingdom, down in the cellar and away from the heat. The body was lying on the table, stripped down to the flesh.

'There,' the doctor said, indicating the dark line at the neck. 'That's your killer, inspector. Someone garrotted him with wire.' He peered closer. 'It wasn't too thin.'

But Harper was staring at the dead man's face. There was a large bruise on his right temple, by the hairline. King followed his gaze.

'A heavy blow,' he said. 'From the look of it, enough to knock him out.' His fingers examined the wound, moving and probing with surprising gentleness. 'He was probably unconscious when the wire went around his neck. He wouldn't have known a thing about it. That's something, I suppose.'

'Is there anything else you can tell me?'

'Nothing you won't already know. He's well-fed, heavily muscled. Whoever hit him must have taken him by surprise.' He picked up the corpse's hands one by one, inspecting the knuckles. 'No contusions here. He didn't fight back.' King nodded. 'Definitely taken by surprise. Does that help you at all, Inspector? It's all I can give you.'

'It tells me something,' Harper said. 'I'm just not sure what.'

'Working it out is your job. All I can go on is what's in front of me.'

EIGHTEEN

'Susan Keeble,' the inspector said to Sergeant Tollman. 'Does the name mean anything?'

The big man stirred himself behind the counter, running his tongue across his lips.

'Receiving stolen goods,' he answered after a few seconds. 'It must have been '85 or '86. Three months if I remember rightly, sir.'

The man always amazed him. He was an encyclopaedia of Leeds criminals.

There was more. 'Her husband was Gilbert Keeble, sir. Do you remember him?'

'Housebreaker?' He had a faint image of the man. An unlikely brother for the wife of a bible seller. But you couldn't choose family.

'That's the one. Fell off a roof as he was starting a robbery and died five years back.'

'Did either of them do business with Archer?'

Tollman pursed his mouth. 'It wouldn't surprise me. I don't recall anything specific.'

'Thank you.' He started towards the office and stopped. 'That lad of yours has the makings of a good policeman.'

The sergeant beamed and puffed up with pride. 'I'll tell him you said that, sir.'

The information on Keeble was useful, but it didn't bring him any closer to a killer. To his copper-haired man. He had to find him before Archer or Gilmore did, or the first he'd know about it would be another body. It didn't feel like a race; it seemed as if he was wading through deep mud.

'You look all in,' Annabelle told him.

'I feel it,' he said with a smile. They were sitting in the bar of the Victoria, all the life of the pub carrying on around them. Mrs Turner from Meanwood Road had shuffled across to natter for a moment and complain about her bunions. Mr Bailey, with the hardware shop a little further up the street, paid his respects.

Annabelle came down two or three times a week, more if one of the staff was poorly. This was her place, her home. All the regulars were old friends; she even knew most of the occasional customers by name, ready to ask after families, to laugh and joke with them. In the Victoria she was the queen.

For many years she'd been down here every night, working behind the bar until long past closing time. Then she'd be up first thing to keep an eye on everything in the bakery and make sure the bread delivered to the shops met her standards. But marriage had changed that. Motherhood even more.

Ellen was upstairs to keep an eye on Mary. Their daughter was already asleep in her crib; her eyes had closed quickly while Harper read to her. Time for an hour down here, a chance for Annabelle to talk, and flirt with all the men she'd known for so long.

'You go back up if you want.' She leaned close and spoke softly in his good ear. 'I'm fine.' He smiled at her and took a drink of beer. 'For a few minutes, anyway.'

'I tell you what, the lass from the Society is good. Bertha Quinn. She'll go places, you mark my words. Picked everything up just like that.' She snapped her fingers, then looked up as Fred Donnell, one of the managers from the ironworks on Mabgate, put another glass in front on her and gave a quick nod. 'Thank you,' she said, raising it in a toast. 'Your good health.'

Harper glanced around the pub. His thoughts turned back to the man with red hair. Who was he? It had to be someone local, someone who knew how things were organized in the city. But for the life of him he couldn't think of anyone from Leeds who fitted the bill. He sighed and tipped the last of the drink down his throat. Brunswick beer. It had been part of his life since he was born. The smell of the brewery in the air when he was a child. His first job there after schooldays had ended. And now it lubricated his evenings. He couldn't escape his own past.

'You go,' she advised, kissing him on the cheek. 'I won't be long. Just a quick word with a few people and I'll be along.'

He nodded. He was ready for sleep. Maybe it would bring him some inspiration.

'I've remembered something, sir,' Ash told him. Even at seven o'clock in the morning, with the windows wide open, the office was still stifling in the July heat.

'What is it?' Please God, Harper thought, let it be something useful.

The sergeant glanced pointedly at the clock. 'Happen it would be a good time for a cup of cocoa, sir. Just to start the day.'

And away from anyone who might overhear and pass it on.

'Well?' Harper asked as they sat in Lockhart's cocoa house on Lower Briggate, steaming mugs in front of them.

'I've been racking my brains, going over everything. I keep thinking there must have been something I never realized.' He took a breath that became a low sigh. 'You know I grew up with Len Tench, sir, and we both became friendly with Ted Bradley when we started at the chemical works.'

'Yes.'

'I'd forgotten all about it, but Ted used to say he knew a proper criminal.'

'Go on.' He knew Ash well enough to be certain it was leading somewhere.

'I lost touch with them all when I joined the force. But the name of this chap popped into my head today.'

'Who was it?'

'I thought he was just boasting. We never met the man or anything, so I never paid it much mind. Always thought he was boasting. But last night the name popped into my head. Bob Hill.'

Hill. George Archer's dead bodyguard. They seemed to be lining up. Harper blew on his cocoa until it was cool enough to sip.

'So we have a connection,' he said slowly. It wasn't much. It was as thin as a thread. But it was something.

'I'm sorry, sir. I should have remembered before.'

'It's hardly your fault. It was a long time ago.' The inspector was working things through in his head. 'Morley claimed that none of them ever told anyone what they'd done.'

'Maybe he didn't have to. Think about it for a minute, sir. That fellow whose son was taken—'

'Cookson.'

'You said that his wife told her sister-in-law. She's Archer's housekeeper. She could have mentioned it to Hill. If there was a description, a name . . .'

'Susan Keeble swears she didn't tell a soul, she was too scared for her nephew.'

Ash shrugged. 'Maybe it's nothing. I just wanted to mention it.'

'It's a link. Perhaps it'll turn into something.' It seemed they were building a web of connections. But too slowly. And he still had no idea who was the spider at the centre of it all.

'Somehow or other, this all turns on the man with red hair,' Harper said.

'We've not had any luck finding him. We've been turning the city upside down.'

'Do you have any ideas?' the inspector asked bleakly. 'I certainly don't.'

'I wish I did, sir.' He was silent for a moment. 'About the only good thing is that Archer and Gilmore aren't at each other's throats.'

Maybe they were too busy. Archer's men were looking for Hill's killer while the Boys of Erin were hunting Declan Gilmore's murderer. Everywhere Harper had gone yesterday, someone else had been there first, asking questions, making threats.

'Perhaps Wharton's found something,' he said hopefully.

He hadn't. Frustration showed on the young man's face. He was still too eager, wanting quick results.

'Sir,' he said after finishing his report, 'I'd like to go out on the Brooker case again tonight.'

'You don't need my permission for that,' Harper told him with a smile.

'I've been thinking about it. I honestly believe it was an accident.'

'But?'

'I want to be certain, that's all. She deserves that.'

Good, he thought. Compassion, too. He'd go a long way.

'Give it one more night. Tell me what you think tomorrow.'

'I'd like to try and find this young man she was supposed to have been seeing.'

Another man with red hair, the inspector remembered. Another mystery.

'One more evening. Maybe you'll get lucky.'

Reed was already at home when Elizabeth returned. For once he'd managed to leave right at the end of his shift, catching the omnibus then walking in the sun along the dusty back streets. It had been a quiet day, no fires, a chance to catch up on all the paperwork and reports on his desk.

He loved his job. Where others saw destruction he'd learned to spot reason. Working out how a fire began, the way it spread.

It taxed his skills, made him think and used all his experience. Every day he learned something new.

She bustled in, a ledger clutched against her chest, and let out a long sigh.

'Busy?' he asked as he kissed her. The tea had mashed and he poured her a cup.

'I've been run off my feet. If I've gone between all the shops once today I've done it three times.'

He eyed the volume she'd put on the table. 'Not done yet?'

'I want to keep the books up to date. It'll only take a few minutes.' She stroked his face. 'You're home early.'

'I was lucky.' He paused. 'Are you still glad you decided to buy the bakeries?'

'Oh yes.' Her eyes were smiling, and there was no hesitation in her voice. 'It's going to be wonderful, Billy. A lot of work, but it'll be worth it.'

'Happy?' he asked.

After a moment she nodded. 'Still scared, but yes. Whoever thought I'd do something like this?'

'I'm proud of you,' he said.

She sat, hands around the mug and shook her head in wonder. 'It's all changed since we met, hasn't it?'

'Yes.' Reed thought of the way he'd been then. The way he'd relished a pub at the end of the day, the drinks to fill the evening. How his dream had been to work as a copper in Whitby. He hadn't thought of that in a long time. Now he had more than he'd ever imagined.

'Did you believe this Keeble woman?' Kendall asked.

'At the time,' Harper answered. 'No reason not to. She wouldn't want to put her nephew at risk. Now I know one of the kidnappers might have known Bob Hill . . .' It was impossible to be certain.

'Are we anywhere close to finding an answer?' the superintendent asked. 'Tell me the truth.'

'No, we're not.' It pained him to admit it.

'The Chief Constable sent me a note this morning.' Kendall's voice was sombre as he tapped an envelope on his desk. 'The Home Secretary has written to him. Unless we resolve this business by the end of the week he's going to bring in Scotland Yard.'

'But—' he began.

The superintendent held up a hand. 'I know, Tom.' Exhaustion filled his voice. 'I thought exactly the same thing when I read it.'

'They won't know how things work here, who's who—'

'Do you think I like it?' He raised an eyebrow. 'We're not being given a choice. The first big crime since Leeds became a city and the Yard has to come in . . . it's not going to look good for us.'

'Then we need to make sure it doesn't come to that, sir.'

'Good,' Kendall agreed. 'But how are we going to do it?'

'We need to push the people again.'

'Go and do it, then. I'll talk to everyone I know once more.' He sighed. 'One last thing.'

'What?'

'Pray for a bit of luck, Tom. It looks like we're going to need it.'

Harper raged out of the station. He needed answers that made some bloody sense. The last thing he wanted was some London detective coming up here, thinking he was better than the provincials. Someone with no clue about Leeds, the people, the way things happened here. He wasn't going to be beaten by some flash bastard from the Yard. He wasn't going to look like a fool who couldn't even tie his own shoelaces.

Wharton had tried to catch him on the way out but he'd brushed by. He needed to think, not to be distracted by other things. Time was running out.

'Sir!' He turned and saw Ash lumbering towards him.

'What?' He was on edge. Spiky. The only company he wanted was his own.

'There's a message for you. Sergeant Tollman tried to tell you.' He hesitated for a fraction of a second. 'Maybe you didn't hear him.' He held out a large hand with a scrap of paper.

'Thank you.'

Come home. Maggie Dawson's remembered something that might help.

He read the note again, then crumpled it into a ball.

'Take Wharton. I want you to start throwing the fear of God into any of Gilmore's or Archer's men you see. We need this man with the copper hair and we need him now.'

'Yes, sir.'

'Noon, back at the station.'

She was in the bakery at the back of the yard behind the Victoria. A boy with a handcart was loading the last of the baked bread to deliver while some of the women sat with a cup of tea before starting on the cakes and fancies.

Maggie Dawson looked exhausted. There were smears of flour across her face and gown, her bony fingers red and raw, hair caught in a scarf.

He nodded at the other women – Jane, Alma, Catherine, Leonora – and tilted his head for Maggie to follow him outside. She rested her back against the brick.

'Hot work,' she said as she breathed deeply.

He didn't have the time for pleasantries.

'Annabelle sent me a message. She said you have some infor-mation. Is it about Declan?'

She nodded her head and tried to wipe the flour from her arms. 'The last time he came to Bread Street he kept looking out of the window. I asked him what was wrong. At first he said he'd belt me if I didn't shut up, then he told me he thought someone was following him.' Maggie stared up at him. 'That was always his way. Threaten first.'

'Did he tell you who was after him?'

'I'm not even sure he knew.'

'What else did he say, Maggie?'

'I think it was more a feeling than anything. He said he'd caught a glimpse of someone once or twice. Someone with red hair.'

Harper felt his heart beating faster. Something useful at last. 'Was there anything else? Please, try to remember, it's important.'

'He seemed different. Not so much scared, but on edge.' She tried to find the words. 'He was like a cat on hot bricks the whole time he was there. Up and down, looking out of the window.'

Declan Gilmore had always been a fighter, never afraid of a scrap. It wasn't like him to be worried. 'I need to know anything you can recall.'

'That's the lot,' she answered as she looked at him with pleading eyes. 'I'm sorry. I know I should have said something earlier, what with all you and Mrs Harper have done for me. I was frightened.'

'It doesn't matter.' He smiled. 'I'll let you get back to work.'

'Does it help at all?' Maggie asked. 'It's not too late, is it?'

'No,' he assured her. 'It's not too late.'

Annabelle was sitting at the table writing in a book, with Mary perched on her lap. He could see her legs moving up and down, bouncing the girl lightly as she worked. On the other side of the table a young woman with dark, curly hair glanced up from a ledger and smiled; she stood up, hand out ready to shake.

'How do you do? I'm Bertha Quinn. You must be Inspector Harper.'

'A pleasure,' he answered. She seemed young, about twenty, cheeks shiny, eyes clear behind a thick pair of spectacles. 'My wife says you're a great help.'

Miss Quinn blushed, her whole face turning red. 'I just try to do what I can.' She glanced from one of them to the other. 'Why don't I make some tea?'

'Did you see Maggie?' Annabelle asked once they were alone.

'Yes.' Her hair was gathered on top of her head and he kissed the back of her neck. Mary giggled; he leaned further and brushed his lips against her forehead. The little girl smelled of milk and powder and innocence.

'Was she helpful?'

'She was.' But even that couldn't take away the frown.

She put down the pen and stared at him. 'Come on, something's wrong. It's right there on your face.'

He told her.

'The Met?' Her eyes widened. 'From London?'

'The Home Secretary's orders. If we don't wrap this up by the end of the week they'll send someone up to take over.'

Her eyes flashed angrily. 'What the hell can he do that you can't?'

'Nothing,' Harper said. 'Absolutely bugger all.'

'But you have until the end of the week?'

He nodded. 'Until the end of Sunday. Maybe not even that long.'

She stood, hoisting Mary in her arms, her expression set. 'We'd better get to work, then.'

'We?' At first he thought his ears had fooled him again. 'What do you mean?'

'If you think I'm going to let you do it on your own, you've got another think coming.'

'This is police business.'

'That's fine. You attend to that.' Her voice brooked no argument. Annabelle started gathering things: a parasol, a bag. 'Who do you think sees and hears everything that goes on in the city, Tom?' Before he could answer, she continued, 'The women, that's who. I'm going to talk to them.'

'But—'

'No.' He could see the determination on her face. 'I'm not having some toff from London come and tell us how to do things. And I'm certainly not going to have someone who probably couldn't detect his way out of a paper bag come and try to make an idiot of my husband.'

'What about your work?'

'Blow that,' she told him. 'It'll still be here tomorrow.'

For a moment he didn't know what to say. This was *his* work. He was good at it. He didn't need her help.

But it was time to admit that he'd got nowhere on this case. He was groping around in the dark. The only way to solve it before the man from the Yard arrived was to take every scrap of help he was offered.

Annabelle believed in him. She loved him.

'Thank you,' he told her.

'Now you get going. If I find something I'll send you a note.' She smiled. 'Don't you worry, we'll make sure they don't have the chance to gloat down in London.'

He left feeling confident. She'd just given him the thing he'd been missing in all this: hope. Harper jumped on the tram and climbed upstairs, feeling the sun on his face. Glancing down, he saw the door to the Victoria open. Annabelle came out, pushing the baby carriage and disappearing into the back streets of Sheepscar.

NINETEEN

'Red hair,' Harper said. 'And don't lie to me, Harold.'

'I already told you, I don't know anyone like that,' Harold Chamberlain told him. 'The only ones with red hair I *know* are the Gilmores, and Declan's dead.'

Harold Chamberlain had a room in Waterloo Court, behind the Yorkshire Pride public house off Kirkgate. Even on the warmest day the building never saw the sun. The man coughed and spat into a tin bucket by the bed. A small, old terrier, half its fur worried away, stirred in its sleep on the floorboards.

'That's *know*. I'm talking about *seeing*. Come on, you get around.'

Chamberlain owned a handcart, a rickety thing held together with wire. He made his money delivering items around town. Over the years he'd sold to the police a few tiny snippets of information. Never anything big. But right now the inspector was willing to look in every corner.

'There were one thing.' Chamberlain scratched at his thinning hair and picked something off his scalp, rubbed it on one of his remaining teeth then threw it on the floor. 'Probably nowt.'

'Come on . . .'

'I saw Bob Hill the day he was killed.'

'Where?'

'In the Bull and Mouth on Briggate.' He spat again and ran his tongue around the inside of his mouth.

'Was he alone? Bloody hell, Harold,' the inspector said, 'don't make me drag it out of you?'

'No, he were with someone I didn't know. A bloke with red hair.' Chamberlain glanced up. 'But dark red, you know, like copper. Not a carrot top.'

'Are you sure?' Suddenly he could hardly breathe. A connection.

'Course I am,' Chamberlain said with contempt. 'I en't blind, am I?'

'I want to know everything you remember.'

He shrugged. 'I only popped in for a quick one. They were sitting there when I arrived and still sitting there when I left, that's all I can tell you.'

'Did they look friendly?'

'Mebbe. They had their heads down, talking to each other. You know, quiet like, so no one else could hear. But they didn't look too happy.' He reached down and stroked the dog. It moved its leg but didn't wake.

'Could you make any of it out?'

Chamberlain shook his head. Harper bit down on his lip. He needed to think fast, to learn all he could.

'This man with red hair, what did he look like?'

Chamberlain fell silent, as if he was trying to conjure the face into his mind.

'He had a little scar.' Harold raised a hand to his right temple and traced a small line. 'Right there. I remember that.'

'Was he big? Small?' He could hear the insistence in his voice.

'He weren't as big as Bob.'

Hill had been a tall man, heavily muscled.

'What else?' Harper asked urgently. 'Come on, Harold. How was he dressed?'

'A suit and tie. Modern, you know, like you. None of them wing collars and that.'

'Beard? Moustache? Sideboards?'

'Sideboards,' Chamberlain replied with certainty. 'Not great big ones, just down in front of his ears.'

'Good,' Harper told him approvingly. 'How old was he?'

The man looked doubtful. 'I'm no good with that. He wan't a young 'un, but he wan't that old, neither. I don't know, thirties, forty maybe? I'll tell you summat for nowt, he didn't look scared of Bob and there's not many as can say that.'

That was true. Hill used his fists and size to intimidate and make sure George Archer got everything he wanted.

'What else? What about a name?'

'No. Never heard one.' He spat for a third time, the phlegm landing neatly in the bucket. 'He wan't anyone I know, though.'

Harper tossed a florin on the dirty bed. The information was worth every penny.

'Why didn't you tell Archer all this?'

'He din't come and ask me,' Chamberlain said as if it was the most obvious thing in the world.

'Find me next time you're up before the magistrate for moving stolen goods,' the inspector said. 'I'll have a word.'

Finally he had something solid. The red-headed man had been seen with Bob Hill. That was valuable.

The others listened as he recounted everything Chamberlain had told him.

'I'll go down to the Bull and Mouth,' Kendall said. 'I know the landlord.'

'Thank you.' Harper turned to Ash. 'What have you found?'

'Nothing, sir. If Gilmore hasn't been there first, George Archer has.'

Harper had been lucky with Harold Chamberlain; he knew that. But after scrabbling for days he was due something.

'Go around the pubs. Anything at all. Even if it doesn't seem relevant, I want to know.'

'Yes, sir,' the sergeant nodded.

'Tom,' Kendall said as they prepared to leave. 'A word with you.'

He sat down again, waiting until the door had closed and they were alone.

'This came from the Yard.' He opened the top drawer of his desk, took out the telegram and slid it across the wood.

SENDING ROBERTSON ON MONDAY STOP HAVE ALL PAPERS READY FOR HIM STOP HAVE YOUR OFFICERS READY TO ASSIST STOP

'Do you know what I'd like to do with this?' Harper asked.

'The same thing I would, I expect.' The superintendent sighed. 'Robertson. They're sending the artillery.'

'We'd better not give them the chance. We have a few days yet.'

'Then we'd better make them count. I met Robertson once.'

'What's he like?'

'He thinks he's cock o' the walk because he solved some case with a duke or an earl or something. He'd last about five minutes up here.' Kendall stared. 'I don't want him in my station.'

*   *   *

Elizabeth bustled through the door, dropping her packages and unpinning her hat. Her face was flushed from the heat of the day, cheeks bright pink, a sheen of sweat on her forehead. Reed looked up from his newspaper. It was his day off, a time to sleep late, to catch up on little jobs around the house – fresh putty around a loose pane of glass, stopping the drip in the tap.

She leaned over and kissed him. He felt the warmth coming off her skin.

'I saw Annabelle down in Meanwood today. You won't believe what she told me, Billy.'

'What?' He was curious. It had to be important. He'd expected her to be full of the business, what a day it had been in the shops, another plan for the future.

'Scotland Yard's sending up a detective to take over Tom's case.'

'You're kidding.' He couldn't believe his ears. 'They can't.'

'That's what she said.' She bustled around, taking a loaf of bread and some cakes from her basket then pulling out the ledger. 'She's furious.'

'I don't wonder.' The close friendship he and Harper once enjoyed might have withered, but he still felt sorry for the man. Something like that . . . it was humiliating. 'What about Tom?'

'Going round with a face like thunder and doing everything he can to solve it. If it's not done by the end of the week, some detective from London will be here to take over.'

All Reed could do was shake his head. 'I hope he can manage it. Give the Yard a black eye.'

'If Annabelle has anything to do with it, he will.'

Wharton was waiting in the office, attempting to look busy. But the pen in his hand hadn't written a word on the page and he kept glancing up.

'Come on, you look like you've got something on your mind,' Harper said.

'It's about Miss Brooker, sir.'

The inspector settled in his chair. 'Well?'

'I went out walking again last night. Just down from the wharves I saw a man. Red hair, young. I don't know why, I can't explain it, but I just thought he had to be the one she'd been seeing.'

'Was your hunch right?' Of course it had been; they wouldn't be sitting here otherwise.

'Yes, sir.' He flushed with pride. 'They were supposed to meet on the night she died, but he had to work late. By the time he arrived there was no sign of her and he thought she'd given up and gone home. He went back the next night and the two after that, but she didn't appear. It was all secret so he couldn't go to her house. The first thing he knew was when he read the newspaper.'

A sad tale, but life was full of those and nothing they could do about it.

'Very good,' Harper told him. The young man's face reddened more. 'Did you check where he worked to be certain he was telling the truth?'

'On my list, sir. I haven't had time yet today, what with everything else going on.'

'Early in the morning,' he ordered. 'Perhaps we can finish one thing, anyway.'

By the time Harper trudged back to the Victoria, late darkness had fallen. He'd spent the evening in the public houses and the beershops, talking, listening, pushing hard with his questions. There'd been one or two snippets, but that was all they'd been: fragments of information.

On the way back he'd stopped at Millgarth. Superintendent Kendall was there, drinking tea from a cracked cup as he pored over some of the paperwork on his desk.

'Any luck at the Bull and Mouth, sir?'

'Not so you'd notice.' Kendall ran a hand through his hair. The deep circles stood out under his eyes. 'John the landlord is straight as a die. He was working when Hill was in but he swears he hadn't seen this copper-haired man before or since.'

'We'll find him.'

'When, Tom? You know what'll happen once the papers get a sniff of someone from the Yard taking over, don't you? That's it for you and me. We'll never see another promotion. We'll be lucky if we don't end up back on the beat. There's even talk that the chief will have to resign if Robertson comes.'

'It's not the end of the week yet.'

'No.' His eyes looked haunted by the prospects for the future. 'Go home. Sleep. Fresh eyes in the morning.'

'You should as well, sir.'

Kendall pointed at the pile of letters waiting for his attention. 'Once I've gone through this lot. I could paper my house three times over with it.'

The night was warm, heavy with the stink of industry. The door to the pub stood open, the noise of the men inside leaking out to the street. Harper made his way through, waving to Dan the barman, then up the stairs. He felt as if the day had been too long. Bed, rest, start again and hope.

Mary was asleep, no breeze to stir the curtains in the room. Annabelle was bent over her ledgers with a nib in her hand; she turned with a smile as he entered.

'I was hoping you'd be back before it was too late.' She was already rising as he moved towards her. 'Don't take your hat off, we're going out again.'

'Now?' he asked as she pecked him on the cheek and picked a bonnet off the back of a chair. 'Where?'

'I said I'd find you information.' On the landing she called up the next flight of stairs and Ellen appeared in the doorway. 'Can you keep an eye on Mary? We'll only be a few minutes.'

'Course I can, love.' The woman wiped her hands on her apron. 'Take as long as you need.'

The street lamps were glowing as they walked arm in arm up Roundhay Road. She kept to his right, close to his good ear.

'Where are we going?' Harper asked.

'I told you I was going to ask around. I went and talked to all the gossips and the women who run the corner shops and the pubs. By now it should be all over Leeds.'

He was exhausted but he'd keep going. Annabelle had hope. The belief that everything could work out.

'Who are we seeing?'

'Mrs Johnson. She runs a rooming house just up past Roseville Road.' He turned and gave her a curious glance. 'She sent me a note. It sounds like she had an interesting lodger last week.'

Harper felt his heartbeat speeding up. 'With red hair?'

'It could be something or nothing,' Annabelle told him. 'She said to come any time.'

'Do you know her?'

'Only slightly. But it's enough. She's the kind who likes a nosey around everything. I'll warn you now, she can talk the hind leg off a donkey if you give her the chance.'

The house was one of a respectable terrace of three-storey villas close to Spencer Place, no more than a few years old, the brickwork still new enough to have a ruddy shine. Mrs Johnson was a compact, neat woman who showed them through to the kitchen. Everything was scrubbed and gleaming, and a book lay open on the old oak table.

'You sit yourselves down,' she said, pulling a shawl around her shoulders in spite of the warm night. 'How's that little one of yours, luv?'

'Growing every day.' Annabelle smiled.

'Next thing you know she'll be bringing a young man through the door. I remember when my—'

'My wife said you might have some information for me,' Harper interrupted. He was tired and ragged. He needed information but he was long past the point of small talk.

'Yes. Sorry, luv.' She sniffed and frowned then composed herself. 'I had a gentleman staying here. He left on Saturday.'

'Did he have red hair? A scar near his hair?' Harper leaned forward, elbows on his knees, staring at her.

'He did that,' she replied, surprised. 'He's good at his job, your husband, isn't he?'

'Very,' Annabelle agreed.

'What else?' Harper asked.

'The scar, it were over here.' She indicated with a finger.

'What was his name?'

'Mr Lamb. He didn't tell me his Christian name; I don't encourage that.' Mrs Johnson pursed her lips. 'He was an odd one. I was glad when he left.'

'Odd?' He cocked his head. 'How?' He knew he sounded desperate.

'There were twice he stayed out all night.' She sniffed once more and straightened her back. 'I tell my guest the rules when they arrive: no noise, no young ladies in the rooms, and I lock

the front door at ten o'clock every night. If they come back after
that they're out of luck. He did warn me it would happen, that
he had to be out on business. But it struck me as strange. Who
has honest business at that time?'

'When did this happen?' He held his breath.

Lamb had been gone on the nights Len Tench and Tom Bradley
died. Now Harper was certain he was after the right man. The
two of them, then Bob Hill. Whoever Lamb might really be,
whatever he intended in Leeds, death walked right beside him.

'Did he say where he'd come from?' Harper asked. 'What was
he like?'

'He were polite enough, I suppose,' she said grudgingly. 'It
were always Mrs Johnson this, Mrs Johnson that, and please and
thank you when he needed something. He weren't local, I can
tell that. Said he was from Manchester, but I don't know.'

'Is there anything else you can tell me? Anything at all? Did
he talk about himself? What type of work brought him here?'

She talked, but after five minutes of this and that he knew she
had nothing more to add. It didn't matter. He was closer now.
Still a few days behind the man, but gaining. Things were starting
to lock into place.

Finally he thanked Mrs Johnson and stood. 'You've been very
helpful,' he told her gratefully. 'If he comes back . . .'

'I'll be sure to send a message to Mrs Harper. And don't you
worry, luv, someone like him doesn't scare me.'

He smiled. 'You're safe enough.'

They walked back along Roundhay Road. The night seemed
still and quiet. So many houses and factories around them and
there could still be silence.

'I'll pass the word about anyone called Lamb,' Annabelle said.

'You've already been a godsend,' Harper told her.

'Don't ever underestimate women.' She smiled, reached on
tiptoe and kissed him. 'I've told you that before.'

'Have you been to see Elizabeth?'

'I ran into her today. I thought I'd keep my distance for a little
while. Give her a chance to put her stamp on the shops. She
knows where I am if she needs me.'

His stomach rumbled.

'Have you eaten today?' Annabelle asked sharply.

'No.' He'd been too busy, rushing from pillar to post.

'There's some kettle broth at home. I'll heat it up for you.' She paused. 'Was Mrs Johnson really helpful?'

'More than you can imagine.'

'They're not going to beat you.' She squeezed his arm in hers. 'I'm not going to let them.'

Them, Harper thought. He wasn't even certain who the real threat was any more, the criminals or Robertson of the Yard. Defeat on one hand, humiliation on the other. Hobson's choice.

Annabelle picked up her pace. 'Come on, let's get you home and fed. You mark my words, there'll be more of the women coming forward tomorrow.'

He hoped she was right. 'Have I told you that I love you?'

She arched an eyebrow. 'Not often enough, Tom Harper.'

TWENTY

'At least we know where he was last week,' Kendall said. It was only one small victory but there was a note of triumph in his voice. 'We're after him now.'

'I've telegraphed Manchester to see if anyone knows him,' Harper said

'Copper hair and that scar. People are going to remember him.' The superintendent rubbed his hands together. 'What about you two?' he asked Ash and Wharton.

'Something that puzzles me, sir,' the sergeant began slowly, rubbing his chin. 'If this Lamb fellow's from Manchester, how did he know who to contact here? Killing Len and Ted took some planning, we're agreed on that.' Harper nodded. 'He must have had people in place for a while.'

'It's a good point,' the inspector agreed. He'd considered it himself, riding along on the early tram into town and staring out of the window at the grim faces of men on their way to the morning shift. 'Either he's working for a gang in Manchester that's looking to expand over here—' he saw the superintendent grimace '—or he's doing something on his own. Neither is good for us.' He pulled his watch from his waistcoat pocket. 'I hope we'll hear back very soon.'

'I'll have the bobbies on the beat check all the hotels and lodging houses.' Kendall scribbled a note. He turned to Wharton. 'Have you found anything?'

'Sorry, sir. Nothing.'

'Keep trying.'

'We've tied him to all the murders,' the inspector said. 'We want him. But Ash is right. He has to have some friends in Leeds who are helping him. The question that keeps coming back to me is why he started with Tench and Bradley. Why he didn't kill Morley and finish that job? There's got to be something in that.'

'Morley's in there somewhere,' Ash agreed. 'I'd lay good money on it.'

'Well, we haven't managed to get anything from him,' the superintendent pointed out. 'Gilmore and Archer have people watching him so there's nothing more he can do.'

'And the truce between the gangs is still holding—'

'For now,' Kendall muttered darkly.

'—so we don't have to worry about them. Not yet, anyway.'

'Do you think they know about Lamb, sir?' Wharton asked thoughtfully.

'I don't think so.' Harper gave a small sigh. 'Let's hope not, anyway. We're sunk if they do.'

'Let's get to work, gentlemen,' the superintendent ordered. 'Just a word with you first, Tom.'

The door closed, leaving the two of them in Kendall's office.

'Time's ticking away.'

'I know, sir. We're making progress, though.'

'They're small steps. We're going to need a lot more than that to solve this before the end of the week.'

The spectre of the Yard and the disgrace that would come with it hung heavily over them both.

'Believe me, I know.'

'What do you want me to do?' Kendall asked.

'We know what Lamb looks like now. We know what he's done.' He shrugged. 'All I can think of is the same as before. Go back, talk to people. We have the description, see if it rings any bells.'

The superintendent nodded. 'Seen with Bob Hill, and the mother of one of the kidnap victims talking to this Mrs Keeble . . . we still have that connection to Archer, don't we?'

'To the people around him,' Harper answered with care. 'I really don't believe George is involved. What does he get from killing one of his own men?'

'Hill with Lamb,' Kendall said slowly. 'Archer could have found out that Bob was plotting against him.'

'If that was true, he wouldn't be looking all over Leeds for whoever killed the man.'

'Then what about the housekeeper?'

What about Susan Keeble, he wondered? Could she be involved? He'd believed her when they'd talked. But she might be worth another visit . . .

'I'll go out there.'

Before he could continue there was a tap on the door. Tollman.

'Sorry to interrupt, sir, but there's someone on the telephone. From Manchester. A Detective Inspector Clark.'

He'd used the instrument a number of times, but he never felt comfortable with it. Even with his good ear pressed hard against the receiver, it always tested his hearing; he could never be certain he'd understood correctly. A bad line and it was painful.

More than that, the idea of talking to someone miles away seemed impossible. He knew it was the future, more and more people had them. Just not for someone like him. At least Annabelle hadn't suggested one for the Victoria yet.

'Hello?'

'Harper? This is Clark in Manchester.' A brisk Lancastrian voice, dour and dry. 'You wanted to know about someone called Lamb.'

The connection was so clear that the man could have been in the same room. Thank God for that, at least.

'Do you know him?'

'Oh aye. Ken Lamb. You know he has red hair, don't you? A darker colour, very noticeable. Everyone just calls him Red. We've had our eye on him since he was a nipper.'

The same man. 'Scar on his temple as well?'

'That's the one. What's he done over your way?'

'We think he's murdered four people.'

Clark let out a low whistle that came through the telephone like static. 'We've had him pegged for one or two killings in the past but never found anyone who'd testify against him. Four? Bloody hell. What's happened to him?'

Harper explained in a few short sentences. The chance to talk to anyone familiar with Lamb was priceless.

'I don't see him doing work like that for someone from Manchester,' Clark answered after a moment. 'I've not heard of any of the gangs looking for new horizons. And Lamb's a bit of a loner.'

'Is he clever?'

'Smart as a bloody whip. He knows how to use people. I'll warn you, he's violent, too.'

A few moments of silence as that sank in. He could feel the blood pounding in his neck, the beginnings of an ache in his head.

'Do you think he could be trying to take over the gangs here?'

'He's always been ambitious, has Red. But bloody hell . . . this is a leap, even for him. He's clever, but you don't manage that on your own, do you?'

'That's what I thought.'

'If you get close, watch yourself,' Clark warned. 'He's good with his fists, used to be a boxer. If he's desperate enough he might kill a copper.'

'A boxer?' the inspector asked sharply.

'That was a few years ago. He wasn't that good, by all accounts. I can send his file over on the express if you'll have one of your men meet it. Everything we know is in there. Hold on a minute.' Suddenly all sound vanished. For a moment Harper thought they'd been cut off. Then, 'I started asking around before I rang you. No one seems to have seen Lamb for two months. That's plenty of time to lay some groundwork over your way.'

'It is,' Harper agreed. 'I appreciate all this.'

'You're welcome, if it helps you catch him. Just something between you, me, and the doorpost.' Clark's voice quietened. 'If you get the chance, kill the bastard. You'll be doing us all a favour. Good luck, Inspector.'

He replaced the receiver. Without thinking, he rubbed the ear that had been listening so intently.

Ken Lamb. Red Lamb. He'd know a lot more once all the information arrived. But the little he'd learned made him certain. This was the man behind it all. And he'd been a boxer once . . .

'Boxer?' Kendall said. 'Do you think he knows Morley?'

'I've no idea. But it could explain why the man's still alive when his friends are dead.'

'I want Morley down here sharpish. You know him, you handle that one yourself.' The superintendent gave a fleeting smile. 'Since you're pals maybe we can avoid brawling in the street. I'll arrange for someone to meet the Manchester express.' He hesitated for a second. 'The inspector really said that? Kill him?'

'"Kill the bastard. You'll be doing us all a favour." Exact words.'

'Let's see when we find him.'

Somewhere above the smoke and the clouds the sun must be shining, Harper decided as he strode along Lovell Road. The heat pressed down, and people looked miserable as they trudged along. He saw two men idling outside the stairs to Dooley's Gym, trying to keep themselves in the shade. Morley's shadows. In a few minutes they'd have a surprise.

The air inside was sharp. There was a ripe scent of sweat and the faint iron tang of blood, all mixed with the heat. Men in leather boxing gloves pounded heavy canvas bags. In a makeshift ring at one end of the room two fighters were sparring, landing light blows on each other.

Morley was in front of a mirror, watching himself move quickly. A combination of blows, feet constantly in motion. No one in their right mind would want to be facing those fists, the inspector thought. He waited until the boxer stopped to catch his breath then approached.

'The bout's soon, isn't it?'

'A week and a half.' Morley dipped his hands into a bucket of cold water and sluiced it over his head. 'There's always bad news when I see you.'

'Then I'm not going to disappoint you today, Eustace. I need you to come to the station with me.'

'No,' the boxer answered. 'Not until I've finished my routine. I have to train.'

'How long will that be?'

'Another half an hour or so.' A smile crossed his face. 'Unless you want to spar with me?'

The inspector shook his head. 'I daresay you'd enjoy it, but I wouldn't.'

'Pity.' Morley held up his fists and moved closer. The smile was fixed in place but something had shifted behind his eyes. Harper saw Morley feint, felt the air from a blow that passed too close to his face then a second that stopped a fraction of an inch short of his belly.

'Very impressive.' But the boxer was still weaving in front of him, hands up against his face. Ready. Another move and his fist snaked forward and hit the inspector on the chest. Soft, little more than a love tap.

'This is my place, so it's my rules,' Morley said through gritted teeth. 'You get to fight like a man. That's what they say, isn't it?'

'Is it?' All around, the sounds of the gym were fading away. No more grunting or sharp yells as people stopped to watch.

The boxer was moving on the balls of his feet, up and down, his hands ready to lash out. One proper blow, one swift, short combination and he'd be on his back. If Morley put his weight behind a shot he'd be out cold.

But he was a police officer. He couldn't run away.

'Enough of the games, Eustace,' he said quietly.

Morley shook his head. 'Training.' The hand flew, stopping less than an inch from the inspector's eye. For a fraction of a second he could see the knuckles so tight they were white. 'Do you understand?'

'And you're good at it.'

'I am. I'm going to be the best.' His voice was hoarse, concentrated.

The boxer moved again, his feet fast. Slipping from side to side, coming a little closer, sliding back. His arms were like quicksilver, a rush of darts and jabs that could have connected wherever he chose.

Harper knew he was being slowly pushed back. Much longer and he'd be up against the wall of the gym.

Morley's knuckles were white, sweat running down his face

and chest. Hate filled his face. This was beyond a game. The boxer was breathing hard. There was murder in his eyes. The inspector was trapped. All he could do was edge away, step by slow step.

'Morley.'

The voice filled the gym, loud and sharp enough to make the man pause and turn his head. Dooley, the owner, rushed through the room, his face set, shirtsleeves rolled up over a pair of thick, hairy arms. 'For God's sake, don't be an idiot. You don't mess with a copper like that.' He slapped the boxer's face hard and pushed him away.

Morley shook his head as if he was coming out of a daze. Maybe that's what it was, Harper thought. A killing trance.

'I was just showing him what I do.'

'You're a boxer, not a bloody fairground act.' Dooley was yelling, still pushing Morley away until he was against the wall on the far side of the gym. Around him, men were working once more, punching at the bag and each other as if nothing had happened. The excitement was over, everything was back to normal.

Very slowly, Harper let out a long breath. It had been close. Another minute . . . He stuck his hands in his trouser pockets to hide the shaking. He'd never seen anything like that. It was as if some switch had been turned and changed the man. He'd become something that wasn't quite human, but still with enough control, enough sense, enough power to destroy him with a few blows.

Dooley was still talking to Morley, his mouth close to the man's face, his voice too low now to catch.

Finally the owner turned and marched across to the inspector.

'I'm sorry about that.' Dooley shook his head. 'His mind's too much on the fight.'

'It doesn't matter,' Harper lied. 'No damage done.'

'Once he gets something in his head he can't turn off easily. Never been able to. It's what makes him so good, really.' He grimaced. 'What do you want with him, anyway? He needs all the time he can get here.'

'I need to take him down to the station. More questions.'

Dooley sighed with exasperation. 'Can't it wait?'

'No.' And definitely not now, he thought.

'If you have to, then.' The man sighed again. 'Don't worry. He won't give you any trouble now.'

'Thank you.' There was real gratitude in his words.

The two men set to trail Morley followed them through town. For the first time Harper was glad to have criminals close behind him.

Morley seemed brighter, alert, acting as if nothing had happened. Had he really gone to some strange place in his head? Or was he sly, far cleverer than the inspector had imagined? He'd stopped just shy of assault, no more than a hair's breadth short. Now he was talking easily, all the intensity and violence vanished. The talk ranged over the weather, the upcoming fight, all the money that had been bet on him.

People on the pavement saw him coming and moved aside. The boxer didn't even appear to notice. At Millgarth he pushed the doors open and entered as casually as if it was his own home.

'You make a very good liar,' Harper said when they were settled in the room. A constable stood by the door, the biggest man Tollman had been able to find. It was at times like this that he really missed Billy Reed. The man would have made Morley talk, by hook or by crook.

'About what?' The boxer looked bemused. He sat with one leg crossed over another and lit a cigarette. 'What do you mean, lies?'

'How many red-haired men do you know?'

'One or two, I suppose.' He shrugged. 'Charlie Gilmore. I knew his brother a bit. I've never thought about it. Why?'

'How about someone called Lamb?'

Morley shook his head. 'Doesn't ring a bell.'

'Small scar near his eye.'

'No.'

'He used to be a boxer.'

'Not around here,' the man said. 'I'd have heard of him.'

'Perhaps you should have. He's the one who murdered your friends.' Harper watched the man's face very closely. Just a tilt of his head in curiosity.

'Have you arrested him?'

'Not yet.'

'I don't see how any of this makes me a liar.' Morley was smiling genially.

'Because I think you know him.'

The boxer shook his head. 'The first I've heard is what you just told me.'

'What would you do if you found him?'

'I'd kill him.' He made the promise matter-of-factly.

'Pity you didn't do it when you had the chance, then.'

'What chance? I've just told you, I've never heard of the man.' His voice started to rise, fingers gripping the arm of the chair. 'I know I've never bloody met him.'

'Like I said, Eustace, you're a good liar.' Harper stood and walked towards the door. 'We'll carry on in a while.' To the constable he said, 'Keep your eye on him.'

Kendall had gone out; the office was empty. He asked Tollman if the copper had returned from the station with Lamb's file. Not yet; the train was due in ten minutes.

Let Morley wait a little longer, he decided. Allow his anger to build. Harper wanted to take a look at the file on Lamb and see if there was any connection.

The small café at the market was almost empty, the traders busy at their pitches, shouting their wares as the crowds moved around. The inspector sat with a cup of tea, all too aware of the minutes ticking by and the shadow of the detective from the Yard hanging over them. Growing larger every second. And here he was, doing nothing.

But sometimes you needed to spend a little time to gain much more.

Once he had the chance to learn about Lamb he hoped he'd have the ammunition to pry more out of Morley. If there was anything to learn. The boxer could have been telling the truth. It was becoming impossible to tell. He'd give it a few more minutes of questioning.

Things were moving, he was certain of that. It was all too slow, though. Annabelle had helped, but he couldn't pin his hopes on the idea she might be able to do more.

A quarter of an hour passed. He pushed the empty cup aside

and idled on his way back to Millgarth. A thick folder was waiting on his desk.

Amos Kenneth Lamb, known as Red Lamb. Thirty-three years old. Six feet tall, thirteen stone and five pounds. He'd started out with a gang on Oxford Road, making his name as a hard man. Tried his hand as a boxer in his early twenties; he'd won three and lost eight before giving it up as a bad job.

There was much more detail, fleshing out the bones Inspector Clark had given him.

Lamb had received a few small convictions when he was young, enough for the police to keep an eye on him. Once he'd grown, though, he'd proved impossible to convict. The old, old story: people too afraid to testify against a big, violent man.

But intelligent, too. He'd run this and that for other bosses and made a success of everything he did. He thought ahead. He anticipated problems and difficulties and worked out ways around them. For the last six years he'd sold his different talents to the highest bidder, keeping himself in the background but always dangerous.

The last note had been written two months earlier. Nothing more than a sighting in a beerhouse on Deansgate.

That chimed with what the Manchester policeman had told him on the telephone. What had made Lamb come to Leeds? Had someone told him there were opportunities here? He'd managed a great deal in such a short time. The man definitely had brains, the inspector thought. Just two months in Leeds? No wonder the police didn't know about him. But someone did. Someone was helping him.

'Let's try this again, Mr Morley. Three wins, eight losses.'

'What?' At least it caught his attention before he sneered. 'If that's a fight record it's a walking disaster.'

'Not in your class?'

He snorted. 'Not even close.'

'That was what Lamb did as a boxer.'

'I hope he's retired. He'll be lucky to have any brains left after that. But I've still never heard of him.'

He still had nothing to tie Morley to Lamb. The man in front of him was no more a fool than Lamb himself.

'He's been in Leeds for two months.'

'So?' He shrugged. 'It's not like we're short of people here, is it?'

Harper was about to say more when the door opened and Tollman appeared, giving an urgent nod.

Annabelle was standing by the front desk, with Mary sitting up in her carriage, gazing around in wonder. 'The Cobourg Arms,' Annabelle said breathlessly. Her faced was blotched and pink, a film of sweat on her upper lip. 'He was there until yesterday.'

'Lamb?' he asked quickly and she nodded.

'Mrs Ingram, the landlady, sent me a message. I told her who you were looking for and she knew him right off. I came running over here.'

So close now, the inspector thought. Close enough to smell the bastard.

'Did she know where he was going?' He wouldn't be leaving Leeds. Not yet.

'He told her he had business in town and he needed to be closer.'

Harper turned towards Tollman. He was standing behind the counter, listening intently.

'I want every officer on the beat asking at rooming houses. They should already be covering the hotels,' he ordered. 'We're looking for a big man, copper hair, with a scar on his temple. He'll probably be calling himself Lamb. I need them all checked today.'

'Yes, sir.' The sergeant hurried off to pass the command.

From the corner of his eye the inspector saw Wharton pass, gazing silently at the scene.

'You've managed more than me,' he told Annabelle with a smile.

'I told you, never underestimate women.'

'You were right,' he admitted. 'She won't say anything to any of Archer or Gilmore's men?'

Annabelle gave him a pitying look. 'I told you, Tom, women have been keeping secrets from men for as long as we've been on earth.'

He kissed her softly. Never mind that it was in public. 'Thank you,' he whispered.

'Well, we don't need a London detective cluttering up the city, do we? Come on,' she told Mary, 'wave bye-bye to your da.' He held the door for them. As she passed, Annabelle whispered in his good ear: 'Now go and catch him.'

*   *   *

'Are you going to keep me here all day?' Morley complained when he returned.

'And all night if I have to.' Harper paced around the room. He didn't have time to play these games. He needed something now.

The boxer lit another cigarette, the smoke sitting in a cloud below the ceiling. The room was hot and airless, uncomfortable. Tempers frayed easily in a place like this. And that was when the truth leaked out.

'What you mean is you can't prove a thing.' He smirked.

'I will, Eustace. And that'll be the end of your career. Unless Charlie Gilmore or George Archer get hold of you first. Then you'll be dead.'

'They like to see me fight.'

'Happen they'll watch as you fight for your life, then.'

'I don't believe a word of it. Neither will they.'

'We'll see, Mr Morley.' Harper raised a hand for the constable. 'Take him down to the cells.'

'You can't bloody well do that!' the boxer protested.

'Watch me.'

He went searching through the station. Wharton had gone out. Ash was in the office, filling out a report.

'Come with me,' Harper told him.

TWENTY-ONE

'Where are we going, sir?'

'The Cobourg Arms.' They pounded along the pavement, eating up the distance. 'We've had a tip. Found anything on Lamb?'

'You'd think he'd never existed from the looks I've had.'

'Do you believe them?' Harper turned up Woodhouse Lane, the sergeant at his side, easily keeping pace with his long legs.

'The thing is, sir, I do.'

The Cobourg Tavern dominated the corner of Claypit Lane. Dirty brick, clean windows, a proudly donkeystoned step at the front. Harper pushed open the door and walked in.

A woman assessed him from behind the bar, arms folded
across her chest. She was perhaps just the young side of forty,
with a few strands of grey in her dark hair. Not heavy, but definitely firm. Brassy, strong.

'Well, I know Fred.' Her eyes twinkled. 'That means you must
be Annabelle's husband. She came and told you, then?'

'Hello, Nellie,' Ash said, a faint flush of embarrassment
crossing his face. 'How are you?'

'Right as rain, luv.' Her eyes turned back to Harper. 'I can see
why she married you. I might be tempted meself if I was a few
years younger.' Then she laughed, a throaty, husky sound before
her face became serious again. 'You want to know about Ken Lamb.'

Normally he'd have loved all this, the back and forth. Now
all he felt was the breath of next week on his neck.

'Whatever you can tell me,' he assured her.

'He moved on yesterday, like I told your missus. Said he
needed to be close to town, as if five minutes' walk isn't near
enough. Here nearly a week, paid by the day.'

'Was he out all night at all?'

She shook her head. 'Always in before closing time. I lock
the doors when I've turfed everyone out from the bar and I don't
unlock them until morning.'

'Did he say much? Did you talk to him?'

'I always try. Some of them can be a right laugh, the salesmen
and them as stop here regularly. Mr Lamb was polite enough but
he didn't want much conversation.'

'Did he come in the bar for a drink much, Nellie?' Ash asked.
'Have a word with someone, maybe?'

'I suppose he spent a bit of time down here,' she replied.
'Can't say as I saw him with anyone, mind. But once it's busy
you don't have time to look.' She glanced at Harper. 'Your
Annabelle would know what I mean.'

'Is there anything you can think of about him?' the inspector
asked. 'Something he might have said, or done?'

'Not really.' She bit her lower lip. 'He's the kind of guest
everyone likes. No trouble, pays on time. But as soon as he's
gone you forget he was ever there.'

Not a bad talent for a criminal, Harper thought. 'He had a
scar.'

'Right enough.' She nodded. 'I asked him about it. All he'd tell me was that he'd had an accident when he was young.'

'If you remember anything else . . .'

'I'll send word, don't you worry. I will tell you one thing before you go, though.'

'What's that?' he asked with interest.

'I hope you realize what a treasure you've got in Annabelle. If I hear you've been messing her around, I'll give you what for.'

He grinned. 'There's no danger of that. Thank you for your help.'

As they were leaving she called out, 'And Fred, don't be a stranger.'

'A stranger?' Harper asked with a lopsided grin as they walked back along Woodhouse Lane. 'Fred? Nellie?'

'It's not what you think, sir. We've known each other for years. She loves to tease, does Nellie.' He gave a small cough. 'At least we're closer to him now.'

Without warning, Harper pushed Ash into the shadow of a building.

'Watch,' he said.

They stayed in the shadows as a man moved through the knots of people on the pavement, marching out purposefully until he reached the Cobourg then pushing open the door. On a mission.

'Who is it, sir?'

'Davy something-or-other. He works for Archer.' The inspector kept his gaze on the pub. A few seconds later the man came tumbling out and Nellie Ingram stood in the doorway. He didn't need to hear the words as she sent the man on his way.

'Looks like she's put a flea in his ear,' Ash said with a chuckle.

'We should be glad of that.'

But it meant that Archer knew who Lamb was. And it would be a few hours before reports started coming in from the men on the beat.

'Back to Millgarth,' he decided. 'I want you to question Morley. See if you have more luck than me.'

The constable had barely set foot in the office before Harper said, 'Mr Wharton.'

'Sir?'

'Did you check at the factory this morning about Miss Brooker's young man?'

Wharton smiled. 'Yes, sir. He was telling the truth.'

'That's an end to the matter, then. Have you written a final report?'

'It's in the file for the inquest, sir.'

'Very good.' He waited until the young man nodded, then asked, 'I was looking for you earlier. Where did you go?'

'Out trying to find leads on Lamb, sir, the way you and the superintendent wanted.'

'Did you come up with any?'

'Not a thing, sir.'

'You have the makings of a good detective.'

Wharton beamed. 'Thank you, sir.'

Harper tilted his head. He wanted to be absolutely certain he heard every word.

'It's a pity you'll never have the chance to make it happen.'

For a second the man stood in shocked silence. 'You mean my work's not good enough?'

'I mean you're passing information to George Archer,' the inspector told him.

'I never—'

'Only two people could have heard my wife tell me about the Cobourg earlier – you and Sergeant Tollman. On my way back here I saw one of Archer's men going in there, and getting thrown out again for his pains.'

'It must have been coincidence, sir.' He sounded desperate.

'How much has Archer been paying you?'

Silence.

'How much?'

Wharton didn't reply. He was still standing there when Kendall arrived.

'What's going on?' he asked.

'I think we've found one of the men passing information to Archer,' Harper said.

The superintendent turned sharply, his face looking old and hard. 'Is this true?'

The constable stared at the ground in front of his boots.

'When did it start?' Kendall's face was beginning to turn red with fury. 'In plain clothes or on the beat?'

'When I was still on the beat, sir.' His voice was small and fearful.

'How much did he pay you?' The super was curling his hands into fists and opening them again.

'Two guineas a month.'

Kendall snorted, his mouth in a snarl. 'He must have thought his ship had come in when you became a detective.' No reply. 'Get out. Leave everything on your desk and go.'

'Yes, sir. I'm sorry, sir.'

'Get out,' he repeated. As Wharton began to walk away, shoulders slumped, Kendall spoke to his back. 'You're a disgrace.'

The door closed, the young man gone, and the silence grew.

'I thought you'd have him arrested,' Harper said quietly.

'We'd only end up looking even bigger fools in court.' Kendall was still staring at the door and breathing slowly. At least the anger had faded from his face. 'I'll tell you this, Tom. If I have my way he'll never get a job within fifty miles of here.'

'It's a pity. He really had talent.'

'How did you find out?'

Harper explained, fitting it around the information Annabelle and Nellie Ingram had given him.

'At least we're still ahead of Archer,' Kendall said when he'd finished. They had to put the business with Wharton behind them and keep their eyes on what mattered. 'We've got a good sniff of Lamb now. I've just been talking to the chief. He's going to try to get the Yard to hold off for two more days.'

A small weight lifted, at least for a while. A little more time, a few more yards on the lifeline.

'We're close,' the inspector said. 'I can feel it.'

'You've read Lamb's file. Do you think he's behind everything?'

'He's supposed to be bright and ruthless. That fits. Still . . .'

'What?'

'He had help here. He must have. He's only been here two months. He'd have needed friends.'

'Morley?' Kendall guessed.

'If it is, I can't pry a damned word from him. And I still don't see how he fits in, not with his friends dead. Maybe it was Bob Hill, then Lamb decided to use him to bait George Archer.'

'We need Lamb. Then we can begin unravelling everything.' The superintendent took out his pipe and began to fill it. 'At least Gilmore and Archer are keeping the peace.'

'Let's hope it stays that way.' He glanced at the clock. No word from any of the beat men yet. Anything would be better than just sitting and waiting. 'But it wouldn't hurt to reinforce things.' He stood, straightened his tie and reached for his hat. 'You did the right thing with Wharton, sir.'

'What I did wasn't what I really wanted to do.' He gave a wan smile. 'Maybe it's just as well or I'd be in court myself.'

Only one man stood guard outside the Sword, sweating in his thick wool suit, a brown bowler hat perched high on his head. He kept his eye on Harper, giving the merest nod towards the door. The man he wanted was there.

There was no pleasure on Charlie Gilmore's face. The bar was empty, none of his men in sight; none of the regulars who used the place either. Only the barman reading his newspaper and Charlie alone at the big table.

The last few days had been unkind to him. His face was hollow, gaunt, as if he'd barely eaten. Harper sat and faced him.

'When's Declan's funeral?'

'Tomorrow. Mount St Mary's at eleven.' He raised his head and a sly look passed across his eyes. 'Why, are you thinking of coming, Inspector? It's going to be the biggest the Bank has ever seen.'

'I don't think you'd welcome me, Charlie.'

'Have you found his killer yet?' His words were slightly slurred.

'We're close. And it's no one who has anything to do with George Archer.'

Gilmore turned his head and spat. 'I know that. Why do you think nothing's happened between us? And he understands I had nothing to do with his man being murdered. We've been exchanging notes, Inspector.' Harper couldn't hide his astonishment. 'That surprise you? We're both chasing the same quarry.'

'Not both, Charlie,' Harper corrected him. 'Three of us. And I'm going to find him first.'

'Why? Because you have the women working for you?' It came out as a sneer.

'Maybe the question you need to ask is why they're not working for you.' He gestured at the empty pub. 'If they love you so much around here, why aren't they queueing at the door with tips? Maybe they're sick of one of their own trying to rule them with fear. Have you thought about that?'

'It'll take a better man than you to goad me, Inspector. Perhaps you'd better run to your wifey to do your job for you. And I daresay George will tell you the same.' He turned away. 'Good day, Inspector.'

He'd hoped for better but expected worse. He could take insults; God knew he'd experienced enough of them as a copper. But the news that Gilmore and Archer were working together was interesting. Worrying, too.

Smoke from the factories laid a blanket over the city and the streets felt like an oven. The July heat showed no sign of breaking. All the faces he passed on the pavement looked on edge. Thoughts of violence hung over their heads. Another day or two and there'd be fights. Men would beat their wives over nothing at all. There'd be woundings and killings in the pubs and beershops.

Archer was exactly where he'd hoped to find him, in the office of his accountant, above a shop in New Briggate, the windows facing the Grand Theatre. He visited twice a week, keeping a close eye on all his enterprises.

Roger Harrison the bodyguard filled the landing with his smell of bay rum and cheap cigars. He didn't try to stop the inspector squeezing past them. The door opened and he saw George Archer sitting in a leather chair, studying a balance sheet. He glanced up, annoyance turning to anger as he saw the inspector's face.

'Out,' he ordered. 'This is a private meeting.'

'And this is urgent,' Harper said. 'Do you want to know or not?'

Archer chewed his bottom lip for a moment. 'I need five minutes, Ben,' he said to the accountant. 'Do you mind?'

They waited as the man closed his ledgers and returned them

to a drawer, taking time to lock it with ink-stained fingers. Finally they were alone.

'You've got brass balls, I'll give you that.' He sounded amused. 'Marching in here like that.'

'Do you want to talk or not, George?'

'What I want to do is hang you out of the window by your ankles. Maybe even let you drop.' He stood, menace on his face. 'Do you want to tell me what the bloody hell you're doing? Dragging my housekeeper away? My bloody housekeeper!'

'Are you done?' He'd had enough of posturing and poses and people with something to prove. 'I've already been threatened by someone much tougher than you today. Wharton's gone, you won't be getting any more information from him.' He studied the man's face but it gave nothing away. 'So are you going to listen, or do you love the sound of your own voice too much?'

'Go on.' Now Archer sounded curious.

'It's as simple as this. I'm the one who's going to catch Lamb.'

'If you can.'

'The police can.'

'No.' The man's voice was firm. 'I owe Bob Hill. He'd been with me a long time. He was like family.'

'You won't win.'

'Don't put money on that.'

'I will. Even if you and Charlie Gilmore are working together.'

Archer raised an eyebrow but didn't reply. He took out a cigar, cut the tip with a knife from his waistcoat pocket, then lit it. 'I'll tell you something. Once all this is all over, I'm done. I'm out of the game completely. Most of my money's in legal stuff these days. I'm going to keep it that way.'

'Do you think you can stay respectable, George?' Harper didn't believe a word.

'I do.' He nodded. 'I'm getting too old for this. Used to be I'd relish the idea of a hunt and a scrap. Not these days. And I don't want a war with bloody Charlie Gilmore. I made sure we nipped that in the bud.'

'What about all those little schemes that have been filling your bank accounts for years? What are you going to do about them?'

'Get rid,' Archer replied wearily. 'Gilmore can have them if he wants. We've been talking about it. There's no future in this game.'

Harper leaned against the door jamb. 'Do you want to know what I think?'

'You're going to tell me anyway.'

'I think Lamb's working with someone to take over from you and Gilmore.'

'Fine. Let him. He'll have no fight from me about it.' He shrugged and shook his head. 'But when I catch him I'll make him pay for Bob. That's one thing I have to do.'

'He was seen talking to Lamb the day he died.'

'I don't believe you.' Archer kept his voice steady but his eyes were filled with fire. 'I knew Bob all my life. I know what he'd do and it's not that.'

Who ever really knows anyone else, Harper wondered. 'Walk away now, George.'

Archer shook his head. 'I can't. Not from that. That's a debt of years.'

'Then you know what I'll do if I catch you.'

'Your lot haven't managed it yet.' The ghost of a smile crossed his mouth. 'Do your worst, Inspector.'

Back at Millgarth, there was no more word about Lamb. Many of the constables had reported back, nothing to find, nobody fitting his description in the hotels and rooming houses. The rest still had to return or send a message.

He paced the office. He was drained. Absolutely empty. But there were still things to do today.

The hackney dropped him off at the end of the drive to Lakeside. It had been a bone-rattling ride, the cab jouncing and bumping along the road. He stretched, breathing in the cleaner air. Fresher, too, away from the smoke.

From the plain back door of the house, the tradesman's entrance, he could stare down over the big lake. A pair of anglers sat by the path, hunched over their rods. A couple walked arm in arm towards Barran's fountain on the hill. Everything looked so peaceful, so ordinary.

He turned away and knocked on the door.

* * *

'You're telling me you never said a word to Bob Hill or anyone else?'

They were in the housekeeper's parlour. Susan Keeble sat in the chair, staring daggers at him.

'That's exactly what I'm telling you. Same thing I told you two minutes ago and the last time you were out here. You're not that stupid, are you? I'm not going to do anything that means my nephew could end up dead.'

'Evidently Bob Hill used to know one of the men who did the kidnapping. You could have had a quiet word with him, it rang a bell, and he decided to do you a favour.'

She snorted. 'Happen he could. *If* I'd had a word. But I didn't.'

'We know who killed Hill,' the inspector told her. 'A man called Lamb, from Manchester. Does the name mean anything to you?'

'Never heard of him.'

'No?' he asked. 'That's funny. Hill was seen talking to him before he died.'

'What's that got to do with me?'

'You tell me, Mrs Keeble.'

'You're off your head, you are.' She started to rise. 'I've given you ten minutes, that's all you're getting. I have meals to look after. The girls won't do a thing if I don't keep my eye on them.' Mrs Keeble looked him full in the face. 'I don't know what you wanted to find, but it's not here.'

Waiting for the electric tram down to Sheepscar he could smell his own sweat in the thick woollen suit. Women fanned themselves, wilting in their dresses, pinched by their corsets.

The vehicle moved slowly, the windows down to try and catch a breeze. Along Roundhay Road, from the green of trees to smutted brick, the houses growing smaller, more closely packed together, the people poorer.

The cobbles were dry and dusty as he alighted at the terminus. Not a breath of wind. Smoke from the factories along Meanwood Road – the chemical works, the bootmakers, the tanners and God knew what else – hung low, in clouds coloured from storm grey to dark green.

The bar was no cooler than outdoors. Just a handful of drinkers were scattered around the room. He waved a greeting to John

Willis, sitting awkwardly on his chair. No more than thirty-five and his life over after losing half his left leg when a boiler exploded at work. His face was puckered and livid where the water had scalded him. Now he was unable to do much but sell bootlaces around the neighbourhood, pushing himself along on crutches.

The door to the cellar was open; Dan was probably down there if he had any sense, where things were cooler. The inspector climbed the stairs. Miss Quinn sat at the table, tracing a column of figures with a fingertip. He waited until she'd finished, nodding her head in satisfaction.

'I don't know how you do that,' he said. 'Keep it all in your head, I mean.'

She gave a small laugh. 'I don't either,' she said, a hint of surprise in her voice. 'I just do it. Maybe that's the trick, not to think about it.'

'Are the books making sense yet?'

'Bit by bit.' She started to gather her things. 'I'd better pack everything away. I should have left an hour ago.'

'Is Annabelle here?'

'She's just changing Mary. I'll be out of your hair in a minute.'

Her movements were brisk and efficient, sliding bookmarks into the ledgers and piling them neatly on one side of the table. She finished just as Annabelle emerged from the bedroom, putting Mary down and watching the little girl's face light up as she ran across the floor. Every day she was growing. Each footstep more confident than the last. For a second he believed that she'd be grown in a heartbeat.

'I told you your da was home.' She grinned. 'As soon as she heard your voice she was squirming.'

He picked Mary up, nuzzling his nose against hers.

'Back tomorrow?' Annabelle asked Bertha.

'Yes, in the morning,' the young woman answered. She winked. 'You were definitely right.' She pinned a straw boater to her hair.

As the footsteps faded he turned to Annabelle. 'Right about what?' he asked.

'Never you mind,' she said, leaning over and kissing him. 'Woman's talk. Did Nellie help?'

'Yes.' He told her, watching her laugh when he added the part about her seeing off Archer's man.

'I've not heard from anyone else.' It almost sounded like an apology.

'I'm grateful for everything you've done. We're closer now.'

'Will you be able to find him? Before anyone from the Yard comes up here, I mean.'

'I promise.' And he hoped he was right.

The early evening was too hot, too heavy to eat anything. They played with Mary until the little girl's bedtime. Later, sitting together on the settee, Annabelle told him how a man from the local Labour party ward had arrived to ask her to do their books for them; he'd heard about the work she was doing for the Suffrage Society.

'What did you tell him?' Harper asked.

She grinned. 'I asked if he'd have me as a delegate at the party conference. He hummed and hawed and then said it wouldn't be possible. I told him if I'm not good enough for that he can stuff his books.'

It was dusk when they stirred. Still too warm outside. It was going to be a poor night for sleeping, he thought.

'It's been a month, you know.'

'Has it?' he asked, although he knew to the day.

'You remember what the doctor said.' Every four weeks, pour warm olive oil in his bad ear and keep it in overnight. It might help, the physician said as he pocketed his money.

It hadn't. But nothing would. It was a waste of time. Yet Annabelle insisted, as if she believed some miracle might happen. And once a month he submitted. She was already bringing out the small bottle from the chemist and warming a few drops in a teaspoon over a candle.

TWENTY-TWO

'What do you want to do about Morley?' Kendall asked.

'Leave him in the cells for now,' Harper decided. He stared out of the open window, down at the yard behind Millgarth, where a troop of new recruits was parading for a sergeant. During the night a breeze had risen, blowing the worst of the closeness away. The air felt clearer, a little crisper. That would change soon enough as the factory chimneys belched out more of their smoke. But even a small respite came like blessed relief. Friday, not even a handful of days before Robertson of the Yard arrived. Unless something happened.

'We still don't have any sign of Lamb,' Kendall said.

None of the constables had found the man. Between them they'd covered the hundreds of hotels and rooming houses around the city centre, from the grandest to the lowest lodgings in the courts.

Harper pictured the map in his mind. 'South of the river,' he suggested. 'There are places in Hunslet and Holbeck that are close enough.'

'I'll talk to the division over there. They'll do it today.' The superintendent's voice was grim.

'There's something else we haven't considered, sir,' Ash said.

'What's that?'

'If Lamb's behind all this—'

'He has to be,' Harper said.

'Listen to him, Tom,' Kendall said with interest. 'Go on, Sergeant.'

'If Lamb's behind all this, what's he going to do next?'

The inspector felt their eyes on him and saw the reflections of their faces in the glass.

'He's probably wondering what the bloody hell happened. By now Archer and Gilmore should have been at each other's throats and ready to be taken.'

'Could he have left Leeds, sir?'

'No. There's a man at the railway station keeping watch,' Harper said. 'And the staff in the ticket office have been alerted.'

'Time's running out,' the superintendent reminded him.

He nodded. They all knew. He could almost hear the clock ticking in his head.

New jobs. Back to the snitches and the informants. Even Kendall was out working with them. From the grandeur of the Griffin Hotel on Boar Lane to the sour ruin of the beershops at the bottom of Kirkgate.

By now they all knew Lamb's name and what he looked like. Word had spread like a wave among the criminals. Half of Leeds believed they'd seen him, but they were all wrong. Harper spent the morning following this tip or the next. Every one was wasting time.

He didn't stop for dinner. Back at Millgarth Sergeant Tollman handed him a fistful of messages. The inspector riffled through them. One caught his eye and he slid it into his jacket pocket.

'Anything else?' he asked.

'The boxer, sir. What do you want to do about him?'

'Nothing.'

'Leave him down there?'

'For the moment.'

He cut through the streets, and crossed the river over the Victoria Bridge. Holbeck spread out ahead of him, tall chimneys meant to look like Italian church towers, but as dark and dirty as everything else here.

The Cross Keys stood on Water Lane. Inside, there was a pleasant coolness to the air. The pub was quiet, too early for the shift men from the mills and factories to be in. Percy Gillthwaite tossed a damp towel down on the bar and gestured with a turn of his head. Out into the yard behind the building. Harper followed.

'Your missus has been talking to people,' Gillthwaite said. He was a man who'd never married, had no time for women.

'I know,' the inspector said.

'I'd rather have a word with a man.' He pushed his hands into his trouser pockets.

'I'm here now, Percy. I got your note. What do you have to tell me?'

'You didn't hear it from me, right?' That was his way, disavowing everything. But he'd passed on a few good tips in the past.

'Go on.'

'That man you're all looking for. With the copper hair.'

'Lamb.'

Gillthwaite nodded. 'That's him. You know the bottom of Bath Street, down by the allotments behind Marshall's Mill?'

He tried to picture it. Nothing came to mind. 'No.'

'Well, he's down there, staying at number seventeen.'

For a second he didn't dare believe it. 'He's there *now*? We've been checking all the rooming houses over here.'

'It's not a rooming house,' he said patiently. 'It's Mrs Simpson. She's a widow woman, sometimes lets a room when she needs a little extra money. Puts a card in the shop and Bob's your uncle.'

'Are you sure? Who told you?'

'Bloke who lives next door to her drinks here.'

'When did he move in?'

'Day before yesterday.' It fitted. Gillthwaite's gaze moved restlessly. With his bushy, greying hair and long, thick sideboards, he looked like a man quickly going to seed.

'He's still there?'

'Unless he left this morning.' He shrugged.

Harper brought out a florin and laid it on top of an empty barrel. 'More if he's there,' he promised.

He needed men with him. Ash would be ideal, or Kendall, but God only knew where they were. It would have to be someone from the Holbeck station house.

The duty sergeant listened carefully. He could almost have been Tollman's twin, large, round, but with a fierce intelligence behind his blue eyes.

'I can let you have two lads, sir. Bruisers, the pair of them.'

'I'll take them.'

'Bottom of Bath Street, you said? They'll meet you at the top of the road and you can tell them what you need.'

He waited until the constables arrived, anxious in case Lamb tried to leave. A pair of brothers named Bradshaw, every bit as large as promised.

'I know Mrs Simpson,' one of them said after he explained the plan. 'She'd never take in anyone she knew was a criminal, sir. Christian woman, Temperance, lives by her bible, she does.'

'Then we'll won't have any trouble, will we? Let's go.'

The man who knew the woman stayed with him, the other positioned himself outside the yard at the back. As basic as it came, but it would serve.

Mrs Simpson's grey hair was caught in a neat bun at the back of her head. She was small, barely five feet tall, and thin, with wattles of loose skin on her neck. But her gaze was clear and calm.

'Hello, Davy,' she said to the bobby, then nodded at the inspector. 'What can I do for you gentlemen?'

Harper's nerves were screaming. He tried to breathe slowly. Be here, he thought. Just bloody be here. Let's be done with this.

'You have a lodger, Mr Lamb,' he began, but she was shaking her head.

'He left first thing. Went out to buy a newspaper, came back all agitated and began packing his bag. You're welcome to take a look, but he's gone.'

He nodded to the constable and waited as the man went through the house.

So close. He'd come so bloody close. 'Did he say where he was going?'

'He told me something had come up urgently. He'd paid for the week, too. I tried to give him some of the money but he told me to keep it.'

'Did he say anything else while he was here? Anything at all?'

'He'd barely got his foot in the door. But he seemed pleasant enough. Polite.'

Bradshaw reappeared, shaking his head.

'How long ago did he leave?' Harper asked.

'Couldn't have been more than two hours,' the woman replied, eyeing him with curiosity. She cocked her head. 'What's he done?'

'I believe he's killed four men.'

Her hand flew to her mouth. He could almost see her thoughts – a murderer in her house, and the chill of a close escape. She could have been a victim.

'He wouldn't have hurt you,' Harper told her. 'He had his targets. Criminals.' She nodded but her face was still white with shock. 'Take her in and make her a cup of tea,' he said to Bradshaw. 'Make sure she feels safe.'

'Yes, sir.'

Two hours. Two bloody hours. He wanted to smash his fist against the wall. Back on Bath Street he glanced around, as if Lamb might have left a trail. All he saw was a woman trudging along with her shopping bag.

By five o'clock he felt frantic. There had been no more sightings of the man. Kendall returned to Millgarth looking defeated.

'I'll try again tonight,' Ash offered. Even he looked weary, no more than a flash of hope in his eyes.

'Two days,' Kendall said. Harper didn't need the reminder. Monday and he'd be meeting the London train. Maybe Wednesday – maybe – if the chief could negotiate it. 'Go home,' the super ordered. 'Every man on the force is looking for him.'

'But—' Harper started.

'Rest. We'll all come at it fresh tomorrow. And we'll catch him.'

It was a good idea but he paced around the parlour, unable to settle. He played with Mary, helping her assemble blocks until she became bored and turned her attention to a doll propped against the toybox in the corner. Once she was asleep the evening seemed to chafe against him.

'You're making me dizzy,' Annabelle told him. 'Up and down like a jack-in-the-box.'

'I'm sorry.'

'I know.' She reached out and took his hand. 'It's not over yet. Just remember that.'

'Yes.' He kept trying to convince himself. But deep inside, all he could see was failure. What could he do tomorrow that he hadn't done today?

Sleep didn't come easily; it was gone one by the time he finally dropped off. There was just enough of a breeze to make the night comfortable, but his thoughts wouldn't give him any peace. It seemed as if he'd barely closed his eyes when something was shaking him.

'Tom.' Her voice hissed in his good ear. 'Someone's hammering on the door.'

Almost half past four, according to the alarm clock, partly light outside. Bleary-eyed, he padded down the stairs and drew back the bolts on the front door.

Constable Stone. The man who always seemed to be sent to wake him.

'What is it?'

'A fire, sir.' He paused. 'The Sword's burning. The pub Charlie Gilmore uses.'

'I'll be there as soon as I can.'

TWENTY-THREE

By six the firemen were rolling up their hoses. All that remained of the building was charred beams and burned bricks, everything steaming in the morning sun. The crowd who'd gathered to see the blaze had gone, on their way to work or back to their beds.

'What do you think?'

'Arson,' Reed said without hesitation. He'd appeared not long after Harper, still buttoning his tunic and watching the crew work on dousing the flames. 'I could smell it right off. Paraffin, it's always a giveaway.'

'You're the expert, Billy.'

'That's what they tell me.' Reed smiled. He nodded at an approaching figure. 'Your man's back.'

Charlie Gilmore, flanked by his men. He'd been here an hour before, watching helplessly as the Sword was consumed.

'I'm burying Declan today and now this,' he said. 'Nowhere for the wake.' He stared at Harper. 'I'll kill whoever did this.'

'No, you won't.'

'Like hell I won't.' Gilmore was raising his fists. 'I know who it was, too.'

'Who?' the inspector asked, praying he wouldn't say George Archer. That was the last thing he needed.

'Lamb.' He curled his lip around the name. 'The one you can't seem to find.'

'Seems like neither of us can.'

'Then he'd better pray you or whatever weasel they send up from London catch up with him first.' He spat on the pavement.

'Go and mourn your brother, Charlie.'

He watched them leave. Gilmore kicked at some embers, sending sparks flaring into the air.

'Who's Lamb?' Reed asked.

'I'll buy you a cup of tea and tell you all about it, Billy.'

The market traders came and went from the café. Harper talked, Reed listened. When the tale was finished, the fireman let out a low whistle.

'You've got quite a job on your hands. But that arson at the pub was amateur work. Just luckier than the warehouse where that man was killed. The alcohol meant everything caught well.'

'Bradley. That was the man in the warehouse.' Him, Tench: their deaths seemed distant now.

'That's the one. My men could smell it wasn't right as soon as they arrived at the Sword. It looks like everything started by a back wall near the kitchen. Sneak around in the dark and it's child's play.'

'I've got two more days to find Lamb and unravel whatever's going on.'

Reed stared at him. The man's face was filled with ghosts. The good friendship they'd once had was gone, but all he could feel was sympathy. 'I wish I could help.'

'You have enough on your plate. It's not your problem. How's Elizabeth getting along with the bakeries?'

'Busier than ever now she's taking care of everything.' He gave a small chuckle. 'I'll tell you something: Tom, she loves it. I can see it in her eyes. She's got her chance and she's taking it.'

'She'll do well with them. You've got a good one there.'

'You're right,' he said quietly. 'How does Annabelle like her new job?'

For a moment Harper didn't answer. Then, 'She's setting the whole world in order. That's right up her street.'

Harper stayed in the café after Reed left to examine the ruin of the Sword again. He nursed another cup of tea, eating bread and dripping to fill his empty belly. Whatever happened, it was going to be a long Saturday. He needed something to sustain him. Something to help him think.

'You look like a man who's spent too long staring at the devil.'

Maguire sat down opposite him.

'The only devil I'm looking for has red hair.'

'Not me, I hope.' He gave a lopsided grin. His face was still gaunt, the skin pale, but there was a twinkle of life in his eyes. His hair was greasy and lank; he looked uncared-for. If he really had a summer cold it hadn't all left yet.

'You don't have the proper scar,' the inspector told him.

'You're looking for a man by the name of Lamb?'

'What?' Harper looked up. His heart was beating faster. If Maguire knew where he was . . .

'I talked to your wife yesterday. She told me.'

'Have you seen him?'

'No. But anyone who wants to bring Charlie Gilmore down must have a little good in his soul.'

'He's killed four men here in Leeds. Maybe more.'

'I know.' His voice was serious as he drained the cup and stood. 'I wish you luck.'

The superintendent was already in his office. He waved Harper through, looking as if he'd been in the station for hours and filling the air with the comfortable fug of his pipe.

He pushed a piece of paper across the desk. 'Came half an hour ago.'

Not me. Archer.

Short, to the point. But it said nothing he didn't know. George Archer wanted peace now, not war.

'We're safe. Gilmore already knows Lamb set the fire. He's burying Declan today, too.'

'Busy day for him, then.' There was no sympathy in his voice. 'Lamb,' he said, shaking his head. 'Bloody Lamb.'

'We were just hours behind him.'

'Even minutes are too long right now.'

'I know,' Harper answered with a nod. 'I know.'

Ash arrived, looking as weary as Harper felt. 'I thought I had a sniff of him last night,' he said. 'Someone told me about a red-haired man at the Albion Hotel.' He gave a small, wan smile. 'It wasn't him.'

'You heard about the fire?'

'Yes, sir. Trying to up the ante, isn't he?'

'Trying. At least it's not working.'

'We're talking when we should be searching,' Kendall interrupted.

'I'd like you and Ash out there, sir. All we can do is ask and listen. I'm going to kick the boxer out.'

'Why?' the superintendent asked.

Harper looked at the pair of them. It was a sudden decision, but there was nothing more to be gained by keeping him in the cells.

'When you're out there, start saying that Morley's told us everything. Just that.'

'Use him as bait, you mean, sir?' Ash asked.

'Why not? We've tried everything else. Don't forget, one way or another he was involved in the murder of his friends. Your friends.' He kept an eye on the sergeant, seeing his face harden. 'If Lamb hears, maybe it'll bring him out of the woodwork.'

'Fine,' Kendall agreed, reaching for his top hat. 'Back here at noon.'

It took another ten minutes of glancing through reports for the tiniest hint of Lamb before Harper was ready to leave. He'd just walked out of the station when a boy dodged around him, pushed open the door of Millgarth station and ran inside.

The inspector wasn't fifty yards down the road before Tollman was shouting his name loud enough to make him run back.

'Have a listen to what the boy says, sir.'

It was the lad who'd swerved past him, breathless and red-faced. 'Please sir, the lady at the bakery in Sheepscar said can you come now?' He paused, closing his eyes and concentrating. 'She says the man with red hair is there.'

A hackney was dropping a customer down the street. Harper sprinted for it, tossing the boy a coin as he went.

'Sheepscar.' He pulled out his warrant card. 'Police. As fast as you can, please.'

The cabbie looked at him and nodded. 'Yes, guv'nor.'

They made good time, and the horse was flecked in sweat when they arrived. He dashed towards the shop. The sign still read Harper's Bakery, but it was Elizabeth he saw on the other side of the window.

'How long?' he asked.

'No more than half an hour.'

Even closer now. But it might have been yesterday. In the streets around here it was easy to disappear.

She was pale, shaken. The two women behind the counter just stared. The inspector led her into the room at the back and sat her on a stool. The teapot on the table was still warm. He poured a cup for her, added milk and sugar and put it in her hand.

'Tell me about it,' he said gently.

'As soon as he came in I saw his scar and I knew.' Elizabeth looked up at him and sipped the tea. 'Annabelle told me what he looked like. But he seemed so ordinary. All he wanted was two teacakes. Said please when he asked for them buttered.'

Mundane, he thought. But life often was.

'What then?' he asked her.

'That was it.' She shook her head. 'He paid and left and I sent a boy to find you.'

'Which way did Lamb go?'

'Down to the end of the road, then he turned left. I didn't see after that. I'm sorry.'

'It's fine,' he assured her. He was picturing the streets in his mind. What was the man doing out here? It was nowhere near the city centre. A thought came to him. 'How did he look?'

'What do you mean?' She didn't understand.

'Was he rested? Worn, what?'

'Oh. There were smudges on his face and clothes. Just faint, but . . .'

'Thank you.' He smiled at her. 'You were always safe. Really.' He took out his notebook, scribbled on a page and folded it. 'Can you find someone to take this to Millgarth?'

At the end of the street he turned left and stopped. Too many choices. In the distance he could see the chemical works on Meanwood Road. Where all this seemed to begin. Was Lamb going there? No. The place had nothing for him.

Where?

Any direction was going to be a gamble.

Lovell Road. Dooley's Gym. It was still early, not yet eight. Men and women would be counting off the hours until Saturday dinner and the end of the working week. Then the engines would shut down, the smoke would cease. At least they'd have fair weather for their leisure. Still warm, but comfortable, not oppressive.

Inside, no sign of Morley. Just men moving, fighting, training. The rank smell of sweat. Back on the steps the sun made him blink. Had Lamb come up here? It was possible.

The inspector started back down the hill, gazing around carefully as he walked. Something down the ginnel next to the building caught his eye. He slipped through to look.

Harper pulled the police whistle from his waistcoat pocket and started to blow.

Now he knew where Lamb had gone.

'Will he live?' Kendall asked.

'Maybe. That's as far as the doctor would go,' the inspector said.

'So nobody really knows.'

Lamb had been battered. He looked as if every bone in his face had been broken. Blood spattered everywhere. A metal bar lay close by, but fists had done all the damage. It looked as if Eustace Morley had kept his promise.

'He's cuffed to the bed by his ankle and there's a constable at his bedside. Just in case he should wake.'

'If he ever does,' the superintendent said. There was relief in his voice, but who could blame him?

'I talked to one of the nurses, sir,' Ash said. 'She reckons he won't last the day.'

Harper knew he should have felt a sense of triumph. But it didn't seem like any kind of victory.

'Doesn't matter either way,' Kendall told them. 'The Yard's off our back now. I've already sent the telegram.'

The case was over. No London detective would arrive to show them how it should be done. That was some small consolation, some satisfaction. But they hadn't been the ones to find Lamb. Someone else had done the job for them. They'd failed.

'It's not finished yet,' Harper said quietly. 'We already know he wasn't doing all this on his own. There's still someone else out there.'

'No, Tom.' The superintendent's hand clapped him on the shoulder. 'That's it. Everything bar the shouting. Even if Lamb pulls through we'll have him in court for murder. If he up and dies, it saves us the money and the trouble. Whatever anyone else planned is over now. They needed Lamb to make it work. Without him it all falls apart. The only thing left is to find Morley. And that's a job we can handle ourselves. Unless something else happens, we'll leave the rest of it be. It's done.'

'I checked Morley's lodging, sir,' Ash said. 'He hasn't been there. And Dooley said he hadn't been in the gym this morning. He swears none of the boxers there were involved. I'm inclined to believe him. If someone had given out a beating like that his knuckles would be swollen. Couldn't hide it.'

'Tell Tollman I want every copper looking for Morley,' Kendall ordered, 'but warn them he's dangerous.'

'Yes, sir.'

'We're going to leave it at that and be grateful. With Lamb out of the picture we won't have any more trouble. Once we catch Morley it's all mopped up. It's done, Tom.'

'Is it?' Something wasn't right. He couldn't put words to it, just the feeling in his gut.

Kendall pulled out his pocket watch and glanced at the time. 'Right now they're putting Declan Gilmore in the ground. He's gone, and there's nothing left of the Sword except a few charred pieces of wood. It's going to take Charlie a long time to recover from all that, if he ever does. And Archer—' the superintendent almost spat the name '—is intent on making himself whiter than white. It's done.' He gave a small chuckle. 'In the end Lamb got what he wanted anyway. The power's all gone.'

'If it was him.'

'It's over,' the superintendent insisted. He clicked his watch shut and replaced it. 'We'll find Morley. Go home. We won.'

'Barely.'

'It doesn't matter, Tom. We still won. You did a good job.'

'That's the thing. I don't believe it's really over yet.'

He could have taken the tram, but he needed to walk and think. By the time he reached the Victoria he'd been moving for an hour. Here. There. Everywhere. He didn't even notice. Trying to make sense of the picture they had. Whichever way he looked at it, the thing was still full of holes.

They'd kept the Yard at bay. That was success. Gilmore and Archer would never be powers in the city again. But someone would replace them. It was human nature. Then they'd start all over again.

But someone was behind all this. Someone they hadn't found yet. Harper was certain the person was closer than they knew. Lamb couldn't have had the local knowledge to bring down two gangs. He'd been involved, yes. He'd been important. But someone else was pulling the strings.

Things would only be finished when they were behind bars. But for the life of him he couldn't see who was doing it.

He opened the door to the parlour in the Victoria, hearing the low buzz of women's voices. Annabelle and Miss Quinn, heads close together as they studied a page in a ledger.

'That can't be right,' Annabelle said as she shook her head. 'It just can't.' She turned her head to gaze at him, her frown becoming a smile. 'I heard.'

'All of it?' he asked. Suddenly he felt exhausted.

'The fire at the Sword. Lamb. It's all over, isn't it?'

'Most of it.' He gazed around the room. 'Where's Mary?'

'Sleeping.' She rolled her eyes. 'A good job, too, she was fractious all morning. And we still have something to sort out here.'

Harper sat in the bedroom, the door closed, a mild breeze through the open window. His daughter was on her back in the cot, eyes closed, her breathing soft and even, arms splayed on either side of her head.

So perfect, so innocent.

He lay back, trying to ease all the thoughts from his head, to empty his mind. Maybe Kendall was right; Lamb was as good as dead; he should accept it was done. But he knew he couldn't. He wasn't made that way.

Someone was shaking him gently. He blinked his eyes open.

'You were snoring,' Annabelle said.

'Mary . . .?' He began to sit up.

'Still fast asleep.'

It was the shank of the afternoon. He could feel the heat of the day all gathered around. God only knew how he'd slept, but now he was awake his thoughts were already churning.

'Did you sort everything out?' he asked.

'Not really.' Her gown rustled as she perched on the bed.

'What's wrong?' He propped himself on one elbow.

'The sums don't add up. I've gone over them, Bertha's gone over them, then we went through them together.' She sighed. 'We're off by the best part of twenty guineas.'

His eyes widened. That was a hefty sum.

'What? Was it stolen?'

'No. I think it was Miss Frobisher. She's old. She must have made some mistakes. We found a few, but . . .' Annabelle rubbed her eyes. 'It doesn't matter, we'll sort it out next week. Come on, I want to hear it all.'

By the time he finished, Mary was awake, sitting on the rug and playing a game that seemed to involve two of the blocks and the doll. He watched her for a while, but couldn't make it out.

'Why did you say it's not over?' Annabelle asked. 'It sounds final to me.'

'Because it doesn't make sense this way. Not to me.'

'Then you'd better do what you know is right.' She reached out and squeezed his hand.

Reed had barely given the Sword another thought after his crew left the ruin of the building. Definitely arson, but Tom Harper seemed to know who'd done it; he could look after that. Now he listened intently as Elizabeth told him about Lamb coming into the shop.

'I was that scared I must have been shaking. I could hardly say a word.' She pushed her palms against the table top.

'But he's in hospital now?'

'That's what everyone's saying.'

'It's all done, then.' He smiled at her. 'Put it behind you, eh?'

'I . . .' She shook her head. 'I know. You're right, Billy. It's happened, it's history.' At the stove she placed the kettle on the hob to boil. 'I've done the figures.' She turned, her smile proud. 'After everything's paid, I made almost five pounds this week.'

'Five!' He could hardly believe it.

'That's after another five for Annabelle to start paying everything off, and the wages and supplies.' She was grinning, wide-eyed with joy. 'Can you believe it, Billy love? Five pounds.'

TWENTY-FOUR

Sunday and he was awake early. Annabelle gave a small grunt and shifted in the bed as he rose. Mary slept on, heedless.

There was a half-light through the curtains. In the bathroom he washed, shaved in cold water, and dressed. There was nowhere he had to be. He was off duty until Monday. But he'd go in anyway. The pub was silent. Somewhere he sensed the creak of a pipe, but no voices, no words to disturb him.

He felt as if he'd hardly rested. All the things troubling him bubbled just under the surface.

The streets were empty. The skies had cleared, the smoke of the working week drifting away to show patches of blue. A gentle warmth dusted his face. The sound of his boots echoed off the buildings. All the grand offices were empty today. A single copper stood guard outside the Town Hall, barely glancing up as he passed.

The central court at the Infirmary was empty. Beyond the doors the hospital would be busy, patients awake, nurses moving around with their pills and ointments.

He remembered the room. They'd put Billy Reed in here after a beating that left him close to dead. A year and a half ago? Could it have been that long?

Harper pushed open the door. The bed was empty. Pillow plumped and waiting. Sheets a pure, clean white, the blanket drawn up. No policeman standing guard. In the corridor, he checked to be sure he had the correct room.

'The man who was in here . . .' he asked a nurse as she bustled past.

'Talk to Sister.' She pointed towards the ward as she dashed away.

Sister Smith was a woman with a plump face and a ready smile.

'Where's the man who was on his own in the room? The prisoner.'

At his question she frowned. 'Who are you?'

'Detective Inspector Harper, Leeds City Police.'

'He died a little after midnight.'

'I see. Thank you.' He started to wander away.

'Inspector?' She held up a parcel wrapped in brown paper and tied with string. 'His effects. They forgot to take them with his body.'

With the package under his arm he walked through the streets to Millgarth. Somewhere a faint peal of church bells began, then another started, like an echo. In the distance others joined in. How many people would answer the call, he wondered. His parents had only gone to weddings and funerals. He'd only been in a church a handful of times in his life. Sunday was a day for home, for family. Going out if the weather was good, filling the parlour in winter. His parents had never made any mention of God. He didn't even know if they'd believed.

At his desk he took a penknife, cut the string and unfolded the paper. Boots, scuffed, soles worn, a white shirt with a ring of grime at the neck. A suit of good wool, nicely cut, thick and heavy, the type made to last, perfect for a working man.

An old wallet, the shine gone from most of the leather, holding a train ticket from Manchester to Leeds for May the fourteenth. A little over two months before. That fitted with all he'd learned.

No paper money, but a little over two pounds in coins, enough to weigh down the man's pocket. A handkerchief, a cheap watch and chain. And a letter, folded away in an envelope, addressed to Mr K. Lamb at an address in Manchester.

> Dear Ken, I sed things wood be in place for us. Close now you shud come to Leeds. Well meet and make our plans, all of us. Dirty wurk but the best reward at the end! Let me know when your arriving. Bob

Bob. It had to be Bob Hill. Dead in an empty house on Somerset Street. Murdered by his new partner. He read the letter again. The words were half-formed. Not an educated hand. But Hill had never been a clever man. Not the person to devise a plan to bring down the two big gangs in Leeds.

All of us. Who else, he wondered? How many? All. That meant at least one other person. Someone from Gilmore's gang? Declan? Had he wanted to depose his brother, to become the leader of the Boys of Erin? He'd always been ambitious as well as violent. Now he was dead, too. If they'd been scheming together he'd have let Lamb come close, lowered his guard. The perfect chance to kill.

Had Lamb sensed the opportunity to have it all for himself? Could Kendall be right?

'Good morning, sir.'

Ash hung up his battered bowler hat and glanced down at the items on the desk. 'Lamb's stuff?'

'Yes. You heard he's dead?'

'As soon as I walked through the door. Finishes that off neatly, doesn't it, sir?'

'What do you make of this?' He passed over the letter.

'Bob Hill, do you think?' he asked when he'd finished.

'It has to be.' Harper explained his idea about Declan Gilmore.

'That's possible,' the sergeant agreed with a nod. 'Looks like Lamb got greedy.'

'Maybe he did.' He pushed a pen around the blotter on his desk.

'But if it wasn't Declan there's another man out there.'

'Yes.' He exhaled slowly. During the night he'd come up with names. Possibilities. And in the end he'd dismissed every one of them. 'Any more word on Morley?'

'Not yet, sir. He can't stay hidden for long. People round here know who he is and what he looks like. Everyone has their eyes peeled.'

True enough. Men already had their bets down on his upcoming fight. Seats had been sold for the bout. But there'd be none of that ahead. Just a cell and the noose waiting behind the walls of Armley jail.

'I still wonder why Morley wasn't killed before.'

'Because it would be noticed, sir,' Ash said. 'No one cared about Len and Ted. But folk would miss Morley.' He paused and beamed under the thick moustache. 'It would be right if we were the ones to bring him in. Fitting, you might say.'

'You have a tip?' He must have; there was a gleam in the man's eye.

'Not as such, sir. More a possibility.'

'Then why are we waiting?'

Ash reached into a drawer in his desk and took out a polished, heavy truncheon.

'Call it an insurance policy, sir.'

Through the Dark Arches and over the river. Less than two years earlier all this had been rubble and dust after the fire that devastated the railway station above. It was impossible to believe now. Everything was as it had once been, like an underground cathedral with a business tucked away behind the wooden frontage and doors of every arch. Harper read the first few names then stopped trying to keep count.

They emerged into the daylight of the wharf, the stillness of the canal close by. He raised an eyebrow. 'Where?'

The sergeant pointed along the towpath out towards Armley. They'd been walking for five minutes when he asked, 'How did you know about Wharton, sir?'

'After we left the Cobourg and saw one of Archer's men heading there. Wharton had heard Annabelle tell me about Lamb being there. Why?'

'I just wondered.'

'He admitted it.'

'I daresay. Pity. He had the makings of a good 'un.'

A small house with a shed nearby stood close to the canal. With green all around, trees and bushes, birds loud in the branches, it was hard to believe they were so close to the city. Only the dirt in the air gave it away.

'Shed, sir,' Ash whispered. 'That's what someone thought.' He drew his truncheon.

The small building was solid stone, with no windows and a roof of corrugated iron. They arranged themselves on either side of a flimsy wooden door. Harper nodded, drew back his foot and kicked.

The door flew back and they dashed in. Empty. But someone had been here. Sacking had been piled to make a bed in the corner. An oil lantern hung from a nail.

'Hard to tell if anyone's coming back, sir.'

'Yes.' There was nothing personal in the room. But what did

Morley have besides the clothes on his back? 'Who lives in the house?'

'It's storage these days, sir.'

How did Ash know all this, he wondered briefly? But there were padlocks on both of the heavy doors, and the windows were covered with wood that hadn't been peeled away. No one could have sneaked inside.

Harper stood, gazing around. It was impossible to tell if it had been Morley out here. It could have been one of a thousand homeless men.

'We might as well go back,' he said after a little while and exhaled slowly. 'Maybe someone's found him.'

It seemed impossible that a man as imposing as Morley could simply disappear. But he had. No one had seen him, no one had harboured him. Maybe he'd left Leeds. His boxing career was over, that was certain.

A constable was watching the man's lodgings, but it was probably a fool's errand. The inspector spent most of the day going round his narks, searching for any scrap of information. It felt as if he'd done too much of this lately: all chasing and hunting, reacting rather than thinking.

It wasn't the type of policeman he wanted to be. Not the kind he was.

At three he returned to Millgarth. Still no news on Morley. Superintendent Kendall was in his office. The strain of the last week had vanished from his face, but his mouth and eyes seemed filled with a deep sorrow. He pushed a piece of paper across the desk.

'This was waiting when I got back from a meeting.'

A report from C Division. So spare it was nothing more than bones.

Constable 676 responded to a call from a householder this morning. In the privy at the back of the property he found the body of former police officer James Wharton hanging from a beam. There is no reason to suspect foul play.

Sad. A waste. But he'd brought it on himself. He'd taken Archer's money. No one had forced him to do that.

'It's terrible,' Harper said. 'But this isn't our fault.'

'I know,' the superintendent agreed with a sigh. 'Just . . .' He waved a hand over the paper. 'I received an acknowledge-ment from the Yard today. Congratulated us on solving the case without their assistance. I burned it.' He nodded at the charred curls of paper in the ashtray. 'Morley? I want this wrapped up.'

'He's vanished.'

'Then keep looking, Tom.'

But where was there left to search? He needed to talk to both Gilmore and Archer. Charlie wouldn't be in a mood to talk after putting his brother in the ground yesterday. It would have to be George.

The man wasn't in his usual haunts. No one had spotted him since dinnertime.

'I saw him get in that carriage of his and head out towards North Street,' the barman at the Crown said with a shrug. He'd probably gone home to Roundhay. Another journey ahead.

Stepping off the omnibus at Sheepscar he was tempted to leave it until morning. The Victoria was just across the street, his wife and daughter so close. Duty won out, and he walked up Roundhay Road to wait for the electric tram to the park.

He heard the spark of rod against cable as it bumped slowly along the rails and up the street. Out and out, where the houses grew sparser and brick faded to trees and grass.

A few couples were picnicking on the field at the entrance to the park. A pair of nannies gossiped, half an eye on their charges who ran and kicked a ball around. The sun was mild on his back as he walked and the air felt clean as he breathed. Glancing over his shoulder he saw the chimneys rising like needles over the city.

Roger Harrison answered the door, grunting when he saw the inspector, saying nothing as he stood aside to let him enter.

It was five minutes before he heard the sharp tap of boots crossing the floor. Archer appeared, formally dressed in a tail coat and striped trousers, with a wing collar and black tie. The bodyguard was there, too, in the doorway but ready.

'You look like you're set for a court appearance, George.'

'Formal dinner tonight.' He eyed himself in a mirror and

nodded with satisfaction. 'What do you want, anyway? I heard that copper-haired bloke you wanted died in the hospital.'

'I'm after the same thing I always want: some truth.'

'What truth?' he asked sharply. 'I told you everything I know.'

'If you did, you were the only one. How well did you know Bob Hill?'

'We talked about this. I'll warn you again: don't you bloody dare say a word against him.' Archer's face reddened. He balled his hand into a fist. Harper could feel the tension in the air. They seemed to be standing on the thin edge between talk and violence. 'I told you,' Archer insisted. 'I knew him all my life.'

'Is that what you really think? That you knew him?'

'I *know* I did. Is this your new game? Come here and smear the dead?' He took a step closer.

'I don't need to do anything.' He pulled the letter to Lamb from his jacket and held out his hand. 'Go on, read it.' Archer didn't move. 'Read it.'

Warily, as if it was a trick, the man unfolded the note. Harper watched his eyes moving over the words. Once, then again. Finally, without a word, he gave it back.

'Plenty of men called Bob around.' The inspector said nothing. 'Doesn't prove anything.'

'You don't believe that. I can see it in your eyes.'

Archer shook his head. 'It's not Bob Hill.'

'If that's true, why was he seen drinking with Lamb on the day he died? Why did he end up dead in a house by Dufton Court?'

No answer. Instead, Archer glanced back and dismissed Harrison before striding off into a room at the back of the house.

'Well?' he asked as he glanced over his shoulder. 'Are you coming?'

The furniture was dark, old, heavy. There wasn't much. A battered chair that had seen better days. A scratched table, most of the varnish worn away. Cracked plates on a shabby dresser. Quite different from the showy wealth on display in the rest of the mansion.

'This belonged to my mother. All she had to pass on.'

It wasn't a shrine. Instead it seemed like a reminder of where he'd begun and how far he'd come.

'Why in here?' Harper asked.

'Because we can be private. Because . . .' He shook his head, unable to find the words for his thoughts. The window looked down the hill to the iron water of Waterloo Lake.

'It was Bob Hill,' Harper told him softly.

'It can't be.' But all the defiance had vanished from his voice.

'You know it is.'

'All I know is that he's stood beside me since we were nippers.'

'Things change. Maybe he'd had enough of being in your shadow. He wanted his own place in the sun.'

Archer grunted. 'I treated him well.'

'Perhaps he thought you were growing soft. Didn't have what it took any more, too intent on being respectable.'

Archer shook his head. 'I don't buy it.'

'He and the others wanted you and Charlie Gilmore at each other's throats. Then they were going to step in and take it all.'

'Is that what you think?' He snorted.

'I'm certain of it. I think they had someone from the Boys of Erin with them, too.'

'Who?' Archer turned his head sharply.

'Declan.'

Archer gave a short, bitter laugh. 'If I were you I wouldn't tell Charlie that. He loved his brother.'

'I'm not going to say a word.'

'You know, if Bob had said something he could have had it all.' Archer was staring into the distance. 'I meant what I said the other day. It's time for me to give it up. I'm making more money from honest business these days, and it's less trouble. Even got an invitation to a shooting party if I can find the bloody shotgun I had made last year. Bob could have taken it all over with my blessing.'

'Too late now.'

'Yes.' He sighed. 'Stupid bastard.' He started to bring his hand down hard on the table. In the end it became no more than a light slap. 'What about that bloke in the lake and that one in the fire? How do they come into it?'

'I don't know,' Harper admitted. 'Practice, perhaps?' He still didn't understand the reason; maybe he never would.

'I'm going to believe Bob Hill was a good man. That letter doesn't mean a thing.'

'You can if you like. Fool yourself if you want. I wanted you to see what happened.'

Archer waved it away. 'That's coppers for you. Disbelief's like a religion for you lot.'

Maybe he was right, Harper thought. Maybe it had to be. It was time to change the subject.

'One of your informers on the force has died, George. Maybe you heard.'

'Someone else is dead?' He didn't even raise his eyes.

'Wharton. I told you he was dismissed this week for selling you information.'

'His choice to take the risk. He was paid for it.' He turned, holding out his hands, wrists together. 'You going to take me in for that?'

'Not today.' Kendall would have done it with pleasure. Put the cuffs on and marched him away with satisfaction. But Archer's empire was already crumbling anyway. Gilmore's, too.

'You had your chance.'

'Watch your back, George. That's a warning.'

'Bob . . . Declan . . . the other ones.' He counted them off on his fingers. 'It's over.'

'No,' Harper told him. 'It's not. Not by a long chalk.'

He could smell the city as the tram trundled back down Roundhay Road. Acrid, thick. Soot in his nostrils and on his tongue. Out by the park everything seemed clean and fresh, new-painted and shining. Down here it all wore a coat of grime.

But it was his. He alighted at the terminus and looked up at the Victoria with its large portrait of the Queen on the gable. Home. And certainly where his heart was.

Annabelle was on her hands and knees, putting blocks one on top of another with Mary. She glanced up at him, smiling, content. 'You were off with the lark this morning.'

'Too many things troubling me.' He tickled his daughter, laughing as she started to shriek and squirm away from him.

'I don't think you're done yet, either. There's a message on the sideboard. A constable brought it an hour ago.'

He ripped open the envelope.

Morley dead. Body with King.

Kendall

'I need to go out again.'

TWENTY-FIVE

L ate in the afternoon. On a weekday, workers would be streaming away from the city. All the clerks, businessmen and shop girls would be packed on to trams or omnibuses or walking along the pavement. But this was Sunday, and the streets in town were almost empty as he strode along Vicar Lane, cutting past the Corn Exchange and through to Crown Point Bridge. The shriek from the wheels from a horse tram accompanied him down the steps to the cellar at Hunslet Police Station.

The smell of carbolic scraped his throat. King was in his kingdom, bent over a body on the slab, humming a piece of music as he worked. Over the man's shoulder he could make out Morley's face and body, naked and invaded.

'I expected you a while ago, Inspector.' The man hadn't even turned his head. How did he know who'd entered? 'You have a very specific way of walking. Easy to identify. Is this one of yours?'

'He was. Where did they find him?'

King gestured at a folder on the desk. 'That's what they brought with the corpse. I don't like to work on the Sabbath, it's not natural. But the chief constable insisted this one was urgent.'

It was no more than a few words. Discovered in a culvert on Water Lane in Holbeck, down at the bottom with the rubbish. Already dead when he was brought out. Pockets empty. One of the constables had recognized his face.

'What killed him?'

'Simple,' King answered. 'A knife to his stomach. See.' The

doctor moved and pointed. 'Two blows. He must have lived for an hour afterwards.'

'How long ago did it happen?'

'Last night. Don't ask me to be more exact. Not after he'd been in some water.' He raised one of the arms and examined the knuckles. 'He'd been fighting very recently.'

'He was a boxer,' the inspector reminded him.

'I know that,' King said testily. 'I've seen him fight. He had talent, if you enjoy watching people beat seven bells out of each other. But this was without gloves. He gave someone a beating.'

'What else can you tell me?'

'Very little that you can't guess. He was well-nourished, strongly muscled. You'd expect that in a boxer. Plenty of scars, especially on his face and hands. Again, perfectly natural for what he does.'

'Why would he let someone get close enough to knife him?' Harper wondered.

'That's your business, Inspector. They only come to me when they're dead.'

'He probably killed someone with those fists.'

King shrugged. 'I know. The body's on my list for tomorrow. Whatever you have going on, it's bringing me trade.' He stopped, stood and turned. 'And I'd rather it wasn't happening.'

Six dead now. He couldn't remember another case with so many murdered. And now? There was still one man out there. Morley's killer. The last man standing.

And he didn't know who that might be.

Millgarth was empty. The day shift had left, the night constables were out on their beats. Ash and Kendall had gone for the evening.

He sat for an hour, scribbling notes on a piece of paper. By the time he'd finished, all he'd managed was a few questions. Tomorrow, he decided. They'd wait until then.

Mary was still wet, wrapped in a towel as Annabelle tried to dry her. The girl was squirming and giggling, making a game of it all. Water dripped on to the floor as she shook her head.

'You love this, don't you?' She was smiling and laughing as much as her daughter.

He stood in the doorway of the kitchen and watched. For a few minutes he could let all the cares of work slide away. Pretend he had a job that didn't burrow into all the corners of his mind.

'Enjoying it, are you?' Annabelle scooped up a little water and tried to throw it at him. Mary's giggles grew louder.

'Do you want me to take over?'

'You might as well earn your keep.' She stood up, showing the wet patches on her dress. 'I'm soaked, I need to change.'

By the time she reappeared he'd combed the girl's hair. She was dry, powdered, already in her nightgown, a fresh nappy pinned around her.

'If the coppering doesn't work out I'll give you a reference as a nanny.'

'The way things are going, you might have to,' he said with a sigh as he carried Mary to bed, kissing her forehead gently.

'Bad?'

'I'll tell you about it in a little while.' He wanted this oasis, a few minutes of innocence. He read the child a story, not looking up until her eyes fluttered closed and her breathing turned to the soft rhythm of sleep.

Annabelle had made tea, a cup waiting on the table. Even better than beer, Harper thought as he drank gratefully. She listened as he laid out the facts.

'So whoever killed this boxer is behind it all?'

'He has to be. And it must have been someone Morley trusted enough to let him come close.'

'You'll find him.'

'Maybe I should get you to read that in the tea leaves for me.' He didn't want to think about it any more; it just made his head spin. 'What about this pamphlet writing they want you to do? Have they said any more about that?'

'The writing part is Mr Marles's job,' she reminded him gratefully. 'You couldn't pay me enough to persuade me to put pen to paper. But I've done a little reading and I've talked to a few people.' She let out a long, slow breath. 'Do you know how many beershops there are in Leeds?'

'No idea.' Plenty of them, he knew that much. Sometimes it seemed like there was one on every street.

'Nine hundred,' she told him in amazement. 'I knew they were everywhere, but nothing like that. God only knows how they counted them all. And that's not including the pubs and the gin palaces.'

It didn't surprise him. Without even really thinking he could picture over a hundred of them; dark, solemn rooms that offered nothing beyond the escape of drunkenness.

'You're not thinking of getting rid of this place, are you?' he asked warily.

'Don't be daft.' She tapped him playfully on the arm. 'This is home. The only way they'll get me out of here is to carry me feet first. It's something to leave Mary, too. I never want her to depend on a man.'

'As long as she looks after her parents when they're old and helpless . . .'

'That had better be a long time off,' Annabelle said. 'I'm not ready for my bath chair yet.'

'Don't worry, I'll always be there to wheel you around,' Harper told her with a grin. 'If you're lucky.'

'Don't be so cheeky.'

'We're a right pair, aren't we?' He squeezed her fingers gently.

'You get any soppier and I'm definitely going to write up that reference, Tom Harper.'

'There's a piece in the paper about Morley, sir.' Ash placed a copy of the *Mercury* on the desk in the superintendent's office.

It was part-obituary and part-complaint about the lawlessness in Leeds that allowed the city's most promising boxer to be murdered. Harper read it quickly then tossed it back on the desk.

'Come on,' he said. 'We're going back out to Archer's.'

'I thought you were there yesterday, sir.' The sergeant picked his old bowler hat of the desk.

'That was to see George. I've been thinking about it. I want to talk to Mrs Keeble again. Her nephew was kidnapped and the men who did it died. She knew Bob Hill, he's gone. That's far too much coincidence for my liking.'

Maybe he should have pressed her harder the last time. But the slight hesitations in her answers had seemed so natural. Now he wasn't so certain. Still, with two of them working on her, they'd make sure she gave them the truth.

'I'm coming with you,' Kendall said. 'I want to see where this goes. You're right, we need answers.'

At least it meant a hackney, Harper thought. He couldn't picture Kendall riding a tram and tramping across a field. They rode in grim, forbidding silence. As they neared the park he lowered the window, letting clean, warm air into the cab.

Park Avenue was a wide sweep of road, built for carriages. A place to see and be seen. West Avenue was more of the same, large houses set back behind walls and young hedges.

'Which one's Archer's?' the superintendent asked.

'Next one along, sir.'

At the top of the drive Kendall straightened his coat and top hat. 'Well,' he said, 'shall—'

The blast of a shotgun interrupted him. One barrel, then the second. A pause. Another shot.

'That's inside the house,' Harper shouted.

He ran, feeling the gravel crunch under his boots, dashing up the steps to try the door. He pushed against it with his shoulder. It was too solid to give. One more shot, close enough to feel.

'Go to the back.'

Ash was ahead of him, long legs pushing hard as he rounded the corner. Kendall was at his shoulder, breathing hard.

The door to the kitchen was wide open. The sergeant's boots pounded up the stairs. Harper glanced around. Something was wrong. Not the blast. He could smell smoke.

The superintendent dashed past him. Not one of the servants was in sight. Harper didn't move. He turned his head, hoping his hearing wouldn't fail him again. There. A noise behind a door at the end of the hall.

The key was jammed in the lock. He turned it, forced the door back over the tile floor. Four people inside, their faces torn between fear and relief.

'Out,' he ordered. 'Now! The house is on fire.'

They rushed past quickly. Three women, one older man. No Susan Keeble. He moved, hurriedly checking the other rooms, her parlour, opening the door to the cellar.

Nothing.

His throat was dry, the hair prickling on his spine. Move, he told himself. Bloody move. His boots hammered on the wood as he ran up the steps. He could see the smoke, taste it. Sharp enough to make him cough.

Kendall was standing over Archer's body. It lay sprawled across the chequerboard tiles in the hall, eyes empty, a pool of blood growing around him. Already gone.

'Sergeant!' Harper shouted.

'No one upstairs, sir,' Ash yelled from the landing. 'The fire's in one of the bedrooms. It's spreading.'

'Leave it.'

They needed to make sure everyone was out. People took precedence over property. He tried one door, then another. Nobody inside. One locked. He kicked the wood, a second time, a third until it gave, crashing back against the wall. Empty.

Where the hell was Susan Keeble? And Roger Harrison? Had Archer's bodyguard abandoned him?

One last room. The one at the back that Archer had taken him into, with the furniture from his childhood. All the memories. The reminder not to return to those days.

There he found Harrison, slumped but still alive. He moaned and stirred as the inspector started to drag him away.

The man was heavy in his arms. Sweat ran down his chest. The smoke was starting to thicken and billow as the blaze spread. Then someone was reaching over to help. He glanced up: Ash. Between them they pulled and carried, leaving a slug trail of blood across the tiles.

Kendall had unlocked the front door. Sunshine and clear skies outside. It seemed unreal after all he'd just seen.

Tenderly they eased the man down the stairs, resting him on the grass. He groaned, grimaced. Ash knelt over him.

'Don't you bloody die on me, Roger. Don't you bloody dare.'

'Who?' Harper asked. 'Who did it?'

'Susan.' It came out in two cracked syllables, a hoarse whisper. He felt stupid.

It had been right there all the time, in front of him. He just hadn't wanted to see it. He simply couldn't imagine a woman behind it all. She'd spun him into her web. Fooled him without even trying.

He glanced up at the footsteps on the gravel. Kendall. His face was drawn, shoulders slumped. His enemy was dead, but he didn't seem to find any satisfaction in it.

'Sir?' Harper said.

'What?' He saw the superintendent shake his head, trying to clear it.

'It's Susan Keeble. She's the one we want.'

The servants had vanished. Who could blame them? There was nothing more for them here, and who'd want to stay near a charnel house? Flames licked from the top corner of the building, forming a haze in the air. He didn't care. Let the whole damn place burn down.

How much time had gone by since the shots? It felt like a year but it couldn't be more than ten minutes.

She had a start on him. At the bottom of the hill the park spread out, acre after acre of it. All the places she could hide, corners to disappear into.

'Which way?' Kendall asked.

Whatever he said, it would be a guess. 'Try along there.' He pointed to the far side of the lake. 'I'll take this side.'

He skittered and slid down the steep slope, seeing marks in the earth. Tiny piles of dirt, the grass bent and flat. Someone had come this way. Very recently.

She'd used a shotgun to kill Archer. Had he seen it in the house? Harper tried to picture each room in his mind. Nothing.

With every step he looked around, alert for the slightest movement. He passed the empty rowing sheds.

Which way now?

No hint.

All he could do was hope. He followed the dusty path next the water. On the lake a pair of swans glided close by.

Harper could feel his chest rising and falling, the pulse pounding in his neck. To his left, the slope rose gently from the shore. His eyes scanned the trees.

He was a target.

Every step seemed loud.

She might not be here. And if she wasn't . . .

He walked faster.

A single figure ahead, sitting on the grass, dark against the brilliant green.

Harper paused for a moment. A few yards more and he was close enough to see.

Susan Keeble. The shotgun lay across her lap. She didn't turn her head, didn't seem aware he was there.

'Mrs Keeble.' He shouted the name, keeping his distance.

The woman looked up and stared at him.

'Put the gun down.'

She glanced at the weapon, as if she was astonished to see it. But she kept it in her hands.

'Put the gun down, please.'

Keeble moved her head away to gaze over the water. They were close to the spot where Tench's body had surfaced.

He took one step closer, then another. 'Why? Why did you do it?'

She snapped around to look at him again. In one motion the gun was at her shoulder. Pointing. Steady. He raised his arms, not taking his eyes off her.

'Talk to me,' Harper said gently. 'Tell me why.'

One more pace forward.

From the corner of his eye he could see someone on the other side of the lake. Kendall. Too far away to do any good. He had to do this himself.

'Put the gun down,' he repeated, keeping his tone soft, trying to be reasonable. In the distance a group of geese began calling, the sound ceasing as suddenly as it had begun.

She stood, the gun still trained on him.

The sky seemed too blue for this. The sun was too bright.

He stood his ground. She began to move towards him. Small, steady steps. He could see her eyes now, dark and intense.

She stopped no more than thirty feet away. If she pulled the trigger now he'd be a dead man. Pictures flashed through his mind: Mary, Annabelle. If he ran he might stay alive for them. But he didn't turn. This was his duty. If he didn't do it someone else would have to.

'Why?' he asked again.

'To end it.' Her voice was strong, clear enough so that he could pick out every word.

'End what?' He swallowed hard. If he could keep her talking there was hope.

'Everything.'

He nodded towards the lake. 'Why don't you tell me about Len Tench?'

'After my sister told me about the kidnap I talked to Bob Hill. He knew who it had to be. He arranged it all.'

'Where did Lamb come in?'

For a moment she said nothing. Then, 'You know what George Archer did after my Jack died? Offered me a job as his housekeeper. As if being a skivvy and saying yes sir, no sir, three bags full sir was a great reward.' He waited. She'd started, it would all come out. 'I hated him. He'd gone soft. All he wanted was to be accepted. I saw that. I made Bob see it. Charlie Gilmore was weak, too. The pair of them were ready to be taken.'

She lowered the shotgun for a second and he breathed in. Then she brought it up again, aiming straight at his face.

'What about Declan?' he asked.

'He knew Lamb.' There was a deadness in her voice. No inflection. Reciting history. Everything pared away to bald facts. 'Declan knew Charlie had lost his hunger.'

'Why did you let Eustace Morley live?'

'People would miss him. They'd ask questions.' Simple. Pragmatic.

She came closer. Twenty feet. Impossible to miss now.

'When did you decide to get rid of Bob Hill?'

'That was Lamb.' Her eyes glittered. 'He had imagination. He saw that we didn't need Bob or Declan. We could do it all together. Just him and me.'

And when Morley beat Lamb to death the plans had unravelled. Killing the boxer had been nothing more than revenge. Morley would never suspect a woman, so he'd let her get close enough to stab him.

She moved sideways, gesturing to him with the barrel until they were standing right at the edge of the lake. She'd fire and he'd go tumbling into the water. Die from his wounds, die from drowning. Either way he'd be a corpse. Another one to fish out. Another one for Dr King to examine.

Susan Keeble started to speak again. The gun had been lying there. All she had to do was take it and wait. Archer never asked her if she knew where it was. He treated her like she was nobody. When the missus and their boy went out this morning she took it as a sign. Time to put an end to things.

Very slowly, Harper extended his hand.

'You've done it all now. It's over. You can give me the gun.'

She shook her head. 'You don't understand, do you?'

'Understand what?'

Her answer didn't come in words. She turned the gun so the muzzle was under her chin. Before he could move, she'd pulled the trigger. Both barrels. Powerful enough to throw her off her feet and into Waterloo Lake.

He jumped in after her. He didn't even think if she was dead or alive. The sound of the blast rang in his head. Harper broke the surface, gasping at the cold, and saw her just a few feet away. Two strokes and he was there. Arms around her, pulling her to shore. He climbed out, dragging her behind him, up on to the grass.

Her face was gone. Nothing there at all. As if she'd never been.

He settled on his hands and knees, coughing and retching up the water and the fear, pushing his forehead down against the grass. The sun was warm but he was shivering wildly.

'Tom? Are you hurt?'

He hadn't heard Kendall. No footsteps. The man was simply there, standing over him, his long shadow pointing down towards the lake.

'I'm fine.' His own voice surprised him: so steady, so reasonable.

'Can you stand?'

He tried to push himself upright. A hand holding his arm helped. At first his legs buckled but Kendall kept a strong grip, stopping him from falling.

'What about the house?' The thought came into his head.

'Take a look.'

He turned. Black smoke was spiralling up into the sky. A lick of flame rose then vanished. The blaze was in control. By the time the fire engines arrived there'd be nothing left of Archer's dream home.

Maybe that was for the best.

He didn't want to glance at the body beside him but he knew he had to. Where the face had been it was just shreds of skin and splinters of skull. Wet, matted hair.

His sodden jacket clung to him as he eased it off and covered her head. However many she'd murdered she still deserved some dignity.

'Come on,' Kendall said quietly, a hand on his arm. 'The bandstand's just up ahead. We'll wait there.'

Sitting, he put his head back and closed his eyes, resting against the solid wood. Everything came again. The words, the emptiness in her eyes, the barrel of the gun pointing at him, never wavering.

He heard a match strike, then the harsh smell of the super-intendent's tobacco. It was oddly comforting – normal, on a day when the world had turned upside down.

'Did she say anything?'

'She admitted everything. I'd just never believed a woman could do all that.'

'What about today?' Kendall asked. 'Did she explain that?'

'I think . . .' He stopped. Was it madness or desperation that made her shoot Archer and Harrison? Maybe she tiptoed that line between clarity and insanity, one foot on either side. 'She hated Archer.'

'So did I. I'm glad he's dead.' He heard Kendall's long sigh. 'But I'd rather have put him in the dock.'

Somewhere in the far distance he could hear the urgent ringing of a bell. He felt weary, the exhaustion rising through his body.

Perhaps he slept. Perhaps his thoughts simply drifted. He was slowly aware of another voice.

'I got Archer's body out, sir. The brigade's there now, but I don't think there's anything they can do to save it. Our lot are on the way.'

'Take Inspector Harper home, Sergeant.'

He blinked and sat up, seeing the pair of them just a few feet away.

'My report.'

'In the morning,' Kendall told him. 'There's time for it then.'

His shirt and trousers felt clammy against his skin. He walked slowly, as if he wasn't sure he could manage it; every step seemed an effort. They didn't talk. The words would all come later. For now, silence was just fine.

A hackney was letting out a customer by the entrance to the park. Ash waved it down.

'Sheepscar,' he said. Harper could feel the cabbie's eyes on him, the disdain at his appearance.

'I'm not having him inside. Look at the state of him.'

'Police,' the sergeant told him, never changing his tone. 'I said Sheepscar. Or maybe you'd prefer to lose your licence?'

At the Victoria, Ash escorted him through the bar, shaking his head at Dan's worried stare. Then the stairs, and the door to their rooms.

'Tom—' Annabelle began, then saw him properly. Her eyes widened. She crossed the room, taking his face between her hands. 'My God . . .'

'He's fine.' Harper could feel Ash behind him, warm breath on the back of his neck. 'He just needs a hot bath and a long sleep.'

'What . . .?' Her eyes darted between them.

'He's been in Waterloo Lake. I'll let him tell you all about it. I need to get back to the park.'

The clump of heavy footsteps and he was gone.

Annabelle stood in front of him, hands on hips. 'I'll fill the bath. You get yourself out of those wet clothes.' From the corner of his eye he saw Bertha Quinn sitting at the table, a pen still in her hand, trying to hide her curiosity. 'Go on. I'll be there in a minute.'

Until he closed the bedroom door he had no idea of the time. Mary was stretched out in the cot, eyes closed, oblivious. Afternoon already. The day seemed to have disappeared.

Harper stripped, leaving the soaking clothes on the floorboards. His boots were as heavy as bricks from the water. He could hear the clank and hiss from the bathroom. She'd had a geyser fitted the year before, revelling in the luxury. Hot water whenever she wanted. For the first time he truly appreciated the idea.

Annabelle appeared, holding a towel.

'Ready soon enough. Wrap yourself in that, it's been in the airing cupboard.' She tucked it around him then sat at his side. 'Tell me what happened.'

The words came this time. No hesitation. He could see each moment. Smell it. Taste it.

'I'll turn off the water,' she said when he was done. She kissed him. 'Better her dead than you.'

'Yes.'

Annabelle shook her head. 'What did I tell you, Tom Harper? You went and underestimated a woman.'

He smiled. She changed the mood. Pulled him out of the darkness. And she was right. She'd warned him about it before.

TWENTY-SIX

The start of August burned hotter than July. Finally the cooler weather came, bringing nights that offered a chance to rest properly. In the early days of September Harper gave his evidence at the inquests. Everything simple, straightforward. No lies. No need to nudge the truth. The newspaper reporters stayed busy in court, scribbling away in their notebooks. The verdicts were never in doubt. Harrison had died in hospital: unlawful killing for Archer and the bodyguard. And for Susan Keeble, a simple suicide.

Harper sat in the cocoa house across from the Town Hall with Kendall and Ash. They'd all been called, all said their pieces. But in the last month they'd had to go over it all so many times. Writing their reports, answering endless questions.

'Looks like it's all over at last, sir,' the sergeant said with relief.

Harper shook his head. 'The bit with the law's done. But the public still has to decide if we're heroes or bloody useless.' He grimaced. 'God knows we cocked it up enough.'

The superintendent sucked on his pipe. 'It's already taken care of, Tom,' he said. 'The chief constable had a meeting with the editors. We're all going to come out of this smelling of roses. It's for the civic good.'

Leeds was still too new as a city to have a scandal like this, the inspector thought. A few words, some sleight of hand and they became saviours.

'Tom?' The voice jerked him back from his thoughts. 'Did you hear what I said?'

'I'm sorry.'

'The chief wants to give you a commendation for facing down Mrs Keeble that way.'

He wanted to say no. Not when she'd turned the gun on herself. He could still hear the boom of the weapon. It woke him at night, and after it came the piercing chill he'd felt from the water in the lake. The first few times it happened he'd paced the parlour until it slipped away and he could sleep again. Now it was easier, fading slowly. Soon it might be nothing but one more bloody memory.

'Please thank him.' There was no other reply he could make.

A few minutes later he walked down Park Row, through the open doors of the fire station. The engine glistened, the brass shining, the hoses tightly wound on their reels. At Inspector Reed's door he tapped lightly on the glass. 'Billy. Do you have a minute?'

'Sit yourself down, Tom.' He took a cigarette from the packet on the desk and lit it. 'I need a break, anyway.'

'I wanted to ask you about that fire out in Roundhay back in July.'

'The big house by the park?'

'That's the one.' He could see Billy searching his memory, picking out the images in his mind.

'It started upstairs – it was Ash who said that, wasn't it? By the time we could get an engine out to the place it was too late to save it.' He shrugged. 'No one dead from the blaze. I looked through it myself. There's a widow and a son, isn't there? They'll receive the insurance money. They won't be going short.'

'I only have one question, really.'

'Go on.'

'If we'd tried to put the fire out ourselves when we were there, would it have made a difference?' It had nagged at him since he'd gone back out to view the ruins of the building.

Reed sighed. 'I can't answer that, Tom. It depends how much of a hold it already had. You're not trained.' He considered for a moment. 'If you really need to know, it probably wouldn't have made a blind bit of difference. The house would still have burned down.'

'Thank you.' Harper stood, extending a hand. They shook briefly.

'The inquests were this morning, weren't they?'

'Unlawful killing on the men, suicide on her.'

'I don't think many people are going to miss George Archer,' Reed said.

'Probably not,' he agreed. 'No one's seen Charlie Gilmore since his brother's funeral either. They're saying he's gone to Ireland for a while.'

'Both gone, eh?'

'Yes.'

On the way back to Millgarth his eye picked out the bulging dome of the York Street gasometer. He'd gone there a few weeks before, the day after Susan Keeble had killed herself, asking for Mr Brooker. Charlotte Brooker's father.

He was a small, diffident man with the look of someone who'd been buffeted and let down by life. And Harper wasn't about to give him good news.

'We've finished our investigation into your daughter's death,' Harper told him.

The man swallowed and gave a small nod. 'Well?' he asked in a quiet voice.

'It looks as if it was an accident, sir. She must have slipped into the water and drowned. I'm very sorry.'

'I see,' the man said eventually. His shoulders had slumped. 'Thank you, anyway.'

Before he could sit down, Kendall waved him into the office. He held up a letter.

'Do you know anything about a commission? More of an inquiry, from the look of it.'

Harper frowned. 'No.'

'I got this from the chief. Seems that Miss Ford has been on to him, you know, the Quaker woman, the suffragist. She's working on a study of poverty and crime in Leeds.'

Harper remembered her saying she'd contact the chief

constable. He never believed she'd actually do it. More fool him.

'She's requested someone from the police to advise,' Kendall continued. 'He's suggested you.'

Suggestion? This was the force; it was an order.

'You know what to do. Take them round, tell them the way things really are.'

'Yes.'

'Easy duty. But it'll look good in the press, too, what with you getting the commendation. You deserve it.' He gave a weary sigh. 'We were lucky, weren't we, Tom?'

'Yes,' he agreed. 'More than we deserve.'

With a grunt Elizabeth hefted the bag on to the kitchen table, then took out the ledger and the shopping.

'I saw Annabelle today. Gave her this week's money. She's working on some inquiry or study or whatever it is. All about the poor.'

'Sounds fancy.' Reed put down the paper. His uniform jacket hung over the back of the chair, and his braces were looped around his shoulders.

'She's moving up in the world is that lass. Mind you, we are too. A little more money each week.' She glanced around the room. 'Maybe we'll be able to afford something a bit better than this next year. I told you the bakeries were a goldmine.'

He smiled at her. 'You were right,' he agreed. 'Speaking of Annabelle, Tom came in to Park Row this morning.'

'He's all over the evening paper. Hero copper.'

'You wouldn't know it to look at him. More like someone with a lot on his mind.'

'Still glad you transferred to the fire brigade?'

'Very.' He put a hand over hers. 'Glad about everything.'

Harper spent the evening trying to teach Mary to say 'dada'. She'd managed something like 'mama' as she sat on her mother's lap, being fed the peas Annabelle had mushed together. Fair was fair.

Now she was in bed, eyes closing as sleep overcame her. He put the story book down and closed the door softly behind him.

The day had fallen away, the first hints of dusk outside the window. Another week or two and the nights would start drawing in. Another year was passing by.

'You're a daft thing, you are.' Annabelle was laughing. 'You know she never said a proper word. Not yet.'

'Well, it sounded that way to me,' he protested.

'It'll happen soon enough. She's growing so quickly.' Annabelle sighed and stretched out her legs, and took a sip of tea. 'I heard from Miss Ford today. We're going to start doing interviews for the study a week on Monday.'

'I know.'

She raised her head to look at him. 'How?' she asked suspiciously.

'She asked the chief for a copper to work with the group.'

'You?' She sat up quickly. 'Why didn't you tell me as soon as you walked through the door?'

'I was busy trying to teach Mary some important words.'

'Honestly, Tom Harper. What am I going to do with you?'

He stared at her, his mouth curling into a smile.

'I'm sure you can think of something.'

AFTERWORD

I t seems that in 1893 there was a trial of a torpedo on Waterloo Lake in Roundhay Park, using the missile to blow up a wooden boat. However, references to the event are quite sketchy, with no real details. Confusingly, the term used for nautical mines in those days was torpedoes; I've stuck to the modern meaning to avoid confusion.

The case of Charlotte Brooker is based on the death of Mary Ann Brook (or Brooke, or Brookes) in 1885. Her leg was brought up by a dredger in the River Aire, and the rest of the body recovered several days later in the canal. At the inquest the jury delivered an open verdict.

The pamphlet that Annabelle will be working on was published in 1894 under the mysterious title of *Hypnotic Leeds*; 'hypnotic' meaning 'blind-sided' or the unseen part of the city. It appeared in part through the help of the new Independent Labour Party and covered many areas of life that affected the poor, but it doesn't seem to have had much effect.

I'm grateful to everyone at Severn House for their belief in the Tom Harper series, to the librarians who order it, all the booksellers who stock it, to those who spend their hard-earned money on these books, and to everyone who takes the time to read one of them. You're all hugely appreciated. But part of the credit should also go to my editor, Lynne Patrick, who always improves my work, and my agent, Tina Betts, as well as all those who give their support and love, especially Penny. You know exactly who you are, and how much I appreciate everything.

Lightning Source UK Ltd.
Milton Keynes UK
UKOW03f0334020617
302463UK00002B/11/P